The Irish Bride

A Gareth and Gwen Medieval Mystery

THE

IRISH

BRIDE

by

SARAH WOODBURY

To my mom
who's always up for a good mystery

Special thanks to my physician sister
for her help with all the various ways to die.
All errors are my own.

A Note about Godfrid the Dane

Godfrid the Dane makes his first appearance in the *Gareth & Gwen Medieval Mysteries* in the first book, *The Good Knight.* He comes to Anglesey at the behest of Prince Cadwaladr, but quickly realizes the deal he's made is not quite what he thought, and Cadwaladr is not worthy of his allegiance or alliance. He takes it upon himself to keep Gwen safe and gives her up to Gareth when he comes to Ireland in search of her.

He and Gareth grow to respect each other, and Godfrid returns to Gwynedd in *The Fallen Princess,* on a quest to find the Book of Kells, which has been stolen, and again in *The Lost Brother,* in search of allies in his conflict with Ottar of Dublin, who has usurped Godfrid's the throne of Dublin. In both instances, Godfrid ends up aiding Gareth and Gwen in their investigations.

In the previous book, *The Viking Prince,* Godfrid is faced with a mystery of his own, at the end of which his brother is crowned King of Dublin and Godfrid is betrothed to Caitriona, his friend Conall's sister.

The Irish Bride is the next chapter in the story ...

Cast of Characters

Gwen – Gareth's wife, spy for Hywel
Gareth – Gwen's husband, Prince Hywel's steward
Hywel – Prince of Gwynedd
Llelo – Gareth and Gwen's son
Dai – Gareth and Gwen's son
Tangwen – Gareth and Gwen's daughter
Taran – Gareth and Gwen's son

Evan – Gareth's friend, Dragon member
Gruffydd – Rhun's former captain, Dragon member
Cadoc – Assassin, Dragon member
Steffan – Dragon member
Iago – Dragon member
Aron – Dragon member

Conall – Spy, Ambassador to Dublin
Caitriona (Cait) – Conall's sister
Dorte – Caitriona and Conall's mother
Godfrid – Prince of Dublin, Caitriona's betrothed
Brodar – King of Dublin
Diarmait – King of Leinster
Rory – Prince of Connaught
Donnell – Prince of Connaught
Jon – Godfrid's captain
Bern – Cait's guard
Sitric – Cait's guard

Prince Hywel's Family Tree

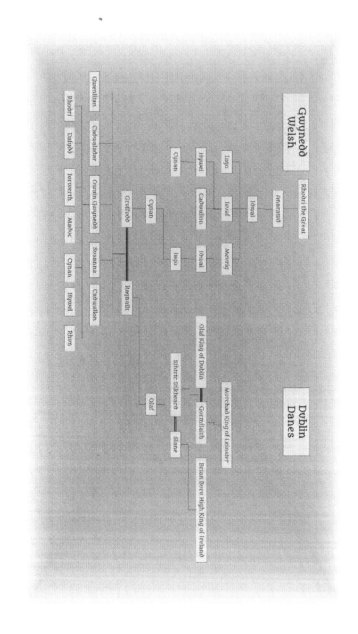

1

Dublin, Ireland
Last days of August, 1148

Day One
Gwen

Gwen fell to her knees on the dock, thankful beyond reckoning to be on dry land again—and heedless of the seawater that soaked the wooden boards and her plain brown dress. She had a better dress, a blue one, to wear tonight for the welcome feast, and a brand new one in a gorgeous green for the wedding day itself. Maybe, if she could be that careless of something she owned, she would pass this dress on to someone who needed it rather than face wearing it again, even for the return journey, which at the moment didn't bear thinking about.

Gareth crouched beside her, rubbing her back. "Give it a few breaths. You should start to feel better soon."

Gwen obeyed, taking in a deep breath that brought her the scents of wet wood, algae, and salt. She'd come to Dublin, not of her own accord, five years earlier and remembered this smell that seemed peculiar to Dublin. With three thousand souls living cheek by jowl here, the city ought to have smelled more offensive. But there was always a breeze in Dublin, especially near the water, as they were, which made the city smell cleaner than it should, like the sea when the wind was up.

"I'm already starting to feel better." She looked up at her husband. "We may have to live permanently in Ireland, my love. How am I going to make that trip again?"

"Don't think about it. Perhaps one of the healers here has a better remedy for your nausea than any had to offer you in Wales. This is a city of seafarers after all."

"Which probably means all of them are better sailors than I am!"

"Don't be so sure. I imagine many a Dane has been embarrassed to admit he doesn't feel the call of the sea and sought a way to disguise his sickness." Gareth kissed the top of her head. "Your color is starting to return."

As she took in another breath, Gwen realized he was right. For the first time since she set foot in the boat the previous morning, she didn't feel like she was going to vomit. She even managed a few sips of water from the skin Gareth gave her. Various people had told her over the years that if only she were to sail more often, her seasickness would abate, which made her feel as if they thought her inability to manage sailing without vomiting was somehow her own fault. It hadn't escaped her notice that such claims were never made by people who actually suffered from seasickness.

What was her own fault was getting on the boat in the first place, even knowing what it would be like. At least she wasn't pregnant like Evan's wife, Angharad, which had precluded her from coming at all. Gwen had been bound and determined to attend the wedding, regardless of the personal cost.

But that was over for now, and she allowed Gareth to help her to her feet. Their daughter, Tangwen, now a precocious three and a half, had disembarked as well, followed by their new nanny, Marged, holding nine-month-old Taran. While their servants who had traveled with them, Beric and Sian, saw to the luggage, Gwen's adoptive son Llelo bounded down the dock. Llelo's brother, Dai, now squire, servant, and general underling to all six of Prince Hywel's Dragons at once, had sailed in Prince Hywel's ship. At sixteen and fourteen respectively, the two boys had become men and embarked on their chosen pathways. Though, as Gwen knew from her own life, only God knew to what end.

Godfrid, bless his heart, had known what the crossing of the Irish Sea was going to do to Gwen and had planned accordingly. He'd sent a ship to collect Gareth and Gwen, sail across the Irish Sea, and when they reached Dublin, to dock several slips down from Prince Hywel's boat, which even now was gliding expertly into place. That was where Godfrid, Conall, their men, and a small crowd of onlookers had gathered to greet the travelers. Only two of the Dragons, Steffan and Aron, had sailed with Gareth and Gwen, while the rest had found berths on Hywel's boat.

With luck, Gwen herself would be entirely ignored until she had a chance to catch her breath and change her appearance to one that was more acceptable for the wife of Prince Hywel's seneschal. With his elevation in status, Gareth had become a lord and she a lady. It was daunting for the daughter of a bard, no matter how renowned. Godfrid had asked that Gwen and Hywel sing at their wedding, and Hywel had composed a song specifically for the two of them to sing together. For once, it was a love song that ended well. Fortunately, Gwen had three days to remember how to be a performer again.

Gwen was quite nervous as well about meeting Godfrid's wife-to-be, Caitriona, and she wasn't too sorry to see that Cait hadn't come to the dock while Gwen was in such a state. At first, when Gwen had heard Godfrid was getting married, she'd worried about the woman who'd finally managed to bring him to the altar. Abbot Rhys's description of Cait's wit and courage—and the fact that she was Conall's sister—had left Gwen breathing a little easier. But still, she would be sorry if they didn't end up friends.

Away down the dock, Godfrid greeted Prince Hywel with great ceremony and gestured that he should walk with him to the palace, which, if memory served, lay in the southeastern corner of the city. That was where Godfrid's brother, Brodar, the new King of Dublin, would be waiting to greet them—along with Diarmait, the King of Leinster and Dublin's overlord, who just happened also to be Cait and Conall's uncle. Cait wasn't quite a princess, but for the brother of the King of Dublin, she was more than close enough.

Gwen could just make out Conall, in large part hidden by the Danish prince's bulk, standing amongst the greeters, as befitting the representative to Dublin from the throne of Leinster. Both Conall and Godfrid were dressed in finery: Conall in a somewhat austere red and black and Godfrid in blue and gold to match his eyes and hair.

This afternoon, after the travelers had been given an opportunity to bathe, change, and rest, they would attend a feast held in their honor. All this Gwen knew because Godfrid had laid out the itinerary in a letter he'd sent with the captain of the ship. Godfrid's wedding to Caitriona was in four days' time, and he wanted everything to be perfect. If anything, he was overmanaging the situation, which was a side of him Gwen had never seen before. The Godfrid she knew best was full of humor and enthusiasm, in between bouts as one of the fiercest warriors Gareth had ever met. Gwen was looking forward to seeing him as a doting husband.

Everyone from Gwen's ship deliberately held back to allow the royal retinue time to leave the dock. But—really to nobody's surprise—Godfrid couldn't maintain the formal façade, even for the time it took to reach the city gate. He glanced back, spied Gareth and Gwen, and reversed course. His long legs ate up the hundred feet between them, and before Gwen knew it, she'd been lifted off her feet in a bear hug. Godfrid set her down somewhat more decorously than he'd picked her up, before enveloping Gareth in a similarly effusive embrace.

"My friends!" Godfrid's voice bellowed out from his barrel of a chest, to be heard all across the waterfront. "It's been too long."

Then, instantly moderating his volume and tone, he crouched in front of Tangwen, who was looking up at him with big brown eyes, and poked her gently in the tummy.

"And who is this gorgeous girl?" He spoke in accented Welsh, but understandable enough to everyone in the party, including Tangwen.

Tangwen's hands went to her belly. "Tangwen."

"I'm very pleased to see you again, Tangwen. You probably don't remember me, but I remember you!"

Then, melting the hearts of everyone watching, Tangwen reached out a hand and tugged on the point of Godfrid's blond beard, prompting a chuckle from the big Dane. He touched her nose gently with his finger and then rose to his feet, his other hand resting gently atop Tangwen's brown curls. His eyes went to Gareth. "You will be beating the men off with sticks in a few years."

"I won't be limited to sticks, my friend." Gareth rolled his eyes. "You are joining the ranks of married men. It won't be long before you have a daughter of your own."

"God willing!" Godfrid swept out his arm. "Come! You will be staying at my house while you're here." He bent to Gwen. "Caitriona can't wait to meet you."

"And I her!" Gwen looked up at him. "Abbot Rhys sends his regrets that he was not able to come, but he didn't want to leave his brothers to their own devices again so soon."

"Or, to tell you the real truth, Abbot Rhys feared his prior was getting too comfortable in his seat and too sure of his own rightness to oversee the monastery." Conall had been standing next to Prince Hywel, waiting patiently a few paces behind Godfrid, and now he stepped forward to greet Gareth with slightly less exuberance than

Godfrid, if only because nobody could match the prince for enthusiasm. He had a kiss on both cheeks for Gwen.

Happily, Gwen was feeling better with every step she took away from the boat—better enough, in fact, to take Tangwen's hand and walk with her underneath the gatehouse tunnel and into the City of Dublin itself.

At that point, however, Godfrid and Hywel, who were leading the group, with Conall and Gareth just behind, pulled up short due to the arrival of a man in churchly garb. The newcomer's hair, which was so blond it was almost white, was cropped close to his head and untonsured, indicating he was either a novice (meaning he had not yet taken his vows), or wasn't actually a monk. He stopped several paces away from the princes, breathing hard.

"Prince Godfrid," he said through heavy breaths, even bending forward to put both hands on his knees. He spoke in French, seemingly because he knew he was talking to a mixed audience. "Please pardon me, I have come from Bishop Gregory. He asks that you bring your companions to the cathedral. He is in need of them."

"My companions?" Godfrid looked bewilderedly around. "Does he mean Lord Conall? Or Prince Hywel?"

The priest managed to stand upright, and he gestured towards the cluster of Godfrid's companions who filled the street behind him. The number included not only Gareth and Gwen and their family and retainers, but Prince Hywel and his Dragons, plus various members of Godfrid's own guard.

"He understands you are today greeting Sir Gareth the Welshman and his wife. It is their presence he is requesting." Then he switched languages to Danish, which Gwen little understood, but she could grasp his last few words, even in his lowered tone. "It is a matter of a dead man."

2

Day One
Gareth

Gareth didn't understand much Danish, but he understood *død mand* well enough and barked a laugh before he could stop himself. "Of course it is."

Conall moved closer to Gareth. "He said they've found a dead man."

"So I gathered." Gareth shook his head.

Godfrid, however, glared at the priest. "You can't be serious. They just arrived."

"I'm sorry, my lord. I am only doing as I was bid."

After Conall translated, Gareth put out a hand to his friend. "It is all right, Godfrid. This happens to us with some regularity."

Godfrid put out his chin. "Not in Dublin."

"Admittedly, that is true. I did not encounter a dead body the last time I was here. I *wish* I had."

As soon as the words were out of Gareth's mouth, he wished he could take them back, but it was too late. The joke was inappropriate. Death wasn't something to be jesting about, not unless one was about to go into battle. And especially not when the young priest was looking at him so urgently.

Still, he couldn't mistake the snort of laughter from Hywel, who knew the dead man Gareth would have liked to have encountered was Hywel's treacherous uncle Prince Cadwaladr, King Owain's younger brother.

Five years ago, Cadwaladr had turned to Dublin for mercenaries willing to kill a king and undermine Owain's rule of Gwynedd. Prince Hywel's grandfather, Gruffydd ap Cynan, had been born in Dublin. Through him, the family was descended both from the great Danish king, Sitric Silkbeard and the even greater High King of Ireland, Brian Boru. Hywel's mother, who'd died at his birth, had also been Irish.

Gareth had traveled to Ireland with Hywel in the early days of their relationship, but neither had ever been to Dublin nor met Godfrid before Cadwaladr had arranged for Anarawd's assassination.

In point of fact, however, none of them had dealt with a murder in many months. But Gareth was only speaking the truth when he said this kind of thing happened to him and Gwen every time they traveled, and Gareth's laugh had been more about the inevitability of being summoned rather than reflecting real amusement—or even surprise.

The cleric had understood nothing of what they'd said, since they'd been speaking Welsh, so Gareth now held his hand out to him and switched back to French. "I am Gareth the Welshman. Of course we will come. Please tell the bishop we are on our way."

If Bishop Gregory hadn't requested Gwen as well, Gareth would have sent Llelo to escort her and the children to Godfrid's house while he continued to the cathedral on his own. But her color was better than it had been in two days, and when he opened his mouth to suggest she leave this to him, her eyebrow arched at what he was going to say. In the end, he closed his own mouth rather than make himself look foolish.

Having dismissed the churchman to run ahead to the bishop with the news of their approach, Conall turned to Godfrid. "My friend, your brother is waiting. It would be no trouble for me to introduce Gareth and Gwen to the bishop while you continue to the palace with Prince Hywel. I speak French, Danish, and Welsh all well enough that we should be able to manage."

The look of consternation that crossed Godfrid's face was almost comical, indicating he was torn between his princely duty on the one hand and the possibility of adventure, even if grim or macabre, on the other.

With a similar amused look, one Gareth had seen on his prince's face more times than he could count, Hywel clapped Godfrid on his beefy shoulder. "I have long experience leaving these two to their own devices. Murder is not for us to investigate—not this time, or at least not in this moment when we have so many able companions upon whom we can rely. We should do as Conall suggests. Your brother awaits us."

Only then did Godfrid acquiesce. While one of Godfrid's men led Gareth's servants and children directly to Godfrid's house, the rest of the large party set off down the main street from the dock gate at a faster pace than they would normally have taken, not wanting to keep the bishop waiting. Under normal circumstances, Gareth would have liked to gawk a bit at the city around him. There would be time for that later, hopefully.

For now, they didn't have to diverge immediately. Nothing was very far away from anything else in Dublin, and the cathedral was a stone's throw from Brodar's palace, so they could all walk most of the way together.

"The two of you look well." Conall was taking long strides, but he still managed to look both Gwen and Gareth up and down as the three of them kept pace behind Godfrid and Hywel. "I see Gwen survived the crossing."

"Barely," Gwen said with a twist to her mouth.

Conall laughed.

And, all of a sudden, the uncertainty and awkwardness that was a natural consequence of being apart for more than a year—and being faced with a murder within moments of their arrival—dissipated like mist on a sunny morning. They'd been through too much together for it to have lasted long anyway, and Conall's laughter had been because he appreciated Gwen's wit, not because he was mocking her seasickness.

Gareth reached forward to put a hand on Godfrid's shoulder. "When we learned from Abbot Rhys that you and Conall had met and become friends, we couldn't have been happier."

"And then to learn that Godfrid was marrying Conall's sister!" Gwen gave a little skip, which told Gareth how much better she was feeling. Dead body or no dead body, he could understand her exuberance, given how sick she'd been up until a quarter of an hour ago. "Abbot Rhys told us a little, but we long to hear the full story as to how that came about."

"It involved a murder, naturally," Godfrid said.

"As it would." Gareth spoke more gravely than he might have a quarter of an hour ago as well. "And we have barely set foot on Dublin's dock when we are summoned by Bishop Gregory to look at a body. How is it possible for him to have summoned us by name? How did he know to do so?"

Godfrid spread his hands wide, turning fully around to walk backwards up the street. "It is no secret you are a friend and were to have arrived today from Wales for my wedding."

Conall's lip curled in amusement. "Your reputation has preceded you, even in Dublin. You can't be surprised."

A grin spread across Hywel's face, one Gareth was very happy to see. These past months the prince had been less light-hearted, carrying the weight of Gwynedd on his shoulders more and more, burdened by the effort to take away some of his father cares and desiring to prove himself. Now, when he smiled, he looked again like the Hywel of old.

"Do you still not know your own reputation, Gareth? The churchman who came for you spoke of *Gareth the Welshman*. I imagine your name precedes you to every castle from here to France. You saved the life of Prince Henry of England. Twice. King Stephen himself might call on you were he not at odds with my father. Even then, he might seek your help if he had a murder on his hands none of his men could solve."

"As Conall, Cait, and I are not in a position to be called upon, I do find it interesting that he sent first for you, rather than Holm, Dublin's sheriff." Godfrid rubbed his chin and turned back around. They were almost at the church, the tower of which was visible throughout the city. "I might have to smooth some ruffled feathers in that quarter later this evening."

Gareth took in a breath. He was not displeased to find his reputation had preceded him across the Irish Sea, but he was far less pleased to learn he might be stepping on someone else's toes. He always tried to maintain a good relationship with whatever local men might normally enforce the law. An uphill battle with a slighted sheriff before Gareth even had seen the body was not a good way to start.

"If murderers were smart, they would run when they learned Father was coming rather than commit the evil deeds they planned." Dai was walking beside Cadoc, the resident archer in the group, who'd taken the young man under his wing.

"Is this your doing, Godfrid?" Gwen asked.

"You forget that five years ago it was a band of men from Dublin who ambushed King Anarawd," Godfrid said. "Gareth led the defense of the caravan escorting Anarawd's body to Aber, and he himself came to Dublin in pursuit of you, Gwen. Your subsequent exploits have not gone unnoticed, even here." He turned to look at Llelo. "And now I hear you are apprenticing in the family trade!"

Llelo bent his head and said quite formally, as was his wont when the subject of his apprenticeship came up. "I am, my lord."

They had reached the church gate. Beyond, the churchman who'd come to find them was waiting for them in the porch. Gareth squared his shoulders, accepting what he couldn't change. Death was always with them, and he and Gwen would always do their best to see that a murderer, if murder was the cause, was brought to justice.

With the promise they would meet up again at Godfrid's house, Gareth, Conall, and Gwen said goodbye to the two princes and turned through the gate that led to the Cathedral of the Holy Trinity, known locally as Christ's Church, which Gareth remembered from his previous visit to Dublin during the aforementioned events five years earlier.

The church itself wasn't as magnificent as some of the fantastical Norman constructions Gareth had encountered in England, but it was certainly larger than average, as befitting a bishop. It was within Dublin's city walls, which meant space was at something of a premium. The graveyard to the south of the church building was full of headstones and looked to be running out of room, and the residential complex, with the dormitory and the cloister, overlooked the city to the west of the church, with only a narrow pathway between the buildings and the churchyard wall.

Conall seemed to be in a speaking mood, and regaled them as they entered the yard. "Since the Council of Reims in March, convened by the pope himself, Bishop Gregory has been working to reform the bishopric, even going so far as to include it within the dominion of the Irish Church rather than Canterbury. Just since Brodar became king three months ago, Bishop Gregory has brought in Benedictine monks to serve as caretakers for the church and the diocese. The bishopric lays claim to many acres of land surrounding Dublin, which these monks now oversee at the behest of the Christ's Church."

Gareth had heard something of what the council had decreed from Abbot Rhys but didn't know the rest. "Where did the monks come from? Are they Irish?"

Conall barked a laugh. "Not if Gregory can help it."

Before Conall could expand further on the topic, about which he obviously knew a great deal, the churchman came forward from the porch.

He bowed first to Conall and said, "Lord Ambassador. My apologies for my initial haste and failure to greet you as I should have." Then he looked to Gareth. "Thank you for coming, Lord Gareth." This was all respectfully done in French, which Gareth assumed he'd be speaking predominantly from now on.

It was a commentary on Gareth's reputation that Bishop Gregory would call upon him even if they were going to be disadvantaged throughout the investigation by their lack of Danish. And then his stomach twisted for a moment at the idea that their lack of Danish was *why* they'd been called upon. For now, he put the fear aside, not wanting to prejudge anything or anyone before he'd even seen the body.

Then the churchman put a hand to his chest. "I am Father Arnulf, the bishop's secretary. If I can do anything for you while you are here, you have only to ask."

Gareth eyed him, reassessing. If he was known as *Father* then he was a priest, not a monk, so not among the new Benedictines who'd been brought in a few months ago. "I can't say it is my pleasure, but I am pleased to be of service to the bishop if I can."

Arnulf bent his head again. "Bishop Gregory awaits you in his private chapel." He hesitated, his eyes going to Gwen and then back to Gareth. "Perhaps Lady Gwen would like to wait in the warming room?"

Gwen gave him a gentle look. "You were the one who said the bishop had asked for me as well."

He'd been looking hopeful, but now his face fell. "He did." And such appeared to be Gwen's reputation too that he didn't argue and instead gestured them through the great doors of the cathedral.

The difference between a church and a cathedral had nothing to do with a building's size. It was all about prestige. A church was called a cathedral when it was the seat of a region's bishop. The Dublin Danes had been Christian since before the Cathedral of the Holy Trinity was built over a hundred years earlier, having become so after Sitric Silkbeard made a pilgrimage to Rome. But the Bishop of Dublin, with Gregory as the most recent occupant of the office, had been ordained in Canterbury rather than Armagh, a deliberate snub to the Irish Church—and an allegiance which apparently was now being reassessed—at the request of the Pope himself, no less.

From the few comments Gareth's friend Abbot Rhys had made on the matter, the pope was hoping the inclusion of the Danes among the Irish bishoprics and parishes would further encourage the reform—and conformity—of the Irish Church to the strictures, precepts, and traditions set by the pope and the Roman church. He wanted the same thing for Wales—though, if Abbot Rhys had anything to say about it, he wasn't getting it any time soon. Gareth couldn't help his stir of pride at the strength of his people. They would not bow so easily to foreign custom and law.

To Gareth's eyes, the cathedral and surrounding buildings looked very much like a monastery, rather than the seat of a bishop. He knew of two such seats in Wales and had been to both: the bishopric of Dewi Sant in Pembroke and the seat of the Bishop of Bangor in Gwynedd. Now that the Normans had taken over Pembroke, they'd consecrated a new magnificent cathedral and what could only be called a palace for the bishop, replacing much of what had been Welsh with that which was English—as the Danes had done with what had been Irish.

If asked, Gareth would have said he cared very little about church politics, except that he cared very deeply for his people and their way of life. He imagined the Irish felt the same. But because both Conall and Godfrid liked Bishop Gregory, for now Gareth could put aside his own private assessments and thoughts and focus on the task at hand. All murdered men deserved justice and were equal in the sight of God, no matter before which king they'd bent the knee.

Bishop Gregory was waiting for them two-thirds of the way down the church. Conall introduced Gareth and Gwen, leaving out Llelo, who as usual was acting as their retainer. Llelo wouldn't take offense, since he'd been silent in the presence of great men before and knew not to speak or call attention to himself unless spoken to.

"Thank you for coming so immediately." Bishop Gregory was a small man, no more than an inch or two taller than Gwen, with kindly eyes, which today were clearly grieved. Past sixty years old, he was mostly bald, with tufts of white hair remaining above his large ears.

He stood in front of the altar that split the cathedral and separated the eastern choir, which was the province of churchmen, from the nave, where the common people worshipped. The cathedral in Bangor in Gwynedd was roughly the same size, but either would have fit into the nave at St. David's (the new Norman name for Dewi Sant). While normally there were rules about where in the cathedral a layman like Gareth could go, today Bishop Gregory simply motioned them past the altar to the eastern end of the cathedral, underneath the great stained glass window that would have admitted the light of the rising sun on the equinox. "This way."

In addition to the sunlight coming through the windows, the cathedral was lit by dozens of candles in candelabra. Bishop Gregory went to a smaller one, with three candles half burned down, and picked it up. He himself then led them into the darkened vestry, the place where priests gathered to dress in their vestments and where the holy relics for the cathedral were kept, and then through a narrow doorway in a side wall.

Although the passage he led them down was open, it could be blocked by a wooden door which Gareth couldn't help hesitating in front of. Made of an unknown dark wood, it bore ornately carved scenes from the Bible.

Behind him, Arnulf said, "It's beautiful, isn't it?"

Gareth could only agree, and as he followed the bishop through the doorway, he realized they'd stepped back in time. Beyond the doorway were five steps down, which led to an unlit stone passage so narrow Gareth's shoulders almost touched the walls on either side. They had to navigate it single file. At the end of the corridor was another ornately carved door, this one closed. When Bishop Gregory reached it, he stopped with his hand on the latch, said a prayer in Latin under his breath, and crossed himself.

Then he opened the door to reveal a small chapel, perhaps eight feet wide and ten long, with a single window above Gareth's height in the eastern wall. As in the corridor, the flagstones had been smoothed by centuries of feet and even hollowed in places, and a clear path forward to the altar had been worn into the stone. The walls were stone as well, whitewashed to add a brightness to the room that was otherwise lit by candles in sconces on the rear wall and two more candelabra.

And upon the simple stone altar lay a man dressed in the full warrior gear of a knight, including mail armor, a white surcoat with a red cross, such as worn by Templars, and a two-handed bastard sword clasped to his chest.

Gareth didn't need the bishop's grave expression to know the man was dead.

3

Day One
Conall

Gareth passed Bishop Gregory and went right up to the body, putting a hand first to the man's neck to feel for the absent pulse, and then resting his hand flat on the corpse's chest.

"I did check." Bishop Gregory made a helpless gesture with one hand. "Every instinct told me I should have my flock remove him, but I thought you needed to see him as I found him."

"Thank you for refraining." Gareth dropped his hand and looked at the bishop. "How long ago did you find him?"

"About an hour."

Conall had let Gareth enter the room first, since he was the professional investigator. And really, Conall saw no reason to get too close to the body just yet. He was more focused on the beautiful little church, which was clearly ancient, and it dawned on him that this must be the first church to be located in Dublin, built by the monks who'd established their community on this spot centuries before the Danes had come to Ireland.

At that time, a very different monastery had been associated with this little church. In fact, Conall recalled from the stories told at night in the hall where he'd grown up, that the Danes had sacked the community multiple times in their initial raids on Ireland, before deciding it was the best place to build their settlement and evicting the Irish monks entirely.

That was how the stories went. In all likelihood, the surviving monks had fled long since, having learned the lesson, belatedly and painfully, that they could not oppose a Viking landing party and live. Ancient buildings and sacred relics aside, monks were no use to anyone—God or man—dying on the end of a Norse blade. Farther inland, the monastery at Kells had chosen to maintain their position, but in so doing had built a high tower, from the top of which it was possible to see for miles in every direction. Its purpose was to provide warning of the Vikings' approach, giving the monks and villagers time to flee. That hadn't prevented Ottar, Dublin's previous king, from sacking the monastery and village three times. But the loss of life had been minimal.

Conall's Irish pride was rising to think of it—along with anger at the Danes who'd built their cathedral and their city over the ruins of this holy place. Conall had been sent to Dublin to help offset the generations of bad blood between the Danes and the Irish—and to evaluate how strong the sentiment against Leinster remained.

It was pretty strong, in truth, but not so much he thought his uncle had to fear rebellion—especially now that Godfrid and Cait were marrying.

But then Conall took in a breath and allowed his emotion to subside. Ottar was dead, and the Danes at Christ's Church were not responsible for the actions of their ancestors, any more than he was responsible for the deeds of his. The men of Dublin *had* preserved the little church, regardless of how they'd come by it, and Bishop Gregory was a man of God—who was understandably anxious about finding a body in so sacred a place.

The man lay like a king lying in state before a funeral. But even a king would be laid on a table before the altar, never on it. It mattered not at all that Christ's Church was a Danish cathedral, or that the bishop was Danish, or that he'd been ordained at Canterbury instead of Armagh. The altar was the site of the Holy Sacrament. It could be used for no other purpose. The sacrilege would reverberate throughout Dublin—and all of Ireland—when it got out. The only reason nobody knew about it already was because the church that had been desecrated was the little one hidden here.

Conall moved closer to the altar, infected by Bishop Gregory's anxiety and appreciative of his desire to remove the body as quickly as possible. Though the dead man's surcoat was akin to a Templar's, upon closer inspection, he was dressed less like a warrior monk or knight than a Danish king of old.

In addition to the massive sword in his hands and the afore-mentioned surcoat, his gear included a full mail hauberk and its padded gambeson, leather bracers on both forearms, leather pants, knee-high boots, and what could have been a real gold torc around his neck. Rather than a feather, his metal helmet sported two ram's horns, an arrangement that would be completely impractical in battle and something Conall had never seen before. Conall didn't know if he wore the horns as a nod to his Danish pagan ancestors or because he had a misguided notion that they were what a Danish knight might wear to war.

Gareth fingered one of the horns. "I've seen this done before. One of Godfrid's warriors had one made, though this is not the same helmet."

What Gareth wasn't telling the bishop was that he himself had once worn that helmet as a disguise when riding among Godfrid's men. Godfrid had made Gareth wear it in order to distract the English in Chester from his real identity. The idea had been that the English would have eyes only for the outlandish horns and wouldn't look twice at the face underneath them.

The deception had worked, though the aftermath had been disastrous. This had been before Conall's time, but he'd heard about it, from both Gareth and Godfrid. The events of that week had resulted in the death of Rhun, Hywel's elder brother, at the hands of their uncle Cadwaladr. The death had ripped apart not only Gwynedd, but King Owain's heart, and elevated Hywel to edling.

Godfrid's men were known throughout Dublin, and Christ's Church was near the palace. It wasn't impossible that the dead man had seen the helmet and copied it, having no idea of its tragic history. In fact, the more Conall thought about it, the more it seemed reasonable that might be the case.

But other than the gear, the man little resembled a warrior. He was shorter than Conall, more the size of Bishop Gregory, perhaps five and a half feet tall, without the bulky shoulders, legs, and arms one would expect to see in a man who'd trained as a fighter. It was as if the dead man had been a youth, playing at war, for all that he appeared to be approaching thirty. They would learn how accurate Conall's assessment was when they got him some place where they could strip off his armor.

"I am most disturbed that the body was placed here, in the very heart of the cathedral, in the holiest site in the city—to both Irish and Dane." Bishop Gregory's hands were clenched in front of him. "Especially with the wedding so close."

"I understand, believe me," Gareth said. "Even knowing nothing about this death but what I see before me, if I can assist in the discovery of how and why this man died, I will."

Everybody in Dublin was referring to the upcoming wedding as 'Godfrid's wedding', but to Conall and the Irish clans who surrounded the Danish kingdom, it was 'Caitriona's wedding'. An Irish woman was marrying a prince of Dublin, thus uniting Leinster and Dublin even more firmly than they already were. That ceremony would take place in four days—barely enough time to cleanse and sanctify the cathedral. The bishop would be loath to move the celebratory mass to another church, however. Christ's Church was Dublin's pride and joy. It wouldn't be fitting to marry Godfrid and Caitriona anywhere else.

Gwen moved to stand beside Conall and said in a low voice, "The fact that the body is in this position does send a very distinct message." It was just like her to have detected the undercurrents in the room, with little knowledge herself of Dublin's current politics.

Bishop Gregory overheard. "It is not a message I could ever imagine Harald wanting to send."

"So you know this man?" Gareth said, rightfully surprised the bishop hadn't opened with that information.

"He is Harald Ranulfson, a monk in the service of the cathedral. He was specifically tasked in the scriptorium, because his handwriting is so beautiful." Bishop Gregory paused. "*Was* so beautiful."

All of them allowed that thought to settle for a moment, and then Gwen said, "I know I don't need to point out that he is dressed as if he is about to go *a Viking*, not as a monk or a scribe."

Bishop Gregory fingered one of the horns on the helmet as Gareth had done, his face drawn and weary. "I could not tell you why."

"You are certain this is Harald and not, perhaps, a brother or close cousin?" Gwen asked.

"It is Harald." Bishop Gregory pointed to a large mole to the left of the dead man's chin. "I would recognize him anywhere. If we were to remove his gloves, I have no doubt his fingers would be ink-stained." He looked over at Gareth. "Do you have some idea how he died?"

"I apologize, your Grace, but I can see nothing amiss from here," Gareth said. "I will have to examine him before I could say more."

Bishop Gregory's expression turned even more doleful. "I suppose I should be grateful the altar isn't covered in blood."

"Is anything else awry or missing in here or in the cathedral itself?" Gwen began to circle the altar, ignoring the fact that it required her to enter the area of the chapel, as in the cathedral, reserved only for churchmen. As a woman and a member of the laity, it was a double offense. Conall was amused that Gwen didn't appear to care. As always, the investigation was all. If Bishop Gregory hadn't realized what calling in Gareth and Gwen entailed, he was learning it now.

Her question seemed to surprise Bishop Gregory, who understandably was entirely focused on the body, but he recovered after a moment and pointed to a bronze box on a little stand behind the altar. The greenish tinge aside, it had ornate carvings along its sides and had clearly been made by a master metalworker.

"The box contains our holy relic, a finger of Saint Patrick. Normally it is kept safe in a strongbox in the vestry. I don't know how it came to be here."

Gwen put a hand to her heart. "The relic is still in the box?"

"It is! After Harald's pulse, it was the first thing I checked."

Conall hadn't known Bishop Gregory ever to lie, but he wouldn't have put it past the bishop to have checked for the relic *first*. Dead body or not, monk or not, the holy relic was more valuable than any other possession—and more important to the Church than Harald's death. To have the little chapel defiled *and* the relic lost would have been a crime beyond reckoning.

"Who *was* Harald, your Grace?" Conall asked. "To you or to your flock?"

Bishop Gregory's expression showed regret. "Until today, I wouldn't have said he was anybody important." Then he put out a hasty hand, realizing how that had sounded. "He was of no more importance than any other man in the sight of God. As I said, as a monk, he worked primarily in the scriptorium."

"You said his handwriting was beautiful," Conall said. "Does that mean he was good at his job?"

"Very good. We have none other here to match him. Maybe none in all Ireland, though I would not proclaim such a thing to my Irish brethren."

"Was he well-liked?" Gwen asked.

"That I cannot tell you. I know each of the men here by name and face, but my duties preclude me from truly knowing many of them well, especially since so many are new to us and to Dublin. Harald came to us a few months ago with the other brothers of his order."

"From where?" Gareth asked.

"Most of the monks are Danish, from small priories between here and Waterford. We do not have so many houses that any could afford to lose more than one or two to us. We asked for those who could be sent and then quested farther afield." Bishop Gregory thought a moment. "I can tell you Harald was born in Dublin, but he found his calling in Denmark, and he was one of several who came to us from there. I suppose you could say his choice to join our number was a way to come home. His mother lives here still." Bishop Gregory paused and said in an entirely flat tone. "I must inform her of her son's death."

"And he was a monk, not a priest?" Conall asked.

"Yes."

"Inducted where?"

"In Ribe, having completed his studies there. He was one of the first of the Benedictines to arrive."

"The wealth represented in the sword, not to mention the mail hauberk, marks him as a rich man. Do you have any idea how he might have acquired his gear?" Gareth asked.

"No." Bishop Gregory wore his emotions on his face, and now he merely looked bewildered.

"You said at first that you discovered the body," Gareth said. "Just you?"

"Yes."

"Can you tell us how it came about that you found him?" Gwen said.

"Of course." He made a helpless gesture. "It was my usual time for prayers."

"Usual in what sense?" Gareth said. "Are you normally in this chapel at this hour?"

"Yes."

"Every day?" Gareth kept his eyes fixed on Bishop Gregory's face.

"Every day I am in Dublin, yes."

"How many other people would have entered the chapel before you today?"

"None." Bishop Gregory coughed into his fist. "It is the innermost part of the Church. None of the other priests say their prayers in here."

"In other words, you reserve it for your private use." Conall tried to keep the judgment out of his tone.

By the gentle look Bishop Gregory gave him in reply, Conall was pretty certain he hadn't succeeded. "I can see why it might appear that way to an outsider. But no one is forbidden to come here. Because the entrance is off the vestry, however, if a lay person wished to pray here, he would have to ask."

"What about a servant or a monk responsible for cleaning?" Gwen said.

"None are charged with this chapel. As a reminder that I am a man like any other, I take it upon myself to sweep and dust every week."

"Is that something most people would know?" Gwen finally turned away from the relic.

"I suppose." Bishop Gregory was more tentative in this answer.

When neither Gareth nor Gwen chose to press him on the matter, Conall spoke again. "*I suppose*, Father, or *yes*."

He still dithered. "I have to say *yes*."

Conall didn't have to ask the meaning of the look that passed between Gareth and Gwen behind Bishop Gregory's back at this admission. It was their practice not to assume anything about an investigation so early in the day, but even Conall could see the reason the body was here at this hour was because whoever had laid poor Harald on the altar had intended him to be found by Bishop Gregory. It was a message, as Gwen had said.

Bishop Gregory realized it too, and he spoke with a mix of awe and grief in his voice. "Someone wanted me to find the body. Someone wanted me to see Harald like this. Someone wanted me to know, *me personally*, that he had defiled my church. The killer."

"I would have to agree," Gwen said. "That is, if Harald was, in fact, murdered."

4

Day One

Gwen

Gwen realized her statement was provocative the moment it came out of her mouth, but it was too late to take it back—and she didn't want to anyway.

"What do you mean by that?" Bishop Gregory's tone showed irritation. "Of course Harald was murdered. How else could he have ended up here?"

Gwen coughed discreetly into her fist. "I apologize, your Grace. My intent was to suggest we shouldn't draw any conclusions as yet."

"Harald was in the prime of his life! I saw him crossing the courtyard yesterday morning. He was as hale and hearty as any man."

Gareth put out a hand, coming to Gwen's rescue. "What Gwen means to say, your Grace, is that there is some question as to how Harald came to be lying on your altar, and until we discover *how* he died, we can't make a judgement as to *why*."

Bishop Gregory made another helpless gesture. "I don't understand."

"It's just that he's wearing armor, Father." Gwen stepped closer. "And I can see from here that he wears a padded shirt under his mail."

"Yes, I see that too. I understand that would be normal."

"It is, your Grace. That's the problem—" she looked at Gareth, helpless herself to explain and worried that the more she spoke, the more Bishop Gregory was closing his ears. She appreciated the fact that Godfrid loved and respected the bishop, but he *was* still a bishop and unused to listening to women.

Coming to her rescue again, Gareth lowered his voice in that commanding but understanding way he had. "I have worn mail most of my adult life. I have also cared for friends and foes who died in battle. It is a struggle to remove gear such as he wears from a dead man, but with help, it can be done. But to dress a man who is already dead—"

"I didn't see it until now myself, your Grace, but I agree it is all but impossible." Conall reached out a hand to lift the man's arm.

Gwen had been tempted to do so herself, and would have if any more time had passed. But she could see from where she stood that the movement took effort, and the body was stiff with rigor. Though she chose not to speak the words out loud, everyone in the room but Bishop Gregory would know it put the time of death in the vicinity of twelve hours earlier. As it was just past noon now, that meant Harald had died near midnight or soon after.

Gareth was still looking into Bishop Gregory's face. "My lord Conall is correct, your Grace."

Gwen thought it safe to add, "To arm a man requires help. That's why knights have squires."

"My son, Llelo," Gareth pointed to where Llelo stood quietly just inside the door, watching and waiting to be of assistance, as he'd learned to do, "aided me in the matter before our boat docked in Dublin."

At Bishop Gregory's glance towards him, Llelo straightened his spine and took up the tale. For a young man of lowly beginnings, he had spoken in the presence of more than one person of power, including Prince Henry himself. Gwen thought Gareth was wise to point Llelo out to Bishop Gregory, since the bishop would find it harder to argue with four people telling him what he didn't want to hear, particularly when one was a clear-eyed young man with no stake in the proceedings.

"The gambeson lies close to the skin and has little stretch to it." Llelo spoke with the authority of one who knew what he was talking about. "It is a struggle to get my father into it every morning, even with his active assistance. Now that I wear armor myself, we help each other."

Bishop Gregory frowned. "Perhaps his gambeson is laced all the way up the back, like a woman's dress."

"It could be." Llelo answered again. "But then the mail wouldn't lie flat against the back, which is part of what makes our gear comfortable to wear all day and protective in the first place."

"What are you saying?" Bishop Gregory's eyes narrowed. "That Harald was alive when he put on this costume?"

"Yes," Gwen said, finding she couldn't remain silent. "That is what we are saying."

"But he didn't place himself here! He couldn't have!"

Gwen and Gareth exchanged a glance, and Gareth made a tiny motion with his hand, down by his right side, telling Gwen he would take care of this.

As Gwen had grown older, she was more impatient with not being listened to, but also more willing to let a slight go. She and Gareth were a team, and there was no shame in recognizing those moments when one or the other would do better questioning a suspect or witness.

Thus, Gareth gave Bishop Gregory's outrage the moment of respect it deserved, before beginning to guide his thoughts again. "When were you last in this chapel, your Grace?"

"Last night, moments before I retired. We have just begun to keep monks' hours here. I say mass morning and evening in the cathedral with the Benedictines, but I pray at noon and at bedtime here, leaving the other services to the prior of the monastery to lead." Bishop Gregory made a motion with his head. "The transition from priests being the custodians of the cathedral to monks hasn't been entirely smooth. Concessions have had to be made on all sides."

It was an admission he didn't have to make, but such was his apparent trust in them that he spoke without hesitation. Churchmen, as a rule, wouldn't come to blows. In fact, Gwen had never witnessed such an occasion, nor heard of one. It was unusual, however, to have a prior, rather than an abbot, lead the monks at a monastery. It was the bishop's job to appoint a monastery's abbot, even as the bishop was overall head of the community, as he was here. Perhaps they were still working out the details of their new arrangement and this was part of the conflict he was referencing.

"What hour would that have been, your Grace?" Conall asked.

Bishop Gregory puffed out a breath. "Nine in the evening, or thereabouts."

"Would there have been anyone in the church between then and dawn?" Gareth asked.

"Our brothers would have met for prayer after the midnight hour. As it is in the dark of night, the office would have been brief." Bishop Gregory made a gesture, indicating the entrance to the chapel, and a man a few years younger than he stepped into the room. Gwen didn't know how long he'd been hovering there and wasn't pleased with herself for not noticing sooner.

The monk was of medium height, a bit portly, with graying brown hair and troubled brown eyes. "I am Prior James. Harald did not attend Matins last night, and he was not in his cell."

"Was that ... usual?" Gwen asked.

"Of late, it had been. The elders in our community had been considering what to do about it. Some counseled patience. His brother had recently died, and his mother lives in the city. Many nights he asked leave to be with her." He made a helpless gesture. "It seemed reasonable not to chide him, but it is clear now he misled us about his activities."

Now Bishop Gregory swallowed hard. "I really was meant to find him, wasn't I?"

"I find it likely," Gareth said.

Prior James moved closer to the bishop, and such was the relationship between the two men that he put a hand on Bishop Gregory's upper arm in comfort. "I am sorry you were the one to find him." James turned to look at the others. "If you are agreeable, may I ask that we make no pronouncements as of yet about how Harald came to be armed as he is and particularly not how he came to lie on this altar?"

Gwen wasn't sure if James was speaking to all of them or just Bishop Gregory, but everyone nodded.

"That is acceptable to me, since we don't know anything about it as of yet," Gareth said. "I appreciate that you prefer not to speculate. That is my preference as well."

But then Prior James gripped Bishop Gregory's shoulder a little more tightly. The two men clearly knew each other very well, with much mutual respect. "Your Grace, if Harald arrayed himself thus and laid himself on the altar in hopes you would find him, that means he may have—" he broke off, thinking better of finishing his sentence.

Gwen wasn't going to help him, and neither was anyone else. They all waited while Bishop Gregory swallowed hard and his jaw firmed. Then he looked up and focused his eyes on Gareth. "As you say, we will not speculate. But I expect you to tell me the truth when you learn how he died—and why he died—whatever that truth may be."

"I will. I promise," Gareth said. "Do you have a laying out room where we could examine the body more closely?"

"Of course. I will arrange it." Bishop Gregory started down the aisle, clearly intending to set off on that quest immediately.

"It would also be helpful to inspect his belongings," Gwen said before the bishop could leave.

Bishop Gregory hesitated and looked at James, who answered. "Harald had a small cell, as does each monk, where he kept a few personal items."

"He didn't sleep in a dormitory?" Gareth came to stand beside Gwen.

"The dormitory holds the novices and monks newer to Dublin." James gestured to the bishop. "We are still working out some arrangements."

"Perhaps Gwen could be taken to Harald's quarters while Lord Conall and I see to the body." He glanced at Gwen, who nodded her agreement.

"Of course." Again Bishop Gregory took a step towards the door, and again it was Gwen who stopped him.

"Your Grace, just to be clear, it is your intent to charge us with this investigation?"

"Yes, of course."

"If that's the case, your Grace," Gareth said, finishing Gwen's thought, "we will have many questions—of you and of everyone else who lives and works around the cathedral."

"And that's just to start," Conall said. "What Gareth and Gwen are trying to do is warn you that once they begin, they will follow the investigation through to the end, whatever that end might be."

"In other words, you will be intrusive and relentless." For the first time, there was a lightness behind Bishop Gregory's eyes. "I did ask for the truth. My friends, I have heard enough about your investigations from Abbot Rhys and from Prince Godfrid that I would be disappointed if you gave me anything less."

5

Day One

Gareth

If Bishop Gregory's urgency hadn't been so contagious, and he didn't have the coming wedding to think about, Gareth might have called a halt to the entire proceedings, now the initial conversations were over, until later tonight—or better yet, tomorrow. The welcome feast at the palace would take place before sunset and was an event they not only *had* to attend, but Gareth *wanted* to attend. He was reminded too, by the discussion about armor, that he had hoped for a bath at Godfrid's house before he spent the evening in Brodar's hall.

Instead, he had a dead body to examine. And, truth be told, dead bodies were better examined sooner rather than later. If he got it out of the way, he could put off asking the hundreds of questions of reluctant witnesses until tomorrow.

He had allowed himself to hope, in the months since the death of Earl Robert and the subsequent events in Bristol, that he and Gwen might never again be called to the scene of an unexplained death. It wasn't that murder wouldn't still happen. That was as old as Cain and Abel. It was *unexplained* murder he was hoping to avoid. And really, if his reputation had spread as far and wide as Hywel claimed, murderers *should* know better.

Fortunately, these days, he and Gwen had a significant number of people they could call upon to help them. And, amazingly enough, most of them were actually in Dublin with them right now. Perhaps if they took the divide and conquer approach, they could discover whatever Harald's death was about and be done with the investigation by this time tomorrow.

Then he chastised himself for wishful thinking and getting ahead of himself. As always, they would face what was right in front of them and leave tomorrow's worries for tomorrow.

Only Llelo had been champing at the bit in the long months of quiet, thinking his grand plan to one day take Gareth's place as Prince Hywel's chief investigator would come to nothing, simply because any murderers in Gwynedd insisted on being open and stupid about their activities. Plus, with Prince Cadwaladr in France in the court of Prince Henry, the intrigue in Gwynedd was significantly reduced.

Gareth himself had also been busy with his transition from serving as the captain of Prince Hywel's *teulu*, his personal guard, to becoming his seneschal. It meant a shift in focus from the martial aspect of Hywel's life to one that encompassed more of a social and fiscal role. It had also made him a nobleman.

Though Gwen was busy most days with the children, he thanked God every day for her level head and the fact that her father had seen to her education as well as Hywel's. It was as if Hywel, by elevating Gareth to be his steward, was getting a second steward in the bargain. Gwen had learned to figure and read as a child (while Gareth had come to both as an adult) and for him both came less easily.

Not that he was occupied much in Hywel's counting house. It was more a matter of making himself familiar with all of Hywel's holdings, tenants, contracts, and alliances, and advising Hywel on every aspect of his life. The next step would be a return to Ceredigion to check up on Hywel's castellan there. Income had been down compared to the previous year, and it was time Gareth knew why.

He had hoped—they had all hoped—that the journey to Dublin would be a welcome break from their day-to-day cares. For him, being the steward to the edling of Gwynedd was a burden he'd never expected to bear. This week, Hywel hoped for a respite from *being* the edling of Gwynedd. In a way, they both were still getting a kind of respite: Bishop Gregory hadn't called upon Gareth as Hywel's steward. It was the investigator he wanted.

And what he would get, now that they were here.

While Prior James showed Gwen and Llelo Harald's sleeping quarters, Gareth and Conall set to work on the body in the laying out house. Gareth had spent countless hours in such rooms, large and small, sized for many bodies or only one. Some were dark, confined places, lit by a few candles and full of incense to mask the smell of death.

This particular laying out room, Gareth was happy to see, was more hospitable than most. It wasn't large, providing space for just two tables—one of which was empty and hopefully would remain so. But the roof was raised on posts two feet above where the top of the wall stopped. It allowed an abundance of light and fresh air to flow freely through the room without anyone being able to look inside unless they came to the door. In winter, it would be as cold as the outside, but with dead bodies to wash and dress, nobody wanted the room warm anyway. Gareth approved of the arrangement.

They started with Harald's sword, which Conall held up to the light from a lantern hanging from the ceiling. "Harald was a monk, which is not the type of person I would have thought would use—or ill-use—a sword."

Gareth stepped closer to look, and just the sight of the nicks and abrasions on the steel had his fingers itching to polish and oil it. A sword without a sharp edge wasn't useless, but it was certainly less useful. "One wonders if it was his personal sword—certainly unusual in a monk—or one he borrowed for the occasion. Did he fight with it? And if so, against whom?"

"All good questions," Conall said. "Regardless, it has not been cared for since it was last used."

"I'm inclined to think it was his own, to match the armor, and he didn't know what to do with it," Gareth said, "but that's my biases talking, and I should stop speculating now."

Together they turned to the man's mail. After some moments of struggle, punctuated by grunts from both of them, Conall said, "I would say removing a dead man's gear is just as difficult as we told the bishop."

"Thank heaven he isn't as large as Godfrid." Gareth glanced at his friend with an amused eye, taking in what he was wearing from top to bottom. "What about you? You're wearing neither sword nor armor. You're rather trusting of the Danish populace, aren't you? You don't think it's possible to be threatened on the streets of Dublin?"

Conall was a nobleman and had a martial past, as all noblemen must, but he'd chosen to deemphasize that history today in favor of what Gareth would characterize as 'court' clothing: shoes instead of boots, a robe instead of armor and tunic, and a knife with an ornately wrought handle at his waist, rather than a sword.

"These days, if someone is going to kill me, it is going to be in secret, with a knife in my back in the dark on the way to the latrine. That or poison in my wine. I confess, I think I would prefer the latter to bleeding out in the yard."

"Such is the power of the King of Leinster," Gareth said.

"Do I detect an acid note in your voice?"

"Not at all!" Gareth laughed. "In a way, I am commenting on my own indenture to Prince Hywel, though, as you can see, despite my new position, I am as fully armed as ever."

"Not enjoying your new employment?" Now that they'd managed to extricate Harald from his gambeson, Conall had turned to examining the contents of Harald's purse, which came to very little: a few coins, a wooden cross on a leather thong, and a tiny knife, like a man might wear within a bracer as a weapon of last resort. It was well-made, similar to those the Dragon Steffan carried on his person. Frowning, Conall laid each item for inspection on a nearby table.

"I am, actually, though Gwen will tell you I complain about it more than my previous job as captain of the guard." This time Gareth's laugh was somewhat more sardonic. "Book work is not my friend. I have two grown sons, and neither appears to want to assist me in *this* particular matter."

"That's what scribes and clerks are for. All you have to do is make sure your man figured right, not do the work yourself! Somewhere there is a smart boy who's terrible at the sword but doesn't want to join the church. You just have to find him."

Gareth looked at his friend curiously. "I wouldn't call you terrible at the sword, but by the tone of your voice, am I right in guessing you're describing yourself, once upon a time?"

Conall scoffed. "Book-learning wouldn't earn me the hand of any lady, not of any station that would have pleased my uncle. And though I soon realized war wasn't for me, the life I found was no better for women."

"So you have none."

"Ouch." Conall shot Gareth a piercing look. "We are marrying off Godfrid so now you think it's my turn?"

"A happy man wants all his friends to be happy too."

"I am happy." Conall gestured to the dead man, whom Gareth had stripped down to his underclothes. "What do we have here?"

Harald was as thin as Gareth had expected from the sight of him on the altar, and his hands as ink-stained as Bishop Gregory had promised. But his body told a different tale from that of a reclusive scribe who spent his days in the scriptorium.

Rather than being genuinely scrawny, Harald's arm and shoulder muscles were wiry, and his belly muscles stood out without an ounce of fat. Gareth was that fit, but this last year, maintaining it took a bit more effort than it had in his youth. While he still trained with the men of Hywel's *teulu*, it wasn't quite as often. Most men as they moved into middle age had to accept a bit of softening about the middle, but Gareth didn't think thirty-three was quite time for that yet.

Harald also sported a dozen bruises scattered all over his body, with the worst on his left side, as if he'd taken a strong blow to the left ribs. His left upper arm had a bandage wrapped around it. Peeling off the wrapping revealed careful stitching, indicating someone other than Harald had sewed up his wound. It wasn't that he couldn't have done it himself, and he apparently had a fine hand for writing, but the angle of the wound was such that it would have been nearly impossible for him to see, much less stitch, without help.

Though the wound might once have been deep, made with the sharp edge of a blade, it had been healing well. Infection hadn't killed him.

"So the armor wasn't just for show." Conall moved to the other side of the table and looked down at the body. "I'm revising your opinion about whether or not he knew how to use that sword."

"As I am—though knowledge didn't stop him from getting hurt."

"Nothing can stop that, as you well know. How many scars do you have, despite your gear?"

"Gwen could tell you."

Conall barked a laugh. "I think I'm safer not asking."

Gareth indicated the arm wound. "We need to speak to the person who tended him."

Conall took in a breath through his nose, his eyes sweeping across Harald's body from head to toes. "It's all very well and good for him to have these injuries, but I see no blood on his clothing. None of them killed him. Internal bleeding?"

"Could be, though if so, I would have hoped to see a spreading bruise across his belly." Gareth let out a *huh* sound. "I have a dead body in front of me with no idea what caused his death."

"His heart could have failed, though that's unlikely since he wasn't even thirty."

"I would have no way to tell that either."

"So what do we say to the bishop?"

"Nothing yet. It's too early to admit defeat." Gareth leaned forward and sniffed at the man's lips, which were closed, and then used two fingers to pry apart his teeth. More than one case had been broken open by what was inside a corpse's mouth. In this case, the alcohol fumes that billowed up had Gareth rearing back. "Whew!"

"I can smell that from here." Conall reached out a hand and pressed on the dead man's belly, sending another putrid waft into the air.

"And maybe we now know the cause of death."

Conall gingerly stepped closer to peer into Harald's mouth where more than just alcohol fumes had come up when Conall had pressed on the dead man's torso. "Did he choke on his own vomit?"

"I wouldn't say there's enough here for that."

"Then what? He drank so much he never woke?"

Gareth shrugged. "I've seen it before, though not often, thank the saints. Men simply lay down and die." Then he frowned and sniffed somewhat more delicately. "I don't recognize the smell of the drink, however. It isn't ale, wine, or mead."

Conall took a similar tentative sniff, frowned, and then said, "Give me a moment." He hastened from the laying out room.

He was gone long enough for Gareth to wish for a drink of his own, though since that wasn't forthcoming, instead he fully cataloged Harald's wounds and went through his clothes. Unlike the sword, the armor had been well cared for, with each link polished until it shone. Gareth himself would have been proud to wear it. If Harald had a squire, he should have been commended. It was Llelo's least favorite task.

Then Conall returned, bringing another man with him, dressed in a monk's robes. "This is the monastery's cellarer."

A cellarer was in charge of all food and drink in the monastery and was the third-highest-ranking monk on the premises. This man was of average height and weight, perhaps forty years old, and was in every way nothing out of the ordinary—except for his blue eyes, which took in the laying out room, the body, and Gareth with undisguised interest.

"How might I be of service?" And then he grinned at Gareth's surprised look, since he had spoken in fluent Welsh. "My father was Welsh. He came to Dublin as crew on a ship out of Llanfaes. He met my mother here, and she sailed to Wales to be with him. After he died when I was ten, she came home to Dublin, to her family." He put his hand to his chest. "You may call me Brother Madyn."

"I am very glad to know you!" Gareth looked at Conall. "Did you know he spoke Welsh when you brought him here?"

Conall was looking a little surprised himself, which gave Gareth his answer before he spoke. "Not at all. I wanted to ask him his opinion about what Harald had consumed."

Gareth gestured to the body. "If you will."

His eyes no more than narrow slits, Madyn approached and hovered for a moment with his face above Harald's. Then he stepped back, frowning. He put up one finger, silently asking them to wait, and left the room. This time, the wait wasn't as long, and he returned almost immediately, bearing a stoppered glass jar designed to contain liquids. The bottle was a nearly opaque light green that was almost white and could be carried by means of a rounded handle.

Madyn uncorked the jar, sniffed what was inside, and then brought the jar to Gareth. "If you can separate what is coming from Harald's mouth from other contents of his stomach, would it smell similar to this?"

Gareth sniffed, and the alcohol fumes were so strong his eyes watered, just as they had when he'd opened Harald's mouth. "Yes." He choked a little himself. "Definitely yes." The back of his hand to his nose, he asked, "What *is* that?"

"*Uisce beatha.* Or, as they say in Dublin, *whiskey.*"

Conall grunted, acknowledging he knew what Madyn was talking about.

Gareth looked from one man to the other. "What is that to someone who doesn't speak Gaelic or more than passable Danish?"

"It means *water of life*, an alcoholic drink distilled by monks throughout Ireland," Conall said.

Madyn nodded. "Though wine is preferred here at Christ's Church, whiskey is often used in the sacrament in more remote areas when wine isn't available, as it very often isn't."

"Harald was a Dane," Gareth said.

"Oh yes." Madyn gave a small smile. "Over the generations, the knowledge of how to distill whiskey has spread beyond the church. You don't have to be Irish to associate with Irishmen, as you well know, my lord. The Danes have been in Ireland long enough to have learned many Irish customs. As the cellarer, I am one of the few monks at Christ's Church who meet with the laity on a daily basis, though as you can see, we are wide open to the residents of the city. Any monk can come and go as he pleases at any time, provided he isn't expected somewhere else. While I can't confirm that any of my brothers frequent local taverns, I know for a fact that a man can order whiskey in several right here in the city."

Gareth rubbed his chin. "I have never heard of whiskey."

"You are Welsh. Your mead is the best in the world. Nobody would drink this when he could have something better, unless—" Madyn broke off, his brow furrowing.

"Unless what?" Conall said.

Madyn thought for another moment before answering. "Whiskey has other uses besides the Holy Sacrament and getting a man drunk. It alleviates pain, for starters, which—" he gestured to

Harald's body, still frowning, "—might have been Harald's reason to drink it. I hurt just to look at him. It isn't as powerful as poppy juice, but enough of it can make a man insensate."

"Where did what you have there come from?" Conall asked.

"We keep a little in the church, in the event the wine has soured or isn't available." Madyn lifted the stopper again to show them the contents. "As you can see, it is three-quarters full. It is the same level as when I last checked it earlier this week."

"So what Harald drank couldn't have come from the cathedral's stores?"

"No."

"But drinking whiskey *could* kill him?" Gareth asked.

"Like any alcohol, it could if he drank enough of it, and whiskey requires less than most." Madyn held up the bottle. "This amount would do it."

"How quickly would it work?"

"That is very hard to say." He gestured to Conall and Gareth. "You have known very drunk men before. Some behave quite reasonably up until the moment they lose consciousness."

Conall nodded. "Just this spring, I fought with men I could have sworn should be blind drunk and staggering, and yet they held the shield wall."

"I am no warrior," Madyn said, "but this is common among Danes, I think? Whiskey is no different from mead in its effects. Certainly, it can take some time for it to overcome mind and body. A surfeit of alcohol is a terrible, but not unheard of, way to go."

"So he could have walked to the church on his own and laid himself on the altar?" Conall said.

Madyn took a long look at the body. "As I said, it would depend upon how much time passed between drinking the whiskey and coming here. If he'd lived, he might not remember anything afterwards. But with the right circumstances and motivation, like the warriors with whom you fought, anything is possible."

6

Day One

Gwen

Gwen had spent an oddly large amount of time in monasteries over the course of the last few years, generally in the company of Gareth in his service to Prince Hywel. Very often, a monastery was the best place for the royal retinue to stay if the palace or castle, which the prince was visiting, was crowded. It had reached a point, in fact, where Gwen almost preferred staying at monasteries because they were the same in every land and she knew what to expect.

Even if she or her children occasionally were on the receiving end of a monk's disapproving glance, she could put up with a few sneers if it meant beds were warm and clean. In general, monks were afforded very few pleasures, so they made sure their food and mead were of the highest quality. And such was the daily sameness of their routine that having guests was a form of entertainment—especially those who, such as Gwen's father and brother, could sing. Gwen was going to sing at Godfrid and Caitriona's wedding, but it would be at the joining of hands itself. Having a woman raise her voice in song during mass was still viewed as a bridge too far.

She had only rarely been given access to a monastery dormitory, however. Christ's Church wasn't exactly a monastery—or had only recently become one—and Harald had a cell rather than a bed among his brothers in the dormitory, so she supposed today didn't count for that either.

Prior James himself had led her and Llelo here, and though it was clear he had business to attend to, he wavered in the doorway. "You will think we are very lax here, though I assure you we are not."

"Father, I make no judgments. Your brothers are grown men who chose this life. If one reconsiders his calling and chooses to step outside the bounds of the Church, that is not your responsibility. Each man is responsible for his own soul and what he does with it."

Prior James canted his head. "My lady, I apologize if I did not greet you as I should have. Do I detect a convent upbringing in your past?"

Gwen smiled. "My father is bard to King Owain Gwynedd, and I was raised at court. But you may know our good friend and companion, Abbot Rhys of St. Kentigern's Monastery in St. Asaph. I have learned much from him."

At the mention of Abbot Rhys, James's eyes lit. "I met him earlier this year. A wise man, and much given to deep thought. Please mention me to him when next you see him."

"I will."

He hesitated again. "I do not know how and why Harald came to be as he was. I am ashamed, in truth, that I don't know, and I wonder now what else has been going on at Christ's Church about which I am unaware."

"All men have secrets."

"A fact I should remember more." He bent his head. "I leave you to your work. Please seek me out if you need anything from me."

Gwen thanked him and turned back to the room. As had been her experience with residents of other ecclesiastical houses, Harald had few possessions. Even from the doorway, she could count his in a quick scan of the room: a basic rope bed with a straw mattress (monks didn't rate feathers), a bedside table with a cup and pitcher for water in the night, hooks on the wall for spare clothing, of which Harald had one robe and one undergown, a washbasin with a cloth for drying beside it, and three shelves containing underclothing, which would be changed daily, and a basket in which to put the dirty clothing once worn.

Throughout, the colors all came from the same palette of cream to brown. Gwen wondered why there were never green monks, or blue ones. Why brown, black, or white? If the natural world outside the door were any indication, God didn't have anything against color.

But if what she saw was all Harald owned, if he kept anything precious in the room, it was hidden.

Llelo had been waiting for her to finish her conversation with Prior James before he began to examine the room. "If the armor he wore was his, he didn't store it here. The sword neither."

"I can't see either going down well with the prior or Bishop Gregory," Gwen said, agreeing.

Then Llelo edged past her with an *excuse me, Mother*, and went to the bed upon which Harald had slept. He lifted up the mattress, and when he found nothing underneath, began to inspect the casing for holes.

While her son got busy with his knife at the mattress's seams, Gwen made a circuit of the room, including the small square window that looked north towards the Liffey. The dormitory and cells were on the first floor above the warming room and chapter house. Though the outside walls were built in stone, the floor was wooden, and she peered through a grate in one corner that allowed her to look down into the warming room. No fire was lit today, but in the winter, the warmth from the room below could provide heat for the bedrooms above. It was an ingenious arrangement, one worth copying.

The grate would also allow anyone above to eavesdrop on those below. Obviously, Harald had kept his secrets to himself.

"If he hid the sword and armor in his bed, uncomfortable would hardly describe it." Llelo grunted as he severed a thread and then pulled the mattress apart to the width of two fingers, not wanting to entirely destroy it if he didn't have to. "The prior didn't know about Harald's activities—unless he's lying?" He shot a questioning look at Gwen, who'd straightened and turned to look at her son.

"Never assume and all that?" Gwen nodded. "The objective is fine as far as it goes, but if the prior—or Bishop Gregory himself—is lying, then we are done for before we've even started. Whatever we find will be hushed up, and then why call us in at all? What would be the point?"

"To get to the truth?"

Gwen smiled at the way her son was so much like his father.

"Bishop Gregory did call you in," a new voice came at the door, speaking in French, and Gwen turned to see a beautiful woman with dark hair and green eyes that could have been gray had she been wearing something else but today matched her dress. She was looking at Gwen with a smile that was amused, curious, and pleased all at the same time. Then her smile widened. "I'm Cait."

Gwen had guessed that already and met her a few paces into the room. "Gwen."

They both paused a moment, and then Gwen threw caution to the winds and hugged her. It was Gwen's nature to be affectionate, and though she was unsure what Godfrid's Irish bride would find comfortable, she felt that an immediate connection between the two of them was necessary—especially with the way the plans for the day had been upended by Harald's death. "Godfrid is so happy. Thank you for making him happy."

Delightfully, Cait hugged her hard. "I've heard *so* much about you!"

"And I you." Gwen stepped back, and both women continued to smile. As Gwen had hoped, her hug had swept aside whatever formality and awkwardness might have colored their initial meeting. She gestured to Llelo. "This is my son, Llelo."

Llelo bowed. "My lady."

"It is a pleasure." Then Cait's smile dimmed a bit. "Though, naturally, instead of us meeting as intended at the palace or Godfrid's house, we are here—" she made a sweeping gesture, "—in the cell of some poor murdered monk."

Gwen made a helpless motion with one hand. "This seems to happen to us more than one might expect."

The smile was back. "So I've heard."

Llelo had straightened to greet Cait, and now he held out his hand to show both women a round wooden coin with the engraving of two crossed axes on one side. "This was hidden in his mattress."

Gwen frowned to see it. She had encountered a similar-looking coin in Shrewsbury as a marker to allow admission to a brothel. By following the coin to its source, they had ultimately discovered Conall and concluded that particular investigation—though not without peril first. The thought of Harald—a monk—visiting a brothel was so horrifying she didn't want to speak of it out loud.

Now, she looked at Cait. "Does the coin look familiar to you? Have you ever seen anything like it before?"

Cait shook her head, though somewhat hesitantly. "Not to look at, though of course I know of such things from Conall. I see from the look of concern in your eyes that you remember it well."

"Not to be indelicate, but are you familiar with the brothels in Dublin?"

"Familiar, no." Cait's lip curled. "I was pretending to be a slave for a merchant on the docks, however, so of course I am aware of them."

Gwen kept her tone level. "Do any of them acquire their patrons through the use of wooden tokens?"

"Not that I know—and I think I would know." At Gwen's initial question, Cait's expression had hardened, but now she paused, her shoulders dropped, and some of the tension left her body. "I apologize for the way I just reacted. You weren't questioning my knowledge of Dublin. You were merely making an inquiry."

Gwen gave her somber smile. "I have been to Dublin only once, and I don't speak Danish, so anything you can contribute would be helpful."

Cait let out a breath. "I am on edge. I didn't mean to take it out on you."

Gwen put a hand on her arm. "Godfrid, Conall, Gareth, and I have been friends for some time. We have saved each other's lives. You are new to us, and it's natural to want to belong and to want things to go well. You don't know me at all, but I can tell you with absolute sincerity that I will never deliberately say anything to offend you."

For a moment, Cait appeared not to know how to reply. Then she tossed her head and laughed. "Whereas I have a bad habit of speaking my mind before I've thought through what I'm going to say."

"So we should get on well together." Gwen grinned. "I'm glad you came, so we could get that out of the way upfront."

Cait wrinkled her nose. "When Godfrid and Prince Hywel arrived at the palace without Conall or you, I knew something wasn't right. I snuck out of the hall as soon as it was seemly."

The she laughed at Gwen's widened eyes. "Don't worry. Godfrid has set two of his men to watch over me. They spend most of their time loitering in anterooms and doorways. It can't be very exciting for them."

Gwen smiled. "I imagine you were used to going about on your own when you lived here as a slave. Gareth never lets me go anywhere by myself anymore, though I have more freedom now that I have my grown up son at my beck and call." She shot Llelo a grin too.

But he wasn't paying attention. While the women had been talking, Llelo had continued to work. He'd moved on to the bedside table, set on the far side of the bed, near the washstand. Gwen had been so focused on Cait she'd almost forgotten their purpose in being in the room.

Now, he picked up a scrap of paper, which had been kept in place by the wooden water cup. "Mother—"

The tension in his voice had Gwen moving around the bed before he'd finished his sentence with, *come look at this.*

The piece of paper was no more than a scrap, one torn from a larger paper, as evidenced by the uneven edge at the bottom. But while the paper was unexceptional, the words written on it in black ink were in exquisite penmanship, albeit in a language Gwen didn't read. Llelo couldn't read it either, and he wordlessly stretched his arm across the narrow bed towards Caitriona.

Cait stepped closer, her brow furrowing, and took the paper from Llelo. "It's a passage from the Bible, written in Danish: *Father, if thou be willing, remove this cup of suffering from me: nevertheless not my will, but thine, be done.*" She looked up. "It's a quote from Luke, but—"

She appeared as much at a loss as Gwen, who finished her sentence for her, "—but in this context, what does it *mean?*"

7

Day One

Gareth

It had been some time since Gareth had felt this particular rumbling in his belly. It was like being hungry, which he was, a little bit, but that hunger was mixed with excitement and tension too. They were on a trail now, and from the sidelong glances Conall kept sending him as they left the laying out room and walked towards the cloister, he knew it too. Madyn had already returned to his duties.

"You are like a cat stalking a mouse. You've grown silent and even your gait has changed."

"We have a mystery, my friend. And if I'm the cat, I just hope my prey is really a mouse, rather than something larger with bigger teeth." Gareth pulled up. "I'm wondering a few more things now as well, and I suspect you are too."

"Of course I am. You go first."

"For starters, and maybe completely irrelevantly, why didn't Bishop Gregory mention he had a Welsh monk among his brothers?

Why didn't Prior James say anything once he learned I don't speak Danish?"

"In the case of the Bishop, perhaps he thought I was adequate to the task. Or it simply could be he doesn't know Madyn. This arrangement with the Benedictines is new. In a way, I'm surprised he recognized Harald on sight."

Gareth considered that for a moment, and then caught sight of Gwen, Llelo, and another woman, who by her staggering beauty had to be Cait. They were leaving the building just ahead of them, so he waved and caught their attention.

While they made their way to him, he said to Conall, "Am I wrong to be sensing an element of discord between the priests and the monks?"

Conall raised one shoulder and dropped it as he watched the women and Llelo approach. "I am not a churchman. I attend mass when I can, but otherwise leave spiritual matters to them and to God." His eyes narrowed. "But I could see why there might be issues. You'll have noted the community has a prior only, and no abbot. The monks have taken over tasks that used to be performed by laymen in service of the priests, who remain in significant numbers here. When the priests had laymen working for them, the balance of power was straightforward: the laymen were servants. But monks are not servants, and even if priests aren't supposed to view themselves as superior to monks, many feel they are anyway. That attitude is unlikely to go over well with any of the monks here. These men are servants of man and God—but not of priests. They would view the differences in their habits and education as a matter of calling, rather than value."

"You know more about the church and churchmen than you think," Gareth said. "And maybe this is why the monastery doesn't currently have an abbot. Or why Bishop Gregory sent us Arnulf, his secretary who is also a priest, rather than Madyn, who speaks Welsh."

"Exactly. Even as bishop, he might feel as if he was treading on the monks' toes to instruct one of their number without first consulting with the prior."

"Who, again, does not have the authority of an abbot."

Conall grunted. "You weren't wrong when you suggested I might have been more scholarly than the average boy. My mother wanted me for the Church, and I attempted to please her for a time."

"You were a novice?" Back in the laying out room, Gareth had made a guess, but he was still staggered to learn he hadn't been far off.

"I never got that far." Conall shrugged. "Becoming a priest might have made sense at fifteen, but by seventeen—" he grinned, "—girls and my uncle intervened."

Then the women arrived. Conall introduced Cait to Gareth, and the five of them moved in silent agreement towards the wall that enclosed the church compound, near where the gravestones began. Here, each related what they'd learned and produced their discoveries. Though few in number, each had profound implications.

Gwen bit her lip. "The whiskey became, in effect, the *water of death*."

Conall studied the words on the paper. "Prior James was worried Harald might have killed himself, and though I was skeptical before, by this are we to conclude he did?"

"While the note wasn't left on his side table by accident," Llelo said, "if suicide was his intent, and he wanted to die in the church, where's his flagon of drink? Wouldn't he have brought it with him?"

"Is it even possible to die on purpose from drinking too much?" Gwen asked. "Even if you drank it all at once, likely you'd vomit it up, wouldn't you?"

"There was no vomit on the floor of the chapel," Conall said.

"Could someone have cleaned it up?" Llelo asked.

"I don't know." Gareth didn't like that he didn't. "If Harald drank an enormous amount in just the right amount of time, his decision to go to the church could have been made before he was so drunk he couldn't walk."

"People do all sorts of things they wouldn't normally do when they're drunk," Conall said.

Gwen shook her head. "But a declaration of suicide would have repercussions in this community and isn't to be lightly asserted, especially on so little information. He drank too much and died. He may have drunk himself to death on purpose, he may have put himself on that altar on purpose, but the why of any of this is hardly self-evident."

"Certainly he wouldn't be the first man who drank too much accidently," Gareth said, "and with his wounds, he may have simply been looking for relief from pain. I think we need to speak with Bishop Gregory again."

"I agree." While Gareth had been speaking, Gwen's attention had been caught by something off to the side, and now she screwed up her face and pointed to the wall near which they were standing. "Is that vomit over there?"

The expression of disgust on each person's face was identical. Conall took it upon himself to edge closer. "Yes." He bent a little nearer. "Fresh as well."

Llelo turned entirely away, his arms folded across his chest. "I, for one, am glad we have no way to match what's on the wall with what's in Harald's stomach."

Gareth chose not to mention he'd found some vomit in Harald's throat and was already guiding the women to a safe distance away, as Gwen was looking a little green again.

Caitriona eyed her for a moment and then glanced upward to check the location of the sun. "Is it really that time already? The feast is almost upon us!"

Gareth shot her a grateful glance. "Perhaps you two should go and prepare."

Gwen visibly wavered, reminding Gareth of Godfrid at the gatehouse, torn between duty and duty, so he added, "Cait *is* the guest of honor."

Gwen put her hand to her head. "I am so sorry! I almost forgot, and we have so much to do. I'm ashamed to be going about wearing something this dirty anywhere near a church as it is!"

"You look fine," Gareth said, meaning it, but then he had to laugh at the withering look Gwen sent him.

"You are no judge." She went up on her tiptoes and put a hand to his cheek. "And I love you for it." Then she tipped her head to Cait. "Perhaps it would be best if you and I adjourn for now and leave these men to their work. Llelo discovered both the coin and the writing. He's perfectly capable of speaking to the bishop of what was found in Harald's cell."

At first Llelo blinked at the accolade, a pleased look in his eyes, but then he nodded gravely, putting on the mask of maturity he wore now whenever he thought of it. "I can."

If anything, he took his duties too seriously, but Gareth knew where he'd learned to do so and could hardly complain about something he and Gwen had encouraged. As the eldest son in the family, it was natural that more was expected of him and a greater weight of responsibility ended up on his shoulders. Gareth tried to allow him room for play. But it was difficult, mostly because Llelo himself wanted more responsibility, and to deny him the opportunity to work as a man would end up making him feel belittled. Gareth well remembered what it was like to be a man by law but not quite be entirely grown up inside.

"Don't be late, brother." Cait shook her finger at Conall. "Godfrid won't want to start without you."

Conall glanced at Gareth. "Assuredly, we won't intend to be."

Gwen took Cait's arm as they started walking away, and Gareth heard her say, "They know. They'll do what they must."

"I am so glad they're getting on." Conall blew out a breath as he watched them go.

"Gwen was determined that they would. I imagine Cait was too."

"It is not in my sister's nature to be jealous, and she knows her own worth, but Godfrid did once ask Gwen to marry him."

Gareth had actually forgotten that fact. He had been insanely jealous himself when he'd learned of it, though it was difficult to be angry at Godfrid for long—especially when it was clear how much he cared for Gwen.

Conall must have seen that memory in Gareth's face, because he clapped Gareth on the shoulder. "You won her away, remember?"

"I did. Obviously, it was the best for all concerned." The men started walking towards the bishop's office, but when Gareth realized Llelo wasn't with them, he turned to look back. "Llelo?"

At sixteen years old, Llelo wasn't a boy anymore, but the expression on his face was comical in its childish horror. "Godfrid asked Mam to marry him?"

Conall's expression turned sheepish. "Sorry. You didn't know?"

"I didn't." Llelo managed to get his legs moving and caught up.

"As you probably could guess, this was during the time Cadwaladr stole her away to Dublin," Gareth said.

"But then you came to get her, and she married you instead." Llelo spoke with some satisfaction, but then he frowned. "If you hadn't, Father, would she have stayed in Dublin?"

"You would have to ask her that. Fortunately, I did come, and she didn't stay." Gareth's expression turned thoughtful. "From what she said at the time, even had I not come, she would not have stayed—or at least not yet. Her family and life were in Gwynedd. Godfrid had more wooing to do, especially since the relationship started with Godfrid throwing your mother over his shoulder and carrying her to his ship."

Llelo's jaw dropped again, as Gareth knew it would, which is why he'd told him that little tidbit.

Conall hadn't heard that part either, and he laughed out loud, though he instantly shushed himself and looked furtively around, not wanting to disturb the quiet of the monastery with laughter. "Really?"

"So I hear. This was immediately after Cadwaladr had announced from Aberffraw's battlements that she was carrying Prince Hywel's child."

Llelo was looking as if his head had just exploded, so Gareth grinned. "I can't believe we never told you this before!"

Llelo shook his head. "You didn't. Nobody even hinted of it, not even Evan!"

"He was there." And then Gareth deflated at the memory of what had happened after that: their archers had killed one of Cadwaladr's men when he'd attacked Rhun, and then Rhun and Hywel had summarily executed two more. It was in the aftermath of those events, after Gareth had gone south with Hywel to take Aberystwyth Castle from Cadwaladr's wife, that Gareth had climbed into the Viking ship to sail to Dublin.

Only Gareth and Evan had realized at the time what a momentous step that had been for Gareth. He'd known it was right—and wanted to do it—but he'd felt caught between love for Gwen and duty to Hywel. Standing on the beach below Aberystwyth Castle, Brodar, Godfrid's brother, had offered him a seat in his boat.

It had been one of those pivotal moments in Gareth's life—the choice to go *this* way instead of *that*—and it had shaped the course of the future from then on. As when Gareth had declined to remain in Prince Cadwaladr's service one more day, he'd known the importance of the decision at the time. It was why he urged his sons to do what they knew was right in their hearts, even if others wouldn't approve. Only they were answerable to God for their souls.

It was the other types of decisions, the ones where he chose by chance or at random or because he felt like it, where what was right was much less clear, that were most likely to haunt him. The meeting with Conall had been just such a decision in that he and Gwen had chosen to ride to the brothel outside of Shrewsbury after dark rather than wait until morning. Because they'd made that choice, they'd saved Conall's life. Had they not, he probably would have died—and thus, he never would have become the ambassador from Leinster, and Godfrid wouldn't have met Cait.

By such choices was a life made.

Now, standing in the yard of Christ's Church, sixty leagues and across the sea from Shrewsbury, he opened his hand to reveal the wooden coin.

"I know." Conall looked down at Gareth's hand. "I have been thinking of that day too."

"My first thought, of course, like Gwen's, was that a coin would gain admission to one of Dublin's brothels. If that is the case, it is troubling to think Harald visited one."

"Perhaps one of the guards at the brothel beat him up, and that's how he received all those wounds," Llelo said.

Gareth looked wryly at his son. "I can't say that notion is any less troubling!"

"Given our experience, it's a perfectly reasonable supposition," Conall said. "But, in fact, I haven't seen a coin such as this in Dublin, ever. I am not aware of any brothel that uses them."

Llelo asked, perhaps with innocence, "Would you be aware?" During the events in Shrewsbury, Llelo had been serving in the retinue of Prince Cynan, Hywel's brother. He hadn't been with Gareth and Gwen that week, but he'd heard about what happened and had met Conall in St. Asaph shortly after his rescue. Gareth didn't think his son had ever visited a brothel, but he'd been around fighting men since Gareth and Gwen had adopted him. He wasn't a stranger to the ways of men.

Conall lifted one eyebrow. "As the ambassador from Leinster, I have, of course, never frequented any such establishments. As Fergus the Sailor, however, it would have been remarked upon had I not joined my fellow sailors a time or two in their escapades." He eyed Llelo for a heartbeat. "If only to drink."

Gareth carefully avoided looking at his son. "How many brothels are there in Dublin?"

Conall thought. "Three, all within a block or two of the docks, to be more convenient for the sailors. Under Brodar's rule and at the behest of Bishop Gregory, slavery has finally been abolished in Dublin, which eliminated a fourth. As it was owned by one of Ottar's staunch supporters, nobody was sorry to see it go."

"But no coins."

"Not that I know. Ottar turned a blind eye to such establishments, and Brodar hasn't been on the throne long enough to determine what kind of threat they pose to our society, if any. Sailors frequent brothels, as you well know, and Dublin is the preeminent port in Ireland. Bishop Gregory certainly would prefer they were closed, but so soon after his victory against slavery, he isn't pressing to reform what happens on the dockside."

"What about the worthy wives of Dublin?"

"Like the church, for the most part they turn a blind eye. In truth, we are all used to doing that. The Danes held slaves for generations. Some of the whores were actually slaves, prostituted by their masters, and those that remain are merely slaves by another name."

On that grim note, it was time to see the bishop. They entered the cloister through the main doorway and followed the pathway around the central grassy space to the Bishop's quarters, which included an audience room, a private office, and his bedroom.

The young priest, Arnulf, who'd run to find them at the dock, was sitting behind a table going through a stack of papers. He looked up as they entered the room and immediately stood. "My lords! I didn't expect to see you again so soon. How may I help you?"

Gareth tipped his head towards the half-open door behind Arnulf. "We would very much like to speak to the bishop if he is available."

"Yes, of course. I will see if he is so disposed." Arnulf went to the door, knocked, even though it was partly open, and entered. He spoke muffled words Gareth couldn't make out, even were they not in Danish, and then returned. "Bishop Gregory would be pleased to speak with you."

They thanked Arnulf and filed past him into the room. It was well-appointed, with tapestries on the walls, heavy furniture, and a fire burning in a grate a few feet from the bishop. The room was illumined by light coming through a large window that faced the churchyard, as well as a half-dozen candles, making Gareth wonder how well the bishop was seeing these days to need so much light to read.

Once inside, Gareth closed the door behind him, not quite in Arnulf's face but solidly enough for his expression to turn to one of surprise. If the Bishop wanted Arnulf in the room, he could summon him, but their topic was a delicate one. Gareth would prefer for now to keep it amongst the four of them.

Then Gareth approached the bishop, who was also sitting behind a table, though his papers had been pushed aside in favor of a metal goblet containing wine and a tray of thinly sliced bread, butter, and cheese.

At their approach, he looked down at the food and said apologetically, "I missed my mid-day meal. While I too am invited to the palace in a few hours, I find in my old age I do better if I eat more small meals throughout the day."

"Please continue." Gareth himself could have done with some food, though he had learned it was best not to examine a dead body on a full stomach, which was why he hadn't asked for anything from the church's kitchen. They'd had the cellarer in the form of Madyn right in front of them, and he hadn't offered either.

"Father, we have some items to show you." Gareth drew out the wooden coin and the scrap of paper and laid them on the table in front of the bishop.

Bishop Gregory picked up the coin first, turning it over in his hands and peering at the carvings. "What is this?"

"We were hoping you could tell us," Gareth said.

Bishop Gregory shook his head regretfully. "I've never seen a coin like this one before. What does it buy?"

"We do not know," Conall said.

"I'm sorry I can't be of more help." Bishop Gregory then picked up the scrap of paper, his lips moving soundlessly as he read the words and then read them again.

"You know the passage," Gareth said, not as a question.

"Yes, of course. In it, Christ is praying for God to deliver him from what he must suffer on the cross." He looked up. "Why is it written on this scrap, in Danish of all things? Where did you get it?"

Gareth wet his lips. "The coin and the scrap of paper were found in Harald's room. The coin was hidden in his mattress. The paper was on his bedside table, held in place by a wooden cup."

"The implication, as we see it, was that it was meant to be found." Conall paused. "Possibly after Harald was gone."

Bishop Gregory's face paled as he came to the same, inevitable conclusion Conall had drawn in the yard.

"Is it Harald's script?" Gareth asked.

"Yes, yes. Of course it is."

There was no *of course* about it, but Gareth didn't contradict the bishop, who was distraught enough as it was.

"Harald wouldn't—" Bishop Gregory stopped, unable to complete the thought out loud. He looked up at Gareth. "You examined the body. Did he really die by his own hand?"

"It appears he died after having drunk a surfeit of whiskey."

The bishop let out a sharp breath. "An accident then."

Conall cleared his throat. "His attire was not, your Grace."

"No. Nor perhaps the location of his demise, though if he was as drunk as you say, he wouldn't have been in his right mind, would he have?"

"And someone could have helped him into the chapel," Gareth said. "We don't know enough at this time to make any kind of judgment about the *why* of it."

"I see. You just think now that you know the *how*." He looked into Gareth's face, his expression turning fierce. "Have you spoken of this to anyone else?"

"Only those of us investigating know of it."

"Good." Bishop Gregory nodded his head in a single sharp bob. "I must ask that you not bandy about anything you learn, not even to Prior James, not until we know more. Send them to me if they ask. Promise me you will not!"

Gareth studied him, not so much surprised at his adamancy as concerned that he would limit their ability to investigate the death. Still, he could not refuse. "I promise."

The bishop sat back in his seat, and his color instantly improved.

Gareth, however, could not let it go quite yet. "Even if we aren't to speak of why he died, and honestly, I agree that any conclusion is premature, we have to consider that Harald knew he was going to die."

The bishop's expression turned grim. "Else why leave the paper there, you mean? Else why write it?"

Gareth nodded. It would have been far easier if Harald had spent his days in some other fashion, counseling the poor, perhaps, or tending to the laundry. Many monks weren't literate and even fewer could write. Harald could do both, and the fact that he was a scribe and such an inflammatory note had been left on his bedside table gave greater weight to the idea that Harald had taken his own life.

If this death was a suicide, then it wasn't really Gareth's business anymore. A man couldn't be brought to justice if he was already dead—and had killed himself.

Gareth wasn't interested in antagonizing Bishop Gregory. He would have much preferred not to have been called to assist in the first place. But if Harald had arranged for his own slow death and laid himself on the altar in full armor, knowing that the bishop would be the one to find him, Gareth very much wanted to know why.

8

Day One

Gwen

Cait walked with Gwen to Godfrid's house, where Gwen found her family settling in. Marged had bathed the children, and Tangwen excitedly showed Gwen all over the house. Taran was happy toddling after his sister long enough for Gwen herself to bathe and change, after which he appeared in front of her, arms upraised, demanding to be fed.

It was Gwen's preference as well, so she swung him into her arms. A few moments later, she was ensconced in a padded rocking chair. And then a cup of mead, along with a roll dripping with butter and honey, appeared on the table at her elbow, thanks to Godfrid's servant with an unpronounceable Danish name, something like Pridborn, but not. Rather than say his name, she just thanked him.

She was stuffing the roll into her mouth when Godfrid came through the door, and the look of surprise on his face had her laughing. "Being a mother means I'm always doing several things at once."

He hastily rearranged his expression and came closer. "I am so glad you found the chair."

"This was your idea?"

"It was." Godfrid had a very low grumbly voice, and Taran was attempting to nurse and look at Godfrid out of the corner of his eye at the same time. Godfrid's voice always attracted Tangwen's attention too. "I confess, this is not a sight I have ever seen before in my own home."

"God willing, it will be the first time of many." Gwen was touched by his attention to her comfort. He had wanted everything to be perfect for their arrival.

He glanced around the room. "Is Cait here?"

"She went to Conall's house to dress for dinner."

"Then I can tell you. I feel I must tell you—" Godfrid pressed his lips together before speaking, and when he did speak, he'd lowered his voice so only she and Taran could hear. "She fears she will be unable to give me children. She had none with her first husband."

It was every new wife's fear. The judgment from others that came with the inability to conceive a child was terrifying and paralyzing. Many a wife had spent years on her knees, praying that it could be otherwise. Armies of women had gone to St. Gwenffrewi's well in hopes of achieving what was otherwise impossible.

"But you are marrying her anyway."

"I am."

Gwen smiled to know Godfrid was just as good and whole as he had ever been. "As I understand it, her first husband had no children at all. It isn't always the wife's fault, you know."

"*I* know that. But she worries." He shrugged. "I have accepted the possibility. Being together is more important."

"I agree, of course. Best not to worry. Best to take what God gives you." She gestured to the door and beyond. "We have two grown sons we never expected."

"That's what I told her."

"And really, you have to learn to master the fear because it doesn't end with conceiving a child. The next fear is that you can't give your husband a son, and the one after that is that the child won't live to grow up. It's never ending. But everyone has the capacity to have a family. We have adopted Llelo and Dai, and they are ours. Gareth will make dispensation for them equally with Taran."

Godfrid nodded, and some of the tension in his expression eased. "That is the Danish way too."

Gwen was glad Godfrid had shared his fears with her. "It's no wonder you were drawn to Cait. She's smart, beautiful, *and* tough. She lived as a slave!"

Godfrid laughed. "Don't remind me!"

Though Gwen had gone out of her way to build a bridge between herself and Cait immediately, Cait's beauty and station did make her less accessible. Gwen herself, especially as she was still nursing Taran and hadn't lost all of the weight she'd gained during pregnancy, felt frumpy and unattractive by comparison. Her husband said otherwise, but he was biased.

Still, there was nothing like nursing a child for making one feel good about the world. By now, Taran had fallen asleep in her arms, and she eased him away from her breast and adjusted her clothing before looking back to Godfrid, who'd chosen that moment to speak with his steward.

At home, she would have laid Taran on a pallet on the floor, but when Gwen arrived in Dublin and tried to suggest to Godfrid's housekeeper that she needn't trouble herself with preparing a bed raised off the floor for the three of them, the look of horror that crossed her face was enough to stop Gwen from speaking further.

Instead, Gareth had found a straight-back chair to act as a guard on the side of the bed, but even with it, Gwen didn't want to leave Taran upstairs by himself, not with the possibility of an unsupervised long fall to the floor below.

Once he was done conferring with his steward, Godfrid found a stool and pulled it close to Gwen, resting his elbows on his knees and studying her over the top of his clasped hands. "So, is it murder?"

"It could be."

"Was it someone I know?"

"His name was Harald Ranulfson. He was a monk who worked in the scriptorium. I genuinely don't know anything more about him except he was born in Dublin, and his mother still lives here. I confess the circumstances of his death are beyond strange." And she told him the details as fully as she could remember.

"A scribe, eh. That would be a good reason to kill yourself right there. To be locked away all day in a room transcribing documents and books ..." He shook his head.

"For you, that would indeed be hell on earth." Gwen laughed. "But Bishop Gregory did not perceive it was so for Harald. He had beautiful handwriting. And suicide is rare enough and so dire for a man's soul that every time it happens it must be questioned and not assumed, especially when the dead man is a monk who should feel in his bones that suicide is a mortal sin."

"I can't remember the last person to take his own life in Dublin. There are better ways to kill yourself without putting yourself outside the bounds of the Church."

Gwen's brow furrowed. "What do you mean?"

"I can see it might be different for a woman, but a man has options." Godfrid rubbed his nose. "He could make a mistake with an axe while chopping wood; he could fall overboard while out fishing; he could trip and fall off the wall-walk. Any of those methods would be aided by becoming insensate with drink, as you say Harald was. A man can come to grief in all sorts of terrible ways, none of which would prevent the priest from burying him in holy ground. But Harald dressed himself in armor, put himself on display, and left a note. Nobody leaves a note."

"Few can write," Gwen pointed out.

Godfrid made a dismissive gesture. "He *wanted* his death to be called a suicide. Why? To shame the bishop? To cause unrest in the monastery?"

"We still have no idea." Gareth came in the door behind Godfrid and approached, Llelo in tow. "And with all you just said, I am not convinced he killed himself." He paused and a curious expression entered his eyes. "It could be it wasn't he who left the note."

"Gwen said it was written in his handwriting," Godfrid said.

"True, but the quote was from the Bible."

"In Danish."

"True again, but I still can't help feeling maybe this isn't what it looks like."

Gwen's eyes met her husband's and they both smiled. It was only the first hours of the investigation, but this was getting to the meat of the issue.

Gareth now made a dismissive gesture with one hand. "Regardless, the bishop begged us not to speak of the possibility of suicide to anyone for now."

Godfrid bent his head. "That probably meant me too."

"I would rather not mar the lead up to the wedding with this anyway," Gareth said. "Harald died. How and why does not need to be booted about."

Godfrid rose to his feet and now hugged Gareth again. "I'm so glad you came. And you too boy—" He pulled Llelo into his embrace as well. Llelo had never experienced a full Godfrid hug before, and his pale skin reddened—whether from embarrassment or from being squeezed Gwen didn't know. He was of the age that too much affection from his elders made him uncomfortable.

Affection from girls was another matter, and though he'd just walked in the door, he was already eyeing Godfrid's steward's daughter, a blonde-haired, blue-eyed Danish beauty. Gareth had spoken to him on the subject of the local girls around their home on Anglesey and in Llanfaes, the palace on the Menai Strait where they'd been staying most recently.

As Llelo's color returned to normal, Gwen studied him, thinking of the coin and where the investigation of it might lead them. She knew of no brothels anywhere in Gwynedd. If they had to seek out the ones in Dublin, Gareth would have to have another conversation with Llelo.

That was a private matter between father and son, however, so Gwen didn't share her thoughts. Instead she said, "Am I to gather from your manner that Bishop Gregory didn't have any insight into the matter?"

"Not to speak of. He was horrified by the note, of course." Gareth emptied his purse on the nearby table, showing Godfrid both the note and the coin.

Godfrid turned the coin over in his hand, as they all had done. "It means nothing to me. And I am disturbed by that fact."

"I'm disturbed by the fact that the coin has meant nothing to anyone we've showed it to so far, not that we've asked many." Gareth sighed. "That and tracing Harald's movements on his last day and night will be the morning's task."

Godfrid's expression turned regretful. "I was hoping to forge better memories of Dublin for you this time! I'm sorry you are faced with a death on your very first day."

"Better than the last day, I suppose. While I hear that you, Cait, and Conall comported yourself creditably on your own, I can't be sorry I'm here if I can follow this investigation wherever it leads instead of adding it to your burdens." Gareth's sorrowfulness dissipated, to be replaced by something a little more intense. "Should I be working with your sheriff? You mentioned you have one."

"I sent a messenger to him. He should be coming by the house in the next hour."

"Which gives you time to tell your story," Gwen said to the big Dane. "I want to hear all about how you and Cait came together ... from the beginning!"

Thus the next half-hour was spent companionably with Godfrid, who regaled them with the story of his spring and summer, including its murder, intrigue—and love. By the end, any lingering concerns Gwen might have had about his relationship with Cait were gone. It was convenient, him falling in love and wanting to marry a woman who was not only the niece of the King of Leinster but the sister of his good friend. But she could see the love in Godfrid's eyes and hear it in his voice when he spoke of Cait. Gwen had already noted the same love in Cait's voice when she talked of Godfrid.

As Godfrid was winding down, a staccato knock came at the door. The steward, who was apparently party to all of Godfrid's secrets, since he'd been in the room for the telling of Godfrid's story, hastened to open the door. Since Gwen had just heard the saga of Holm's elevation to sheriff, his support of Ottar, and his coming to terms with his new allegiance to Godfrid and Brodar, she was very interested to meet him.

As expected, he was her age or younger—middle twenties or thereabouts—with blond hair and blue eyes, as had many Danes (though not all). He was shorter than Godfrid, though most men were, and more slender. At only twenty-five, he might not have entirely grown into his adult shape. In the years between twenty and thirty, Gareth had filled out more broadly, though now he complained that he had a bit more of a protruding belly than he wanted. Gareth was only thirty-three—not exactly into old age—and Gwen couldn't see it. She supposed she wouldn't have told him if she did, any more than he would suggest she wasn't as lovely as she'd been the day he married her.

Holm bowed and then said in stilted Welsh, "I am pleased to meet you."

"We are pleased to meet you too," Gareth said in equally stilted Danish.

Then there was a pause. Gwen had no more proficiency in the language than her husband, and Godfrid had already told them Holm didn't speak French. The Welsh he'd spoken was the full extent of his knowledge, and she gave him credit for learning it, seemingly for the express purpose of greeting them.

Thus, Godfrid took charge, launching into Danish in order to relate to Holm a summary of the investigation, to which Holm nodded and replied after every other sentence. When Godfrid got to the note and the coin, however, Holm hesitated before touching either of them.

Godfrid turned to Gareth and Gwen. "Holm says he knew Harald growing up, and his family has lived in Dublin for several generations. I have no idea if it's relevant, but Harald's brother died following Ottar."

"He was a follower of Ottar or he died among his following?" Gwen said. "They are not the same thing."

"They are not." Godfrid gave a sharp nod. "He was a follower. And I mean that both ways. Toki wasn't a clever man, and he was easily led. He never questioned Ottar's leadership and leapt at the chance to serve him."

"You know this for certain?"

"Many days I sat in Ottar's hall while Toki smirked at me from his post behind Ottar."

Gareth's eyes widened. "You're saying he was a member of Ottar's guard?"

"He was." Godfrid turned back to Holm and spoke a stream of Danish, and they went back and forth, ending when Holm replied in what clearly was the affirmative: "Ja."

Again, Godfrid turned to Gareth and Gwen. "He doesn't know the origin of the coin, but something in the back of his mind is itching—his words—and he will think about where he might have seen one before. Among his men, he thinks. He was raised to the station of sheriff too young, and before that he was the undersheriff. He was never a common guard, so he is still learning their ways."

"You're saying he wouldn't necessarily know what they were up to in their off hours—such as if they were visiting a brothel?" Gareth said.

"That is exactly what we mean. He acknowledges the problem, but he will inquire among his men about the coin and about Toki and Harald. I told him to report his findings to me."

"Since we don't speak Danish." Gwen's tone was displeased.

"You must learn quickly!"

"I am trying, but it isn't easy." Gwen tilted her head. "Do you trust him?"

Holm was standing right there, but as extra protection Gwen had spoken these words in Welsh, which Godfrid could speak passably well.

"I surprise myself by saying it, but I do. In this, certainly."

"Even if it turns out Harald's death has something to do with the fall of Ottar?" Gareth asked.

"Hard to imagine from here, months later, how that might be, but even so, my brother is the rightful King of Dublin. We truly have nothing to hide."

Gwen nodded. "Then I suggest you entrust him with speaking to Harald's mother. She has to be asked about the possibility of suicide, whether the bishop likes it or not. And at a minimum, we need to know when she last saw him and what he was doing. Did she know he had a full set of armor and a sword? Did they belong to his brother? Since her other son served Ottar, none of us here will get the truth from her. But Holm might."

Godfrid nodded his instant agreement and turned back to Holm.

Initially Holm's expression was impassive, but the more Godfrid spoke, the brighter the sheriff's eyes became until he was nodding vigorously. Finally, he bowed to Gwen and Gareth again and said, "Ja. Jeg vil gøre mit bedste for dig." He departed.

Gwen stared after him. "It could be I almost understood that."

"He said he would do his best for us." Godfrid grinned. "He and I have come a long way since that day at Rikard's warehouse."

9

Day One

Cadoc

As a Welshman who'd spent his life amongst foreigners of every stripe and condition, Cadoc was used to being an outsider. But this was the first time in a long while that he'd been somewhere he couldn't communicate beyond hand signals. He spoke Welsh, French, English, and Gaelic. The last was even one of his first languages, because one of his grandmothers had been Irish and refused to learn Welsh. For her entire life, she'd tolerated her family speaking Welsh to her while she replied in Gaelic. He had thought knowing the language might come in handy in Ireland, and it still might, if he had cause to speak to King Diarmait or maybe Caitriona. But so far, all he'd heard was Danish.

Brodar's hall was adorned with trophies from bygone times, acquired, Cadoc assumed, on raids from Galway to St. David's. The average Welshman had no love for Danes, having been on the receiving end of their axes for several hundred years. Like Cadoc's granny, Prince Hywel's mother had been Irish, but he had Danish blood too from his father. And, as Cadoc watched, somewhat grouchily, his prince conversed in Danish with Brodar, having already made his greetings to King Diarmait in fluent Gaelic.

The surprise of the night, however, had turned out to be not this murder Gareth was caught up in, but young Dai, Gareth's adopted son, who was seated beside Cadoc. With a single-mindedness he'd shown in few arenas, Dai had spent these last months, ever since they'd learned of Godfrid's wedding and that they'd all be going, at Cadoc's heels, begging for every snippet of Gaelic Cadoc could impart. Even in one summer, he'd become conversant. Dai had also looked to Prince Hywel for Danish, though with less result, simply because Hywel had less time for him.

Once their journey began, however, Dai had planted himself amongst the sailors who'd come for them in their ship for the two-day journey to Dublin, submersing himself in the language. By the time the ship docked, he could communicate in basic sentences in both languages and understood ten times more than he spoke. For the first time ever, Dai had discovered he was better than his brother at something—better than everyone, in fact.

"What are they saying?" Cadoc nudged Dai's elbow with his, drawing the boy's attention to the group of Danes directly behind them. Tonight, Cadoc wasn't sitting with his back to the wall. It wasn't out of choice but because they'd arrived in the hall too late to claim any of the best places.

Cadoc had worked with Llelo in Bristol and concluded he would ably fill his father's shoes when the time came. But Dai had something about him that drew Cadoc to him. He was less earnest, certainly, but more fiery, questing all the time to prove himself. Likely Dai reminded Cadoc of himself as a boy. Dai had been fortunate enough to have been saved by Gareth at a far earlier age than Gareth had saved Cadoc, which had resulted, miraculously, in a fundamentally sunny personality and hardly any chip on his shoulder.

"Shh. I'm listening." Dai kept his head down, to all appearances completely focused on the trencher before him. "They're talking about the advantages of one weapon over another."

Disappointed, Cadoc shifted in his seat. He missed the wall to lean against. "A bow is best. I could tell them that."

"Bows don't look to be much used weapons of war for the Danes," Dai said. "At issue for them are axes versus swords."

"Swords are expensive." Cadoc pursed his lips. "Maybe the great lords like your father haven't thought of it yet, but that's another reason it's strange for Harald to have had one."

From the age of ten, Cadoc had spent most of his life in martial pursuits, but in regards to Harald's sword, as with the Danish language, he found himself a little out of his depth. While he could appreciate—and wield—a sharp knife when called upon to do so, he was an archer, not a swordsman.

By now the entire Welsh contingent, every one of whom had participated in an investigation in one way or another over the last five years, knew what Gareth and Gwen knew. Each was charged with discovering whatever they could about who Harald was, to whom he confided, why he was dressed as he was, and what impact his gear may or may not have had on his death. The more they discovered tonight, the sturdier would be the foundation of the formal investigation that would begin first thing in the morning.

What nobody had told Gareth was that the Dragons were in the midst of a private competition amongst themselves as to which of them could acquire the most useful and relevant information and be of most use to the investigation. In that endeavor, Cadoc viewed Dai as his secret weapon and had no qualms about using the boy to spy for him.

"That's what one man is arguing, saying a sword is all very well and good in battle, if a man knows how to wield it, but it is quite another thing in the—" Dai paused as the foursome behind them rose to their feet and departed.

"He said all that, did he?" Cadoc said dryly.

Dai's expression turned sheepish. "It isn't as if I understand every word. I let it wash over me, and then I can summarize."

"Can you finish the sentence? In the *what?* Why did you stop?"

"I don't know why he used the word he did."

"What word?"

"Arena."

"You're sure?"

"It's from the Latin word *harena* and is the same in English as Danish. Lots of Danish words are."

Cadoc's eyes widened slightly to hear it. "That's why it's been so easy for you to learn!"

The corners of Dai's mouth turned down, turning his expression truculent. "Others speak English. Father and Mother do. *You* speak English. And Danish hasn't been easy for you."

Cadoc hastened to pat him on the shoulder. "No offense meant, young man. I hadn't learned enough yet to make that connection."

Dai looked slightly mollified. To soften him up further, Cadoc added, "You are better at languages than anyone I have ever met. I suspect you could learn French more quickly if you do what you did with Gaelic and Danish. It's trying to do it with a tutor and books that turns you upside down."

Dai's expression turned thoughtful. "That's what Father said. My French did improve enormously while we were in Bristol."

"There! See! What did I tell you?" Cadoc lowered his voice. "Best you don't let any of these Danes know how good you are. Your eavesdropping could be the difference between uncovering the answers and not."

Dai scratched his forehead, his eyes scanning the crowd. The great hall was packed to the rafters, with everyone who was anyone in Dublin putting in an appearance.

At that moment, Brodar stood and began to speak—in Danish, Cadoc again sourly observed. Dai focused intently on Brodar's face, probably trying to read his lips as well as listen to his words.

But the fact that Cadoc didn't understand more than one word in ten had the effect of shifting his attention away from what people were saying to what they were doing. And while it appeared the majority of the audience was enthusiastic about the union between Godfrid and Caitriona—Dublin and Leinster—here and there appeared faces where the happiness seemed forced. Towards the back of the hall, several men were sitting in a row with their arms folded across their chests. They could simply be unromantic types, but they could also be trouble.

Then Jon, Godfrid's captain, eased onto the bench beside Cadoc and spoke to him in French. "Sorry not to introduce myself to you before. With this murder, I had other duties to attend to. You are one of the Dragons." It wasn't a question.

"I am."

"You do not like my king's speech?"

"I do not understand your king's speech, as you well know."

Jon eyed Dai, who appeared to be speaking to himself under his breath. Jon studied him for another few moments, his eyes narrowing, and then said, "Unlike this one?"

Cadoc put a finger to his lips. "We are keeping that between ourselves for now." And then he decided he liked Jon's tone and attitude and could confess further, "He is my secret weapon."

Jon grinned. The two men were of an age, both veteran soldiers, and Cadoc felt his understanding returned. Then Jon lifted his chin to point to the warriors at the back of the hall. While Jon and Cadoc had been talking, they'd moved apart from one another, as if they'd realized they were giving themselves away.

"Brodar didn't exactly take the throne over Ottar's dead body, since Ottar died in the war against the men of Meath, but he *did* die, and everyone knows Brodar believed Ottar was a usurper. If he hadn't been serving in another part of the battlefield at the time of

Ottar's death, Brodar might have been accused of stabbing him in the back."

The bitterness in Jon's tone had Cadoc looking at him hard. "Ottar was literally stabbed in the back?"

"Yes."

"In the heat of battle, a man can get turned around, especially once a shield wall breaks. It doesn't have to have been one of his own who did it."

"That is what Brodar put out for the few who knew the way Ottar died. We all would stab an opponent any way we could if it meant our own survival." Jon's chin wrinkled. "But the entry wound was narrow, as made by a knife."

"He got close, then."

Jon's jaw firmed. "Good riddance, I say. Brodar was always the better man, and we can see even from the few months he's been on the throne that he is a better king."

Cadoc nodded. "I have been in Dublin half a day, but I can tell what a small community it is. Gossip about the way Ottar dishonored himself, even if it isn't discussed publicly, has to have spread by now."

"You're right, and it hasn't done Brodar any harm that he has refused to discuss it."

"But if Ottar's most ardent supporters, those who didn't fall in battle, are coming to realize who Ottar really was, they might be resentful, even ashamed—and then more resentful because they don't like feeling ashamed."

Jon turned his head to look at Cadoc. "You see all that from a few hours in our city?"

Cadoc gave a little snort. "There is also the matter of the queen. I understand she disappeared with Ottar's son. What explanation has Brodar given?"

"That she didn't want to witness Brodar's ascension and returned to the Isle of Man."

"Is that true?"

"Messages to Man have gone unanswered."

"Ottar's father does rule there," Cadoc said. "He has refused to hear Brodar?"

"So it appears."

Cadoc wet his lips. "That isn't a good start."

Jon took a long sip from his cup. The mead was flowing freely tonight. "The King of Man has not marshalled an army, being busy with his own affairs and threats to his own throne, but we are on alert."

"Which brings us back to Ottar's supporters. Brodar has enemies in his midst."

"Always."

"Could these enemies have had anything to do with Harald's death?"

Other than that one hard look at Cadoc, Jon had been continually scanning the hall, but now he swung his eyes back. "I heard he took his own life."

Cadoc frowned. "Did Godfrid tell you that?" Even had Gareth's people spoken Danish, none would have mentioned it, under strict orders to keep the information secret.

"He did, but only after I asked, having heard from someone else already." Jon frowned. "I think one of the men said something about it earlier this afternoon."

Cadoc let out a *hmm*. "Suicide is one possibility, but a death that looks like suicide provides a convenient avenue for a killer to escape."

Jon waggled his head in a noncommittal way. "Harald's brother did serve Ottar faithfully."

Cadoc had heard that too from Gareth. "The sword Harald died with was not only much-used but well-made. It could have been his brother's, and your prince is sending Holm to find that out from Harald's mother tomorrow. But I don't see why we should wait to discover who crafted it. Any ideas?"

"I haven't seen it yet, but I might be able to answer you after I see it. And if we were to bring it to the castle armorer, he would know more. If the armorer here didn't do the work himself, he should know the name of the man who did."

"I will speak to Gareth."

"And I to Godfrid."

Cadoc smiled as he took a long drink of his mead. Maybe he'd bring Dai along too.

10

Day Two

Gareth

The routine was very familiar, and the only good thing about having to interview a passel of churchmen this morning was that Gareth could start early because the bishop had assured him his community woke at first light in order to begin the day with prayer and song. Gareth himself had woken just before dawn and gone to roust Llelo. But when the young man came up from his pallet with heavy-lidded eyes and his hair standing on end, Gareth thought better of the plan and shooed him back to bed. Llelo had lain back down and instantly fallen asleep again.

Gareth suspected he wouldn't even remember being woken and would then accuse Gareth of working without him.

Gareth *was* working without him, but young men of Llelo's age needed an absurd amount of sleep, which Gareth remembered from his own youth. Llelo had been the one to find both the coin and the paper yesterday. He could rest on his laurels for a morning.

Conall met Gareth a half-step from the church gate. "Thought you'd start without me, eh?"

"I knew you'd come." Gareth shot him a grin. "You couldn't stay away any more than I could."

"The celebrations last night were delightful, but it has been a few months since I had something I could sink my teeth into," Conall admitted. "Being the ambassador from Leinster was fraught with peril and intrigue up until the war with Meath. Since then ..." His voice trailed off.

"Sunshine and roses?" Gareth said. "A little too tame for an accomplished spy such as yourself?"

Conall shot him a mocking look. "You know me too well."

"I'm sure there are other courts to which your king could send you. We would welcome your presence in Gwynedd."

"Isn't Gwynedd almost as tame as Dublin now that Cadwaladr has departed for France?"

Gareth barked a laugh. "You forget we still have Queen Cristina."

Conall's face fell. "That woman frightens me."

"Me as well! Why do you think my prince hasn't returned to Aber in nearly a year? His stepmother has given King Owain two sons. For a time it appeared he might put her aside, having become frustrated by her moods and temper. But he dotes on his boys, and she has used that to her advantage. Both boys were gravely ill this summer and the king and queen reconciled over their sickbeds. These days she is nothing but sweet to King Owain." Gareth's lip curled. "I heard all about it from the king's steward, Taran."

"It happens. You can't be sorry King Owain is happy."

Gareth closed the metal gate to the churchyard a little too forcefully, so it clanged. "Cristina has learned not to drip poison against Hywel in the king's ear. He left her before because of it, but I fear for what she plots in secret. She wants one of her sons on the throne when the time comes. Thankfully, with both boys still toddlers, that is many years away."

"Household intrigue is bread and butter to an Irishman." Conall shook his head. "Wives plotting against wives, sons against sons. The High King's household is a den of intrigue. O'Connor had his own son blinded!"

"Hopefully it won't come to that in Gwynedd," Gareth said dryly.

"You know I will be there if Hywel needs me. As will Godfrid. You or he has only to ask."

"Hywel regrets he wasn't here for Godfrid—but we didn't know we were needed because *you* didn't ask!"

"My king was there, and that was probably better," Conall said. "Dublin has come to the aid of Gwynedd in the past, and we are all family in the end, but sometimes it's best to keep things close to home."

Gareth had to admit—not even grudgingly—that it was true. If King Owain died in the next ten years, Cristina could do nothing against Hywel because her sons were too young to rule or to have a significant claim to the throne. A challenge could come from Iorwerth, as the eldest legitimate son of Owain's deceased first wife, since he was already above the age of manhood. He was not one to foster disunity or intrigue, however, and his best friend was Gwalchmai, Gwen's brother.

Still, as Gareth had said to Conall, if Owain lived longer, until Cristina's sons were in their late teens or twenties, it would be a different story. But they would ford that river when they came to it.

Bishop Gregory had again assigned his personal secretary, Arnulf, the young priest from the day before, to lead them around the monastery. Because of Conall's observations about possible tension between the priests and the monks, Gareth didn't ask for Madyn, the cellarer, or even Abbot James, whom he'd liked on first acquaintance. As monks, both could have given him insight into the community, and Madyn's Welsh might have been helpful.

But Bishop Gregory was a priest, acting for now as the abbot of a monastery, and Gareth didn't want to get involved in whatever was going on between the two factions. He would take Arnulf to start and move on to Madyn, if it became possible, or difficulties arose. Although Arnulf was young, he spoke Danish and French (as well as, likely, Latin). Gareth was fluent in French, as was Conall, so they should be able to muddle through for now.

As Gareth had noticed from the very first meeting when Arnulf had run all the way from Christ's Church to the dock, he was a well-set-up young man in his middle twenties, a bit stocky but not short. He appeared to be more muscular than the average priest, though, before dealing with Harald's death, Gareth wouldn't have said that meant much. He had the characteristic lump on the third finger of his right hand that indicated he spent a great deal of time holding a pen. That wouldn't be unexpected, since he directly served

Bishop Gregory, who likely had a great number of letters and documents he needed written every week.

Given that Arnulf wasn't far off in age from Harald, as they walked to their first stop, the scriptorium, Gareth decided to start the questioning with him. "Did you know Harald?"

Arnulf gave him a startled look. "You're asking me? Why?"

Gareth was surprised that he was surprised, and immediately his attention sharpened, though he made sure not to let Arnulf know it. Answering a question with another question was an instinctive reaction when a person had something to hide. So instead, he merely turned a hand upward. "You are a member of this community, as he was, and approximately the same age."

"He was a monk."

"And you are a priest. Does that mean you didn't interact?"

"I apologize." Arnulf seemed to realize he had come across as somewhat combative because he swallowed and started again. "Of course I knew Harald. I know the name and face of every monk and priest at Christ's Church. I don't know that I can tell you anything more about Harald than that."

"At this stage, anything would be helpful. I know nothing except he is dead and for some reason was wearing armor when he died."

Arnulf spread his hands wide. "I'm sure Bishop Gregory gave you all the relevant information. I don't know what more I can add."

A simple conversation had turned remarkably difficult. Perhaps Arnulf was merely intending to be circumspect. "Bishop Gregory did tell me what he knew," Gareth said gravely. "I was hoping to hear more from you, seeing as how it's unlikely a bishop would interact very much with a monk who worked in the scriptorium."

Arnulf raised one shoulder. "Many here are close in age to me. From what I saw of Harald, he kept mostly to himself." He paused. "I hope I am not speaking out of turn to say that his family supported King Ottar, while mine has always been loyal to King Brodar—and his father before him, of course."

Conall tipped his head. "That a man's family supported one rival to the throne of Dublin over another caused division amongst the churchmen here? I would have thought you would be above all that."

Arnulf gave him a deprecating smile. "Ideally, yes, but we are men, and as such, we sometimes forget ourselves and take on the rivalries and factions of the secular world."

"Would that include you and Harald personally? Did you argue?" Gareth asked.

Arnulf saw immediately the impression he'd given, and he put up both hands, hastening to head Gareth off before he went down that path. "No! No! We never talked about such things. But I felt them between us. Regardless, he kept to himself. I had little contact with him here at Christ's Church. You'd be better off speaking to the men in the scriptorium."

Which was, of course, the plan. For now, Gareth was going to ignore the fact that Arnulf was almost certainly lying to him about something. If he wouldn't answer direct questions, Gareth had other ways of finding out what he wanted to know. And with Arnulf's elisions and avoidances, he'd only piqued Gareth's interest.

Conall clearly felt it too, because he elbowed Gareth in the ribs and said in Welsh, in an undertone. "What does Hywel say? When a man is asked to sing and protests long and loudly that he couldn't possibly, it's an invitation to ask him again."

Because Arnulf was looking at him curiously, Gareth didn't reply to Conall with more than a movement of his hand. But he and Conall had been friends through one of the most trying experiences of their lives, after which they'd investigated another murder together. He didn't have to worry that Conall would feel dismissed. It was the same with Godfrid. From three different peoples they might be, but that didn't stop them from being brothers.

The first man they spoke to was Paul, the *armarius*. His job was to oversee the scriptorium, including providing the scribes with their materials, designating their tasks, providing books for the other members of the community to read, and assisting his abbot—or prior, or bishop in this case—in choosing readings for services. He was Danish but spoke French as well as Harald, which was in large part why they started with him, as well as out of respect for his office since he was the most senior scribe.

Gareth raised his eyebrows at Conall. "Do you mind?"

Again, Conall didn't need Gareth to tell him what he wanted from him, and he urged Arnulf to the far end of the room to begin questioning each of the scribes in the hall. This was a small community, so there were only five.

That left Gareth alone with Paul, which was exactly what he wanted. He began with as open-ended a question as he could think to ask, hoping to elicit more from Harald's supervisor than he'd managed to get out of Arnulf. "What can you tell me about Harald?"

At first it didn't work. "Very little, I'm afraid. As a scribe, his work was always excellent."

"I am glad to hear it." Gareth paused, a finger to his lip. "I know he is dead, and you may be loath to speak ill of him in any way, but I am asking these questions because he *is* dead, and your bishop would like to know why."

"What more is there to know? He killed himself." The armarius spoke bluntly.

Gareth canted his head. "How do you know that?"

"Didn't he?"

"There is actually some doubt on that score."

Paul blinked. "Really? I am glad to hear it. I don't like the idea of him being so beset that he took his own life." His teeth clenched for a moment. "It makes me ashamed that I didn't ask more questions of him."

That was a startling admission, and one Gareth wanted to respect. "He seemed out of sorts to you?"

"Not out of sorts so much as distracted. Recently, he'd been later to his desk than I expected every morning, and when he did arrive, he was obviously exhausted. He also seemed to be favoring his left arm, as if he had injured it."

Gareth knew all about that, of course, but he didn't share his discoveries with the monk. "Did you speak to him about it?"

"I chose not to." He paused before answering the obvious next question, "I feel now I should have. But he was the best at what he did, and it is my policy to give men leeway when they are having difficulties."

"But you couldn't say what those difficulties were about?"

"Like everyone else, I assumed he was grieving the loss of his brother." Again Paul clenched his teeth. "Why didn't I ask? If he was to speak to anyone about it, it should have been to me. Grief affects each man differently, and he wouldn't be the first to lose sleep over a loss. But I thought only to give him the benefit of the doubt."

Gareth didn't have to pretend sympathy. "I'm sorry. Did you discuss him with your prior?"

"Of course." Then Paul shook his head, both dismissively and apologetically at the same time. "Do you know how scribes work?"

"Perhaps you could be good enough to explain, in case I do not."

"The scribe is responsible for all aspects of his manuscript, but each man works differently. We keep the quires at the ready—" here he showed Gareth the folded parchment, already prepared for use, "—but Harald insisted on doing everything himself, barring drying and scraping the parchment." Now Paul held up a pencil. "This is called a plummet."

Gareth reached into his jacket pocket and pulled out his own pencil, causing Paul's eyes to light. "Where did you get that?"

"It was a gift from Abbot Rhys of St. Kentigern's in St. Asaph." Now Gareth brought the scraps of paper he also kept in his pocket and showed the armarius the picture of his daughter he'd drawn yesterday on the boat and then an image of the wooden coin, watching

Paul's eyes all the while for a tell-tale response. He'd given the actual coin to Gwen for her inquiries today.

Instead of recognition, he got a, "But this is wonderful!" Paul cast around the room and then strode towards a corner, returning with a few more scraps of paper, which he thrust into Gareth's hand. "If you need more, you know where to come."

Gareth bent his head. "Thank you."

"Now," Paul was back to the task at hand, "a scribe uses the plummet to line his page before he begins to write. Every book is different, and before anything else happens, a scribe has to ask himself, "How many columns? How many lines? What size the text? He has to plan it all out in advance, you see." As he talked, he showed Gareth page after page in various states of completion, moving among the men who were working.

And Gareth really did see. He'd come to reading and writing late in life and, for the first time, was glad of it. As a result, nobody had ever considered him for the Church. He didn't think he would have had the patience, never mind the skill, to do what these men did.

As Gareth admired one of the books, flipping gently through the pages, Paul stepped to his side. "You can read yourself?"

"Yes."

"Then perhaps this will interest you." He pointed to a piece of parchment tacked to the wall.

Gareth went up to it, surprised to find it wasn't a quote from the Bible, but from Florentius of Valeranica, dated two hundred years earlier:

Because one who does not know how to write thinks it no labor, I will describe it for you, if you want to know how great is the burden of writing: it mists the eyes, it curves the back; it breaks the belly and the ribs; it fills the kidneys with pain, and the body with all kinds of suffering. Therefore, turn the pages slowly, reader, and keep your fingers well away from the pages, for just as a hailstorm ruins the fecundity of the soil, so the sloppy reader destroys both the book and the writing. For as the last port is sweet to the sailor, so the last line to the scribe.

Gareth put a hand to his heart. "I will never look at a book the same way again."

The armarius spread his hands wide. "I don't agree with Florentius, of course. Being a scribe is the best job in the world." He dropped a hand on the closest man's shoulder, a portly monk with a graying tonsure. "Wouldn't you agree, Edmund?"

"Of course, armarius." Edmund spoke in French without looking up. He was working on a lengthy document, and, like Harald in death, his fingers were ink-stained.

The armarius lowered his voice and said conspiratorially, "Edmund tends to be very focused in his work."

"Was Harald close to any of his fellow scribes?" Gareth asked Paul.

"Not that I know. Not that I saw." Again he looked to the nearest scribe. "Edmund?"

Edmund finally paused to look up. But even when he did so, he squinted, as if barely able to make out Gareth's face. "He kept to himself. He made beautiful books." Then the monk's expression changed to one of puzzlement. "I heard he killed himself. Why are you investigating his death?"

Gareth was again displeased to hear the scribe say openly what the bishop had wanted to keep quiet. Cadoc had mentioned last night that the rumor of it was swirling around Dublin, despite their best efforts to contain it.

"From whom did you hear he killed himself?"

Edmund dropped his eyes to his work, as if no longer interested in the conversation—and perhaps he wasn't. "Last evening. I don't remember who mentioned it."

Because he didn't want to let any of these monks know he was concerned, Gareth matched Edmund's tone. "We don't want to condemn a man undeservedly. It is not my job to condemn anyone, in fact, but to get to the truth. All we know at present is Harald is dead, possibly of a surfeit of *uisce beatha*. What the Danes call *whiskey*."

"But he left a note, written in his own hand."

Again, Gareth wanted to ask how he knew that, but decided it wasn't a worthwhile question. Gossip spread through a small community like a monastery in the amount of time it took to turn around. "That it is, in fact, his writing is something we would like you to confirm." He pulled the scrap of paper, much like the armarius had just given him, from his scrip and showed it to the armarius and then to Edmund.

Paul nodded sadly. "Yes, that is his writing. Beautiful, as always."

Then his eyes narrowed as he fingered the edges of the paper. "Odd, though—"

Gareth tipped his head. "What is odd?"

"He wrote this on paper, rather than parchment, which I can understand, since one is valuable and one is not. But, more to the point, he tore it from a larger piece."

"We noticed that. You think it's significant?"

"I would like to find the rest of it, if only for my own peace of mind."

"What about finding the rest would put your mind at ease?" Conall stepped beside Gareth, having finished the questioning of the other scribes. Gareth hoped he'd elicited something, but from Conall's dour expression, he rather thought not.

The armarius drew his finger along the written line of text. "See how the scored line from the plummet is mostly lost and the lettering lies close to the edge of the paper?"

Both Gareth and Conall nodded, having noticed that as well, but didn't speak, not wanting to interrupt Paul's thought.

"If Harald tore the paper first and then wrote the words, he would have written right down the center of the scrap. It would have been easier, if for no other reason than to prevent the pen tip from falling off the paper."

Gareth frowned. "You are wondering if the text wasn't written first and then the paper torn? What about that do you see as significant?"

"It is Harald's writing. Of that I have no doubt, but what if he was writing this line as part of a longer piece? *Father, if thou be willing, remove this cup of suffering from me: nevertheless not my will, but thine, be done,* is from Christ's prayer in the Garden of Gethsemane. I think it is important to find what paper this piece was torn from and if more was written than we have here. If this is really a suicide note, where's the rest of it?"

11

Day Two

Holm

Holm had not believed he was too young for the job of Sheriff of Dublin when he'd accepted the position. Almost every day since then, however, it had been pointed out to him—not overtly, of course, barring the initial cursing by the older men who'd been passed over—but by the curled lips and outright sneers when he walked into a room. He'd realized only after accepting the job that the main reason King Ottar had appointed him was because he *was* too young. The king had wanted someone he could control.

Prince Godfrid had understood this from the start, of course, which Holm had come to realize towards the end of the investigation into Merchant Rikard's death and the subsequent battle against the men of Meath where Ottar had died. That realization had also brought to the fore—and finally explained to him—all whispered gibes and jeers that had been directed at him by the men beneath him since he'd taken office. The comments had never risen to genuine insubordination, thankfully. That would have been something he couldn't ignore.

At Godfrid's suggestion, in the months since the battle, he'd looked for ways to make the men beneath him feel more comfortable and in control of themselves and their positions. And if that wasn't possible, he'd finally worked up the courage to sack them. The men so dispensed had turned out to be just three. Once they were gone, suddenly the barracks were without their poisonous influence, and the world became a much brighter place.

That Brodar had expressed his continued confidence in Holm, at the urging of Godfrid, was humbling, and he had just enough self-awareness by this point to realize that today he was being tested, whether he liked it or not, in a not too dissimilar fashion from his time under Ottar.

Which brought Holm to his second problem: he liked his job. He'd been afraid of it for most of the first two years he'd held it, but he now knew, given time, that he might even become good at it. And he wanted that chance. After Ottar's death, his men had assumed Brodar would appoint someone else, and when he hadn't—when Godfrid himself had come to the barracks to express his confidence in Holm—he no longer woke in the morning with a heavy weight on his heart and a sickness in his belly, and it was easier to get out of bed.

With all that said, by sending him to speak to Harald's mother, a widow named Agnes, not only was Godfrid entrusting him with a piece of the investigation he could easily do himself, since he spoke Danish, but he was letting him do it *alone*.

It had been less than a day since Agnes had been informed of her son's death, so, as Holm walked towards her house, he rehearsed comforting words. Dublin was the largest city in Ireland, with upwards of three thousand people within its walls, but having lived here his whole life, Holm had at least a passing acquaintance with everyone. He and Harald were of an age, but hadn't been friends. He was pretty sure his mother knew Agnes better.

When he arrived at the house, however, he was genuinely surprised not to see any activity around it. Even if Agnes had no children left alive in Dublin, neighbors should have been seeing to her. Resolved to remedy the situation, as a secondary goal to getting whatever he could out of her regarding Harald, Holm knocked on her door and clasped his hands behind his back as he waited for Agnes to answer.

No reply came, so he knocked a second time, again waiting through a count of ten. Just as he was putting up his hand to knock a final time, realizing he'd been foolish to think Agnes wouldn't have gone to stay with a family member or friend, a woman called from within the house. "Trim your sails! I'm coming."

Agnes pulled open her door and stood before him, still in her nightgown with her long gray hair coming out of its braid. "Who wakes an old woman from her sleep?"

Holm took a step back at her hostility. And even though her station was significantly below his, he bowed. "I apologize, mother. I thought you would be awake."

"Why would you think that? Do you see any men to feed? Babies to nurse? No! My son is dead in the church. My other son is dead too, killed in the fighting. His wife is dead. My daughter lives a hundred miles away with her useless husband and screaming brats. What possible reason could I have for waking early?"

Startled by this onslaught, Holm tried to think of what to say, but managed only, "Perhaps I should come back later."

"No, no. You're here now. Come in." She gestured him inside. "I'll get my robe."

At least the house was clean and included a loft for sleeping and a back door, through which he could see the rest of her yard. The space was larger than she needed. But as she'd said, her sons were dead, and now she rambled around the too large home by herself. As Holm stood in the doorway, watching her stir the fire and then the pot above it, he felt her devastation like a physical blow.

He hastened forward to take a stick of wood for the fire from her hand. "Mother, let me help you with that."

Agnes acquiesced, stepping back and saying, "You're Marta's boy, aren't you?"

His back was to her as he crouched before the fire, coaxing it to a better flame. "Yes." He turned on his heel to look up at her. "She sends her regards."

"You're a good boy to come. Marta was here last night. She brought me dinner from the feast and ate it with me."

Holm was suddenly ashamed he hadn't known that—and that nobody official had thought to follow up with Agnes, after whatever priest Bishop Gregory had sent to inform her of her loss had done so. In his experience, churchmen were prepared to tell you at any hour of the day or night where you'd gone wrong, but they weren't very good with the aftermath.

Holm had attended the feast with his family, but his official duties had kept him from their table except in passing. It had been late when he'd returned home, long past the time his wife had settled the children and gone to sleep. That was normal for her and for him, because of his job, and overall they were getting along much better than they ever had when Ottar had been king. His wife herself had commented that he was happier at work and thus more content outside of it. As the saying went, *happy husband, happy home.*

Agnes's hand came down on his shoulder. "You must thank your mother for sending you to me."

Holm rose to his feet, deciding in that instant Agnes deserved the truth, and he wasn't going to ride the tail of his mother's cloak, even for better answers. "I am here as sheriff, mother." He lowered his voice. "I must speak to you of your son Harald."

Agnes's lips turned down slightly, but otherwise her expression didn't change. "I did know that, my dear. Ladle me a bowl of porridge, and I will answer all your questions."

Holm did as she bid, ladling one for himself as well, half the amount, just to be polite, and they sat on stools across the hearth from one another.

"Harald was always a *good* boy."

Holm opened his mouth—but to say what, he wasn't sure. Certainly something agreeable, but then she made a dismissive gesture with her spoon to cut him off.

"I know what they're saying up at the cathedral, but Harald would *never* have taken his own life. It's a mortal sin! When he returned to Dublin, a full Benedictine, I've never seen him so happy and proud. He worked in the scriptorium, you know."

Holm nodded. "Bishop Gregory himself commended his writing."

"Harald was more than just a scribe, of course."

Holm carefully put a spoonful of the flavorless porridge into his mouth and swallowed before following up, making sure his tone was merely curious. "What do you mean?"

"Ever since Harald was a boy, he enjoyed stories. Since he returned to Dublin, he would bring candles and work here until all hours of the night."

To learn information like this was the reason Holm had come, and he didn't make the mistake of asking Agnes to elaborate. She was lonely, and she trusted him (a twinge of guilt there), so he let her ramble.

"Even as a boy, his head was in the clouds, thinking of legends and the days of old. His uncle gave him a wooden sword when he was only three, and he carried it everywhere."

This was an opening Holm had been looking for. "Did he own a sword himself, now that he was a man?"

Agnes frowned. "What would he need a sword for? He was a monk."

"After the battle at the Liffey were you given Tiko's sword?"

Agnes took an unsteady breath. "The captain of the town garrison himself brought it to me." She drew Holm's attention to a sword in its sheath set above the door. "Every day I remember him."

Up until now, Holm had been assuming the sword with which Harald had died had been his brother's. It was the obvious thought, but he was reminded of Godfrid's warning not to take anything about a death he was investigating for granted. "Who came to see you yesterday to tell you Harald was dead?"

For a moment, Agnes looked proud. "Bishop Gregory himself!" Then her expression saddened. "He was very kind."

"Was he the one who told you Harald killed himself?"

"He didn't say a word about it, and I had no reason to think it until my neighbor came to see me with a basket of apples to leave me, along with her condolences."

"How did she hear of it?"

"I don't know. I confess I sent her away with her apron over her face." Agnes stuck out her chin. "I kept the apples."

Holm set aside his half-eaten porridge in order take Agnes's hand. "I have to ask, you understand. If he didn't kill himself, and he didn't die by natural causes, we must discover what did happen and find the man responsible. We can't have a murderer walking free in Dublin! Especially not a man who would murder a monk."

Agnes looked down at their joined hands. "I don't know anything about how or why he died. I do know nobody understood him at the church."

"Why would you say that? I thought Harald was pleased to have become a Benedictine."

"He was! But Harald said to me more recently that he came home because he needed the peace of this house to work."

"How did you feel about that?"

"Toki never more than tolerated him, but I loved having him here, especially since Toki was gone. It was like when Harald was a boy and had first discovered how to read. It was a new world opening up for him." She shrugged. "He tried to teach me, but I never saw the point."

"Do you know what he was working on?"

Agnes shrugged again. "Stories, he said. Legends of our ancestors."

"Will you show me where he worked?" Holm was a little confused about what Agnes meant, but he hoped if he saw Harald's workspace, he would understand. He had a great deal to tell Godfrid already, but he wanted to be thorough.

Agnes stood and led him to the back corner of the house. As Harald had worked late at night, he hadn't needed a window to let in extra light, and the table was littered with candle stubs and wax. Laid neatly to one side were pen and ink and a stack of paper, the latter held down by a smooth stone.

"His work was here." Agnes lifted the lid of a wooden box, two feet wide and a foot high, located on the floor beside the table. Inside were stacks of more paper (not parchment) with writing on them, some bound into books.

Holm knelt before the box, initially in awe at what it contained and the effort Harald had made by collecting the documents—and then made more so by the actual writing on the paper. He scanned quickly through the books underneath and then came back to those on top to read more slowly.

"He tried to share his enthusiasms with us, but neither I nor Toki could ever do more than make a mark for our names. We were poor students. Not like Harald."

Holm himself was no scholar, but still his hands trembled as he turned the pages of the latest book he'd come to. What he held wasn't simply a copy of another book, like the scribes worked on in the scriptorium at the cathedral. It was a translation into Danish of a book titled *Historia regum Britanniae* by someone named *Galfridus Monemutensis*. That part was written in Latin as well as the Danish name, Jófreyr Monmund.

He flipped through the pages, stunned by the effort involved. It wasn't the only book either. There was another that appeared to be the story of Skjöldr, son of Odin and the first king of Denmark. It was a common skald's song but not anything Holm had ever seen written down. At the moment, Harald seemed to be working on a Danish translation of the Book of Luke. Holm had never seen that done either. It hadn't occurred to him that the Bible could be translated into Danish. The priest always spoke the mass in Latin, and for most of the citizens, the words washed over them without understanding.

He turned to Harald's mother. "Has anyone else seen what Harald was working on?"

Marta frowned. "I wouldn't know. He takes a book and brings it back. I don't know if he showed what he was doing to anyone else." Then her expression brightened. "That nice young priest, who came with Bishop Gregory to tell me Harald was dead. He knew."

"You're sure?"

"Of course, I'm sure. Just last week he dropped by to return a book Harald had loaned him."

Holm's pulse quickened. That certainly wasn't something Gareth and Conall had been told the previous day. "Which one?"

"Ach, I don't know. I put it in with the rest."

He realized she was talking about the book not the priest. "Can you show me which one it was?"

She shook her head. "They all look the same to me. Harald always liked to keep the books in a particular order, but I never understood what it was. I went through his things last night and made the books neat."

"Neat? What do you mean by that?"

She blinked, looking surprised as if the answer should have been obvious. "I stacked them so the largest was on the bottom. I think the one the priest brought is somewhere in the middle."

Holm tried not to grind his teeth at how unhelpful that news was. Agnes had been wonderfully forthcoming and trusting, and he didn't doubt she was speaking the truth. He couldn't tell by looking which book was most important, but he knew Godfrid would want to know what he had learned here. Immediately.

"The priest's name?" Holm tried again.

"Arnulf."

12

Day Two

Dai

Early morning found Cadoc, Jon, and Dai standing a few paces from the swordsmith's works within the walls of Brodar's palace. The swordsmith, named Gren, was as big a man as Dai had ever seen—and that was saying something in Dublin where, as far as he could tell, a disproportionate number of men were larger than average. Gren's arms bulged from wielding hammer and tongs all day. His apprentice, by comparison, was half his size, and he ran from bellows to woodpile to water bucket, fetching and carrying at Gren's command—and often without needing any command at all.

Godfrid's captain, Jon, leaned against one of the thick wooden posts that supported the roof and spoke in Danish. "We have with us the sword of the monk who died yesterday. We were hoping you could take a look at it and tell us if you were the one who made it."

Gren shot Jon something of a caustic glance. "What do you know of swords, Jon?"

"Not much," Jon admitted cheerfully. He was typically Danish in that he was all about the axe. Even when deep in his cups, Godfrid's captain could throw his weapon with accuracy fifty feet and hit his target square on—as he'd shown Dai after the feast last night.

"And you?" Gren lifted his chin to point to the great bow Cadoc never went anywhere without if he could help it.

Instead of answering, Cadoc looked at Dai for translation. This was an easy one, so Dai quickly obliged.

Cadoc grinned. "Nothing."

Gren then looked Dai up and down. "You're Welsh, eh? But you speak Danish?"

"A bit."

Cadoc made a motion to get Dai's attention. "What did he ask you?"

"If I spoke Danish."

Cadoc looked as if he didn't want Dai to answer that, but since he already had, it was too late.

Gren continued, "Then what's your story? You're young to be a knight, but the blade you wear is worthy of the name." He'd been looking at the sword at Dai's waist, though how he knew its quality, when it remained in the sheath, Dai didn't know.

Dai found he did better with Danish when his brain didn't get in the way of his mouth, so he just let the words spill out: "My father is a knight, and I am squire to the Dragons. My name is Dai ap Gareth." Holding Harald's sword horizontal to the ground, with his palms up, Dai approached. "This is the sword of the man who died—" he glanced back at Jon. "How do I say *yesterday*?"

"I går."

Dai nodded and looked back at Gren, who gave him something of a side-eye glance. "I går."

"A squire, eh?" Gren took the sword by the handle and walked with it out from under his roof into the yard. The sun was shining brightly for the second day in a row, which likely meant it was going to rain for the wedding. Rain on a wedding day was good luck in Wales. To Dai's mind, the superstition was trying to make the best of a bad job. From what his parents told him, it rained even more in Ireland than in Wales, though he had yet to see it, so likely a wet wedding day was lucky here too.

Dai followed. "Yes, sir."

Gren laughed. "You don't have to call me *sir*. In my time, I was a lowly man-at-arms. Not someone you have to bow to."

"Pardon me, sir—" Dai went right ahead and continued the designation of respect, seeing no harm in being exceptionally polite, especially as he knew his Danish wasn't quite right, "—but I bet you could still wield a sword."

Gren's eyes really lit now and put his free hand on the top of Dai's head and ruffled his hair. These days, at fourteen, with his voice moving in and out of its change, Dai was taller than some of the men in Prince Hywel's *teulu*, but he was still dwarfed by Gren. Dai hoped to eventually surpass Llelo, who seemed to have stopped growing at a finger's width shorter than their father.

"I don't know if I'd want to wield this one." He held the sword on a finger placed under the blade above the hilt, but it took a few tries to get the sword to balance. "Not one of mine."

"Is it not a good sword?" Jon asked.

"Not good enough for me. Not terrible, but not what a knight would want." Gren snapped his fingers at Dai. "Let me see yours, boy."

Dai drew out his sword, which his father had given him on his fourteenth birthday, the day he'd become a man. The sword had belonged to Gareth's uncle, a man Gareth had loved and honored. When Llelo had become a man, Gareth had made him a gift of Gareth's own first sword, the one he'd worn before Prince Hywel raised him to captain of his *teulu*. While that weapon had been special, in that it had been his father's, Llelo respectfully replaced it last November with one bestowed upon him by Prince Henry himself upon their departure from Bristol, because of Llelo's service and sacrifice. It wasn't quite a knighting, which would come soon enough, but it was a huge honor nonetheless.

Gareth could have repurposed his old sword again, now that Llelo didn't need it. The fact that he hadn't, that he'd given Dai his uncle's sword instead of saving it for Taran, his natural child, still left Dai with a twisting in his stomach and heart. Thus, he held it out proudly to Gren, who, gratifyingly, raised his eyebrows at the sight of its quality.

"Where did you get this?"

"It was my great-uncle's."

"He must have been a fine swordsman."

"I never knew him, but so my father says."

Gren's eyes were the most expressive part of him. They'd been bright before, and now they almost twinkled. "You are Gareth the

Welshman's son, yes?" And then at Dai's nod, he added, "When did you learn to speak Danish?"

"This week," Jon said, with a scoffing laugh, before Dai could answer.

"We have a live one here, don't we, men?" Gren now held a sword in each hand. At first, he appeared to weigh them, one after another, and then he started doing two-handed moves that Dai could only aspire to. Dai's sword was in Gren's left hand, and he could see by the way it flashed and moved that it was indeed the better balanced of the two.

In order to work with the swords, Gren had moved twenty feet away from his workshop into a more central position in the palace yard. Others who were about stopped to watch him work through the moves, some of which Dai recognized from his own training.

After working up a sweat, Gren came back to where Dai stood. Flipping Dai's sword around, he returned it to him, hilt out. "Take care of that."

"I will." Dai took back his sword and slid it into its sheath.

"This one," Gren held up Harald's weapon, "was made by a swordsmith, but not an expert one. Regardless, the balance is off, and the hilt is coming loose from the blade. It has not been cared for, either. With oil and sharpening, it could be a useful tool. As it is—" he made a *pfft* sound with his lips, "—I would not take it into battle."

"Do you have any idea as to who might have made it? Or barring that, where he could have acquired it?" Jon asked. "You are the only swordsmith I know in Dublin."

"I am the most skilled, certainly." Gren didn't give the impression of being immodest. He was merely stating a fact. "I would ask Vigo, down by the dock gate."

Jon's expression darkened. "He is not a good man."

Gren barked a laugh. "He is not, but he is an accomplished trader, and he deals in weapons. They are not usually of the first quality, which is why we don't work with him here, even when I am overbusy. If he didn't supply this sword, he is your best bet for finding out who did."

13

Day Two

Gwen

Gwen left Taran and Tangwen in the kitchen with their nanny and Godfrid's cook, who was determined to teach Tangwen a few words of Danish in between popping pieces of honeyed roll into her mouth. At least the cook wasn't feeding her daughter salted herring, which the Danes ate in quantity and served at every meal. Gwen hoped she could manage the rest of the visit without eating any more.

Gareth had returned to the monastery to question the clerics about when they'd last seen Harald and what they knew about him, and Llelo had joined him once he got over his outrage at being left behind in the first place. While Gareth had, in fact, woken him, Gwen decided she'd let Gareth tell Llelo that rather than getting involved. Llelo was a man now, and she was learning (slowly) to keep her parenting and interference to a minimum.

For her part, knowing that churchmen were often reluctant to be interviewed by a woman, Gwen had resolved to leave the monks' and priests' activities to the men to sort out and herself take a different tack. Though Gwen hadn't yet asked Cait about her experience as a slave, she knew the outline of it from Abbot Rhys. Cait hadn't known the origin of the wooden coin or the door it unlocked, but she had lived amongst the lowest levels of Dublin society. If Cait was willing to talk to the people she knew, they might be able to tell Gwen about the wooden coin.

Once at Conall's house, Gwen found Cait standing on a stool with a seamstress crouched at her feet, hemming a shimmering rose silk dress. At the sight of Gwen coming up the stairs to the loft, Cait looked woeful. "You would think getting the dress exactly right wouldn't have come down to the last moment, but inevitably it has."

The woman at her feet said something in Gaelic, and then another woman, whom Gwen hadn't noticed, as she was sitting somewhat in the shadows, spoke from behind Cait. "Introduce me to your friend, Caitriona."

Gwen knew what she'd said because the words were in polished French.

Caitriona gestured in typically graceful fashion herself and said, "This is my mother, Dorte. She arrived in Dublin only this morning. Mother, this is Gwen, the Welsh friend I told you about."

The seamstress stood up, having finished her hemming, at which point Cait shed her dress before stepping off the stool. Meanwhile, Dorte herself rose gracefully to her feet and came forward into the light. She and her daughter looked so much alike, Gwen would have known Dorte was Cait's mother without the introduction, and she understood where Cait had acquired her gift for languages as well as her beauty. Cait's mother was as slender as her daughter, making Gwen feel even dowdier and more awkward than she already did in Cait's presence. Dorte's hair was dark like Cait's, except for two pure white streaks arising from her temples, and her dress was on a par in style and quality with Cait's wedding dress too, though it looked so perfect on her that Gwen supposed she wore such finery every day.

Gwen curtseyed. "It is wonderful to meet you."

"And I you, since I have heard so much about you, not just from Cait but from Conall too. You saved his life." Initially, Dorte had been putting out a hand to Gwen, but then she changed her mind and wrapped her arms around Gwen in a tight hug. Given that Cait was marrying Godfrid, a fierce hugger, Dorte appeared to fit right in. "Thank you. Thank you for allowing my son to come home to me."

Over Dorte's shoulder, Cait smiled, and for a moment Gwen thought she saw moisture in her eyes. "I haven't thanked you properly for that either."

Gwen's upper arms were trapped at her sides, but she bent her elbow and managed to pat Dorte on the back. "Conall is a great friend. Gareth and I think often of that investigation, grateful ourselves we reached him in time."

Dorte stepped back. "It was a close thing, I understand." Then she dropped her arms, and her expression changed to one of embarrassment. "I apologize for being so forward."

"No apology is necessary!" Gwen put out a reassuring hand. "We Welsh are known for wearing our hearts on our sleeves. I am very pleased to meet you and, as I said, Conall is a true friend. We are blessed to know him."

By now, and with the help of a maid, Cait had clothed herself in her day-to-day attire, and she stepped closer to her mother to kiss her on the cheek. "Thank you for your help with the dress."

"It is my pleasure, as you well know. And I did nothing but provide you with my seamstress."

"You chose the color."

Dorte spread her hands wide. "I knew whatever looked good on me would look even better on you." She touched Cait's cheek with the back of her forefinger and followed the seamstress down the stairs.

Cait frowned. "Are you going somewhere, Mother?"

Dorte looked back, her expression suddenly coquettish. Few women nearing sixty could have pulled off such a look, but Cait's mother was one of them. "Your uncle asked me to visit with him at the palace. One of his advisers is a wealthy widower, and he thought I might enjoy meeting him."

"Mother!" Cait was genuinely shocked.

"I mourned your father, Cait, you know that. I observed the rites. But he's been dead a long time. I'm tired of being a widow."

And to her credit, Cait subsided. "I'm sorry I reacted badly. This time I would want the decision of whom and when to marry to be all yours."

Dorte's expression hardened slightly. In a flash of insight, Gwen knew where Cait had inherited her iron will too. "Believe me, it will be. If this one won't do, I will refuse him and my brother until he finds me a man who does suit. No more sister wives for me, for starters."

Among the Irish, instead of mistresses, which was the Welsh and Norman way, lords were allowed multiple wives. Conall and Cait were half-siblings, sharing a mother but not a father. Dorte had married Cait's father after the death of Conall's father, but she'd shared him with two other women—not, it seemed, entirely happily. What Gwen didn't know, not having spent any time in Ireland outside of Dublin, was if the practice was also usual among the common people. It seemed like a practice destined to create jealousy and a situation where there were too few women to go around. But she could see that if the death toll among men in war was very great, the custom could have been created instead because there were too few men.

Personally, Gwen found the policy of allowing Irishmen to have more than one wife at any given time troubling. In her world, interacting with a man who was married was safer for a woman, married or unmarried, than to converse or associate with one who was not. If the fact that a man was already married was no barrier to pursuing another bride, it threw all social compacts into disarray.

Of course, other peoples, the Normans in particular, thought the Welsh law allowing illegitimate children to inherit was an equally disturbing cause of turmoil. But to Gwen's mind, it was one thing to punish a couple for adultery. It was quite another to condemn the resulting child, who'd done nothing wrong.

But that was why allowances had to be made for differences when visiting another place. Northern Welsh felt out of place when traveling south and vice versa. Though Gwen shared more blood with the Irish than the Danes, at times she felt the latter were just a bit more familiar in their policies and customs (other than their love of salted herring), though she would never say so to Cait.

After watching Dorte glide out the door, Cait turned to Gwen. "I hope you are here because you need something from me other than to discuss my mother or wedding dresses."

It was the opening Gwen had been looking for, but now that it came to it, she wasn't sure how to begin. "I am."

"Does it involve going somewhere outside this house?"

"Yes."

Cait grinned. "You can tell me on the way. I need to walk in the sunshine."

Gwen caught up by the time Cait reached the door, but put a hand on the latch before Cait could open it. "You don't even know what I came here for, and now that I can ask you, I'm having second thoughts."

Cait nudged at Gwen's elbow, getting her to pull on the latch and open the door. Warm summer air flooded the room. "Does it have something to do with the investigation?"

"Well ... yes."

"Then what more do I need to know?"

"Are you that anxious to escape your wedding preparations?" Gwen still didn't follow her out the door.

"My mother has them well in hand. As you can see, she is gracious and perfect, and I am not."

Gwen laughed. "I think many would argue with that assessment, including me—and Godfrid, I'm sure—but all right. If you insist: we are in pursuit of the meaning of the wooden coin." She took it from her purse and held it out. "I came here to ask you if you have a thought as to where we might go or to whom we might speak about what it unlocks?"

Cait took the coin. "You are so polite! Let me tell you what you are really asking: I lived as a slave, and I know slaves and members of the lowest social order in Dublin." She looked down at the coin, turning it over in her fingers like everyone who'd held it so far had done. "The last wooden coin like this you saw gained entrance to the brothel where my brother was being held prisoner."

Gwen bent her head. "I apologize for not trusting you enough to speak frankly. You are right, of course. Gareth and Conall spoke to the bishop yesterday and are even now interviewing the monks and priests. Hopefully they will discover something of use today. A churchman might know about the coin, but I find it much more likely that one of your acquaintances will—and it's likely enough that I think we really ought to ask."

"I can see that if a churchman knows what it's for, and it gains entrance to a brothel, they would not be willing to admit it."

"Exactly."

Cait turned the coin around again. "I'm wondering that Conall doesn't know about it either."

"Maybe it's new?"

Cait pressed her lips together, for the first time showing real concern. "That would not be a good thing, because it would be new since Brodar's ascension to the throne—and that means he doesn't know about it because we don't know about it."

"Let's not borrow trouble," Gwen said. "Best simply to ask and await answers."

Cait bobbed a nod. "Thus, you came to me."

"I would ask your brother, but he can't ask questions in his current form, as ambassador to Dublin, and Gareth assures me he shouldn't be asked to become Fergus the Sailor except as a last resort."

"True!" Suddenly Cait's eyes brightened, and she smiled again. "Better not leave this to him. We will do what we can by ourselves." She hooked her arm through Gwen's. "I will take you to speak to my friends."

14

Day Two
Godfrid

Godfrid had intended to make inquiries with Gareth this morning, or at least get to eat breakfast with his beloved future wife, but instead he found himself caught up in another matter entirely—or at least he thought it was another matter when the King of Leinster began talking. "I must speak to you all of Donnell and Rory O'Connor."

The four men—Diarmait, Brodar, Hywel, and Godfrid—had come together alone in Brodar's receiving room. Godfrid could hear the general hum of conversation in the main hall, which he could see through the doorway. The door had been left open so the servants could have easy access to the room with their serving dishes. Two of Brodar's personal guard stood on either side of the doorway, charged with preventing anyone who shouldn't overhear from entering. Hywel's Dragons, barring Cadoc, who'd gone off with Godfrid's man Jon, ate at the nearest table.

"What is the issue, exactly?" As the newcomer to the group, Hywel could get away with asking the obvious question. Godfrid was glad of it. He supposed he should know already, but with the wedding, he'd been very distracted of late and didn't want to guess if the issue was old or new.

"It is clear now that they continue, in their separate ways, to undermine Brodar's rule of Dublin and its relationship with Leinster," Diarmait said. "Just because Donnell's forces were defeated at the Liffey doesn't mean he has given up his efforts."

"And Rory?" Godfrid said.

"He has decided to come to your wedding," Diarmait sad flatly. "I confess, it is a development I had not anticipated."

Hywel tipped his head. "Isn't a willingness to attend an indication of a desire for improved relations?"

Diarmait, Brodar, and Godfrid all spoke the same words in reply. "Not when it's an O'Connor."

Hywel laughed. "I take your point."

Brodar leaned forward, his attention on Diarmait. "We lost many men in the battle, my lord. It will take time to recruit more to fill out our ranks. If Connaught or Meath attacks the city itself, I am unsure if we have the men to defend it."

"I have worried about that too. Enough men of Meath died that they can't be wanting another go any time soon, but—" Diarmait eyed Dublin's king, "—I'm not sure we want to take the chance they won't."

"Or that someone else won't see an opportunity," Godfrid added.

"I could leave a garrison of my men in the city," Diarmait said.

It was as if a bucket of cold water had been poured over Godfrid's head, and he knew without even looking into Brodar's face that he felt it too. Long experience with hiding what they were really feeling allowed both men to keep their expressions impassive, and Brodar said, "It would not be my preference."

Diarmait snorted, not remotely fooled. "You are a proud people. I understand. But I have my interests to protect, and while I am giving you Cait, Leinster itself is not the bride to Dublin's groom."

There were many ways Brodar could have answered Diarmait. Over the last decades, the situation had been reversed, with Dublin the bride, subject to the whims of her husband, Leinster. But neither Brodar nor Godfrid wanted to antagonize Cait's uncle only a few days before Godfrid's wedding.

So Godfrid stepped in, "If O'Connor's men cross the river again, we won't be caught unawares. We will not be giving up Dublin to them, no matter who fights. No matter the cost."

Brodar cleared his throat. "You should know, my lord, that I have already heard from Donnell."

Godfrid shot his brother a sharp look. When Donnell's overture had arrived two weeks ago, they'd discussed how and when to tell King Diarmait about it. Truth be told, Brodar was reluctant to admit any weakness, but he'd spoken the truth about Dublin's lack of fighting men, and if Diarmait knew about that, he had to know about this.

"When?" Diarmait sat up straighter. "What did he say?"

"He offered me the same deal he wanted to give Ottar: more independence for Dublin if we forswore our allegiance and alliance with Leinster in favor of Connaught—specifically him."

"And help him murder his brother, probably, though that wasn't spelled out," Godfrid added.

Hywel scoffed. "Did he refer to the original deal with Ottar, Brodar, which included *your* murder?"

Diarmait's eyes were focused on Brodar's face. "When was this?"

"A fortnight ago."

"Why didn't you tell me earlier?"

"I'm telling you now," Brodar said. "It wasn't something to be put into writing or to come from the mouth of a messenger."

Diarmait eased back in his seat. "No, I can see that. As Ottar learned last spring, we must always be careful about what we put in writing."

Hywel folded his hands and settled back in his chair too. "Why not recruit men from the countryside or the other Danish cities? They owe you allegiance, even if they are reluctant to admit it."

"It would show weakness," Godfrid said flatly. "If we can manage this ourselves, we would prefer to do so."

"They weren't attacked," Hywel pointed out. "And you are all one people."

"Tell that to the men of Waterford!" Brodar managed a laugh.

Hywel now turned to Diarmait. "I have spent less than a day in Dublin, my lord, and I am pleased to see that the populace appears accepting of Cait, but I would hate to see that goodwill vanish in an instant if they knew you were garrisoning men in the city." He shook his head. "That is a *quick* path to unrest."

"Which *I* can ill-afford? We *are* being honest now, aren't we?" Diarmait touched a cloth to his lips and then threw it down beside the wooden bowl that had held his porridge. He claimed that in his old age, his digestion required it. For his part, Godfrid hoped it would never come to that for him. "I hear you are half-Irish, lad. Did your mother's family teach you nothing?"

Hywel's eyes narrowed slightly, but he otherwise kept his expression bland. "They taught me that a single slight can start a war. They taught me to tread carefully when a man's pride is at stake. They taught me that a man can have both Irish and Danish blood, as I do, but be entirely Welsh in his heart."

Diarmait studied Gwynedd's prince for a moment, and then he let out a bark of laughter that appeared genuine. Godfrid hadn't realized he was holding his breath, but now he let it out too, and he didn't think he was the only one who felt the tension drain out of the room.

"You think it would be a mistake to test their loyalties, eh?" Diarmait waved a hand. "I am well aware I am viewed as a necessary evil."

"I wouldn't say evil—" Brodar began.

But Diarmait waved his hand again. "You are a prideful people, as are we. So no garrison for now." Then he looked hard at Godfrid. "I may need my ambassador back, however. Now that the city isn't torn apart by rival claimants to the throne, his skills are wasted here."

Godfrid spread his hands wide. "I am not the one keeping him in Dublin."

"But you agree he has been champing at the bit, wanting a new challenge."

"I do." Godfrid sighed. "Reluctantly, I do."

"After the wedding, then." Diarmait raised his goblet to the other men. "Something must be done about the O'Connors."

Brodar lifted his cup. "As we are being honest, I should say out loud what everyone here knows, even if we don't speak of it: Dublin would prefer to be independent of Leinster. But we also know we are surrounded by enemies. Dublin remains wealthy, but it doesn't have the men to resist all the kingdoms of Ireland." He looked at Diarmait. "You have our thanks for our recent victory. You have our respect. And we have your back. While I am king, we will not defect to Connaught."

The four men touched goblets, but as Godfrid drained his drink and set it on the table, his eyes found first his brother's face and then Prince Hywel's. Both wore almost identical thoughtful expressions. Godfrid believed he could read his brother like an open book, and he'd told King Diarmait the truth. Hywel, however, had looked away rather than hold Godfrid's eyes, and while Godfrid could content himself with not challenging his brother with questions until after the wedding, he wanted to hear what Hywel had to say.

Thus, after the four men dispersed, Godfrid sought out Hywel on the wall-walk, where's he'd gone to look west, over the countryside. At one time, it had been Danish as far as the eye could see.

These days, Godfrid wasn't entirely sure it wasn't Irish right up to the wall.

At Godfrid's approach, the Welsh prince lifted one hand and dropped it. "I was wondering if you would find me."

"You were not pleased with that conversation at breakfast. Why? You have no stake in Leinster's relationship with Dublin."

Hywel turned to look at him directly. "Don't I?"

"Do you?"

Hywel tipped his head. "I can say to you what I couldn't say in the hall. Diarmait is a dangerous man, far more dangerous than I think you realize. Brodar spoke pretty words, but do you really think you can trust him?"

"It isn't a matter of trust. He is our overlord."

"Yes, he is, and as your overlord, as Leinster goes, so goes Dublin."

"That's what we agreed at the table," Godfrid said. "I don't much like the thought of being beholden to another master, however, if that's what you were going to suggest. The O'Connors are no better."

"And very likely worse, in fact," Hywel agreed.

"My brother spoke the truth as well when he said that, while Dublin longs to be independent, we are too few in number these days with fewer fighting men than we should have."

Hywel raised his eyebrows. "There are ways to remedy that."

"It never used to be something we had to remedy. Becoming a fighting man was all every man wanted." Godfrid pursed his lips. "But you're right. As you Welsh train every boy in bow and spear from a young age, we need again to do the same in Dublin, especially since so many fathers and uncles never came home from the Liffey."

"You might not mention such a program to Diarmait. Nobody wants to go back to a time when hordes of Danes descended upon our coasts every summer. The problem with creating fighting men is that, in order to keep them sharp, you have to go to war."

"I suppose that will never be an issue for you with the Normans on your doorstep."

"Sadly, no." Hywel eyed him. "And now you are marrying Caitriona, the niece of the King of Leinster."

Godfrid could understand his skepticism. "It isn't just Cait, of course. Conall is a friend too."

Hywel nodded. "Befriending one's traditional enemies comes at a price."

"As has become clear to me, we have turned into merchants, not warriors. We need warriors to throw off Leinster's yoke." Godfrid made a disgusted grunt. "In truth, it matters little. The reality of our current situation is such that Brodar's and my aspirations for ruling over an independent Dublin once again are as ephemeral as the clouds."

"And I imagine this wouldn't be a friendly topic of conversation over the breakfast table in your household, would it?"

"Cait and I have talked about it." Godfrid took in a breath. "It is true my bride is content with the current relationship with her uncle, but she understands why I am not, and why Brodar and I can never be."

"She sides with you?"

"She says she chooses me, come what may."

"I'm glad for you." Hywel made a dismissive gesture. "That isn't what concerns me the most, however."

The comment put Godfrid completely at sea, and he supposed it showed on his face, because Hywel muttered something in Welsh under his breath and turned again to face outward. "I am far more concerned about the future—not tomorrow, but five or ten years from now. You must have noticed Diarmait is restless, always."

"I have."

"More power. More land."

"It is the way of kings."

Hywel blew out a puff of air. "My concern is what he might choose to do as part of that quest, and particularly with whom he might ally."

Godfrid finally understood where this was going. "You're afraid he'll reach out to the Clares again."

"Does that surprise you?"

"Neither that he would nor that you are concerned surprises me. But what *is* your concern? Gilbert is dead, and Richard is a boy."

"I wasn't a boy at eighteen."

Godfrid pressed his lips together. "I suppose you weren't. I suppose I wasn't either."

Hywel shook his head, not to deny, but in what appeared to be a combination of disbelief and frustration. "You here in Ireland don't know the Normans like we do in Wales. They have never seen a land they didn't want to conquer." He eyed Godfrid for a moment.

"Your people used to be like that. It is my understanding that you and the Clares might even share blood, in fact."

"As I've said, we've grown soft."

"Men like Clare, no matter his age, have not. They have spent the last eighty years attempting to consolidate their hold on South Wales. Kings like Cadell of Deheubarth now must cater to them."

Godfrid's eyes narrowed. "As we do Leinster."

"Like that, yes. Someday the conflict between Stephen and Maud will end, and then Norman eyes will turn to Ireland. If Diarmait seeks to keep O'Connor at bay—or overthrow him—he *must not* look to Clare or Prince Henry or any of these other Normans for help, not if he wants to keep his kingdom. It would be a huge mistake."

"I don't think he'll listen to me. He might listen to Conall. Maybe."

"Eighty years we've been fighting them." Hywel was looking out at the countryside again, but Godfrid didn't think he was seeing it. "There are too many, and they just keep coming. I don't know how long we can keep them at bay." Even though the sun was out, a shadow passed across the face of the Welsh prince.

Godfrid wasn't superstitious. His people had left premonitions and portents behind when they'd converted to Christianity. But even so, he shivered.

15

Day Two
Conall

When Gareth and Conall left the scriptorium, they found Llelo loitering in the yard, his back against the stone wall and his face upturned to the sun. At Gareth's arrival, he straightened and came forward, immediately apologetic. "I'm sorry for sleeping so long—"

Gareth cut him off with a gesture. "I was awake, and you were not. I'm sure there will be some aspect of this investigation which will require one of us to stay up late, and you will be the one to do it."

From Conall's perspective, it was typical of Llelo to apologize rather than be irate at not being woken, and he was glad Gareth rewarded him for it. Conall was not a father, but seeing his friend with his eldest son made him want to be.

The thought brought Conall up short. He had never wanted to be a parent before. Children were ... troublesome. And inconvenient. Certainly they got in the way of doing what needed to be done, and small children, like Gareth also had now, were serious *work*. He probed the notion again, and then laughed to himself: in order to be a father, he would have to find a woman willing to tolerate him, which so far had not happened.

Meanwhile, apparently mollified, Llelo nodded. "Mother has gone off with Cait."

Conall raised his eyebrows. "Are we worried about what they're up to?"

Gareth glanced at him. "Should we be?"

"With Cait, definitely so. I'm hoping Gwen will temper her more terrifying impulses." Conall laughed.

Gareth smiled in response. "Gwen wanted Cait's thoughts on the investigation."

Now Conall *was* genuinely concerned about where the women would take their quest and what they would be doing when they got there. But he reminded himself that Gwen was Gareth's wife and had long experience with investigations, and, in another two days, Cait would be entirely Godfrid's to rein in—or not. Conall had best get used to it.

"What have you discovered so far?" Llelo asked, unconcerned about the vagaries of women.

As they walked to their next stop, Gareth told him about what the armarius had said and added, "Conall or I spoke to every monk in the scriptorium, and none could tell us anything useful regarding who Harald was, what he did in his spare hours, what the coin signified, or anything else relevant to his death."

"Other than the armarius himself, I would add my overall impression that they were resentful of the questions. They were not forthcoming and not interested in being so." Conall glanced at Arnulf, who was walking a few paces away. They'd been speaking in French so as not to shut him out. "Would you agree, Arnulf?"

The priest turned up one hand. "I suppose."

"Do you have a suggestion as to why that might be?" Conall added.

"I really couldn't say." As always, Arnulf's response was vague. It was really starting to irritate Conall.

"Is it because Gareth is Welsh, and I am Irish?" He didn't think that was the reason, but he wanted to give Arnulf a place to start.

Under the gaze of all three men, Arnulf wilted slightly and relented. "No, I don't think that's it. We have many people of all origins here. All men are equal in the sight of God."

Llelo gave a little tsk. "Then why wouldn't they tell Father and Conall anything? They are trying to discover how and why Harald died. Why wouldn't everyone want to help?" He spoke with the innocence of a man unused to intrigue, despite having lived these last four years with Gareth and Gwen and growing up in Gwynedd's court. Conall could have kissed him for being so blunt.

Arnulf sighed. "It's because they're angry to think Harald committed suicide and blame you for bringing the idea to the fore."

"I'm concerned how they even know we're considering it," Gareth said. "Who told them because we *didn't* bring it the fore?"

Arnulf put up both hands as if Gareth was accusing him. "I couldn't say."

"Would that really make them keep information from us?" Llelo asked. "Wouldn't they want to prove Harald *didn't* kill himself?"

"I tried to explain that any little thing might be helpful, and it may be they truly don't know who and what Harald was," Arnulf said. "As I don't."

"I found the note," Llelo said. "Perhaps it's just as well I wasn't there."

"I don't think it would have made any difference to them, in truth," Gareth said. "Nor will it to the healer, who's the next person we're going to see."

Llelo kicked a small rock out of his path. "I don't understand why the note is such compelling evidence anyway. Christ prayed to the Lord in the Garden of Gethsemane. So what? How does that translate to suicide? Christ died on the cross, put there by other people."

"That is the implication. Yes," Arnulf said.

"I still don't understand."

Conall gestured to Arnulf to elaborate further. The priest was actually looking a little brighter now that the conversation had turned to theology.

"We can't know exactly what Harald was thinking when he wrote those words, but he may have viewed his death as a parallel to Christ's in some way, or an act of reparation for Christ's suffering, or even misguidedly believed it was God who instructed him to die."

"He'd gone mad, then?" Llelo said.

"Yes, essentially."

"But if he were mad, then he wouldn't really know what he was doing, right? He wouldn't be in his right mind, so then how could what he did be a sin?"

Gareth's hand came down heavily onto Llelo's shoulder. "Enough, son. Leave it for now. We will speak of this later with Abbot Rhys."

Llelo subsided, somewhat resentfully, Conall sensed—and understandably so. Llelo had always been thoughtful, and he had been asking genuine questions from the heart. But Conall felt bad now in encouraging the boy to speak his mind. His questions were ones many men before him had asked, and a man had a right to his questions.

But now wasn't the time to ask them, and Conall didn't think it would further the investigation to have it get out that Gareth allowed his son such freedom of thought. Both the Welsh and Irish churches had a long history of doctrinal irregularities, which the pope was encouraging Gregory, as the Bishop of Dublin, to stamp out within his jurisdiction.

Arnulf made yet another gesture with one hand, however, seemingly unfussed by Llelo's questions, which was a relief because stricter priests might have warned him against heresy. "Just to let you know, Brother Godwin, our healer, speaks nothing but Danish."

"Then I suppose you will earn your keep with him," Conall said, trying to lighten the mood and further distract from Llelo's questions. At first Arnulf didn't appear to understand, since he frowned. But then his expression cleared, and he laughed. "My French is perhaps not as good as I thought."

"You understood eventually," Conall said. "You know you are fluent in a language when jests don't pass you by."

The healing house was a long room with eight simple wooden beds in a dormitory style arrangement. Three of the eight were occupied. In the nearest, an aged man slept. Two beds down from him was a younger man with bright red hair and a matching nose, indicating he had a respiratory illness. In the last bed, a boy of eight or nine lay curled on his side with a bowl next to his face. Conall supposed the monks were lucky to have only three ill members in a community of thirty. Both the two younger patients looked to have easily-spread illnesses, which could lay low half of Dublin. Not a sight Conall wanted to see this morning.

But such was duty that he didn't immediately turn around and leave the room. Gareth, for his part, appeared to take in the scene and then dismiss everyone but the healer, who greeted them as they entered. He was taller than Conall by several inches, but thinner, with a yellow pallor to his skin that implied either illness or lack of sunlight. According to Arnulf, Godwin had come to Dublin from Downe Priory, located between Wexford and Dublin, a house founded by the Danes after their conversion to Christianity.

Either because he was irked by Gareth's comments about their lack of success with the scribes or inspired by the experience, Arnulf appeared to want to take charge of the interview. He began by introducing them and explaining in detail what they were here for and the kind of information they wanted to know. But before the secretary wound down, the healer was shaking his head. "Harald never came to me, if that's what you're asking. I spoke with him only once or twice since he arrived."

Even working through a translator, Gareth was very attentive to the healer, and Llelo with him, seeming to want to make up for his earlier absence. But Conall had his eye on the healer's assistant, who'd looked at them welcomingly when they'd entered but had found something to keep his hands busy and his back to them the instant Harald's name was mentioned.

Conall drifted over to where he was rolling bandages at a nearby table and said in an undertone. "What's your name, son?"

The assistant looked startled to be so addressed, but Conall found that his Gaelic accent made any oddities about his Danish speech quickly forgiven. "My name is Tod, my lord."

"Well, Tod, do you have something to tell us?"

"I don't know what you mean, my lord."

"I think you do." Conall picked up a vial from the worktable and pretended to inspect it.

Tod rolled another bandage, clearly hoping Conall would give up and leave. When Conall merely set down the vial and picked up another, Tod finally had to answer. "Not here. Please, my lord."

"Where?"

"I don't know."

Conall pursed his lips, pretending to study the writing on the label. "Meet me in the privy by the dormitory. Count to one hundred after we leave the healing house. Say you have an upset stomach. That will be credible, seeing as how you have a fellow sufferer in your last bed."

The assistant reached for another bandage to roll. At first Conall thought he was going to refuse, but then he gave a single nod of his head.

Feigning a casualness he was genuinely trying to feel, Conall returned to Gareth's side and attempted to look interested in the continuing denials coming from the healer. Gareth, being the trained investigator he was, hadn't missed Conall's interaction with Brother Godwin's assistant and had been stalling to give Conall time to finish his conversation. In short order, he made his goodbyes, and they left.

Up until now, Arnulf had walked with a pronounced strut, but the failure to elicit any information from the healer had him stopping in the cloister walkway and asking with true humility. "Where can I take you now, my lords?"

"Rather than disturb your community any further, we will pursue other inquiries this afternoon," Gareth said. "I appreciate your service. We can see ourselves out."

"Of course, my lords." Arnulf tucked his hands inside his wide sleeves and progressed back to the bishop's office.

Once he had retreated around the corner, Gareth turned to Conall. "What are you up to?"

"I have a rendezvous with the healer's assistant, who has something to tell me." As they walked outside into the churchyard, Conall gestured with his head towards the far corner of the church compound. He had never before availed himself of that latrine, but he'd lived in Dublin for a year and often cut across Christ's Church's grounds to get from his house to the palace, so he knew where it was.

Gareth pressed his lips together before saying, "I assume you're thinking Llelo and I should stay away?"

"That's probably best. Perhaps the women have returned, or Holm has learned something from Harald's mother. He doesn't trust me anyway."

Gareth waved his friend away, laughing under his breath. "For good reason, I imagine."

Conall put on a mask of beleagueredness. "I am much maligned." Laughing too, he turned away.

It was a logical division of labor, and Conall appreciated Gareth's willingness to apportion tasks to others besides himself. In truth, these days Gareth had a small army of helpers with some degree of experience with investigating death and murder. It would be a shame to waste any one of them. And while Holm spoke no French or Welsh and Gareth no Danish, likely he could find someone to translate—Cait or Godfrid at a minimum.

Conall approached the entrance to the latrine, which, thankfully, hardly smelled, a result of the skilled builders of the church. Christ's Church wasn't a hermitage or saint's hut tucked away in a hidden valley in western Ireland. The cathedral was the seat of the Bishop of Dublin, who had always looked to England for inspiration. The monks in that country had learned from Rome—and the Romans had built magnificent buildings in England long before the coming of the Normans.

The River Poddle flowed north towards Dublin and circled around the city to the east before it met the Liffey. Near the cloister, a channel ran from the Poddle north through the city until it emptied into the Liffey on the other side. In so doing, it provided fresh water to the residents of Dublin. A branch diverged off the main line directly into the church compound, splitting several more times as it progressed underneath the buildings. One line went to the kitchen, another flowed to the washroom, while a third went to the bishop's quarters. All three lines converged again at the main latrine, washing away the waste accumulated there, before flowing out of the compound headed back into the River Liffey.

One of the few forward-thinking projects Ottar had instigated during his reign was to order the digging of a similar channel to run from the Poddle through the palace and out the other side. The public latrines for the city had all been built over these two water lines, and they were one of the reasons that, despite its overcrowding at times, Dublin was a very livable city and hardly smelled. The arrangement was eminently reproducible almost everywhere in Ireland, with all its rivers and springs.

A bell tolled for the hour of mid-morning prayer, just as the healer's apprentice arrived from the other direction with as anxious a look on his face as Conall had ever seen on any man. That was saying something, and an indication of how fraught with peril Tod viewed this meeting.

"Good." Conall nodded. "You are feeling unwell, and you look it." He leaned against the frame of the door while Tod perched uneasily between two toilet seats. "What do you have to tell me?"

But, as before, now that it came to it, Tod didn't want to speak.

Conall didn't like putting words in an informant's mouth. But in this case, it seemed necessary. "I assume you are the one who sewed Harald's wound? We saw the fine stitching when we examined him yesterday."

Tod ducked his head in a nod of admission, even while he refused to say *yes* out loud.

"How did that come about?"

Tod dithered for another few moments before committing, speaking quickly in the hope that the sooner he told Conall the truth, the sooner he could leave. Which was, in the main, true.

"The first time he came to me he was bleeding badly. While he told me he'd fallen in a darkened street and sliced his head on a splinter of wood, I saw instantly that the wound had come from something sharper, like metal."

"Did you press him on the matter?"

Tod shook his head. "Harald was ever one to keep to himself, though whenever our paths crossed, he was kind to me. After that first time, when he realized I could keep a secret, he came to me whenever he was hurt."

"When was the first time?"

"Shortly after King Brodar's crowning, not long after Harald arrived in Dublin." Then Tod actually volunteered information. "We both lost brothers in the fighting at the Liffey."

Conall didn't know Harald at all, obviously, but it seemed to Conall that Harald might have played up that shared experience, as a way to ensure Tod wouldn't give him away. Conall didn't say anything, however. It would serve only to antagonize Tod, and he wasn't in the business of ascribing motives to dead men without real cause.

"Do you have any idea what he was doing?"

Tod's expression turned sad. "It was obvious he had been fighting—with weapons, it seemed to me. After that first time, he never again had a wound on his face or head, but the rest of him was often bruised. Seeing as how he died with a sword in his hand, I assumed at first he'd been fighting someone and had been wounded to death." He shrugged. "I never thought he'd kill himself."

There it was again. "Any idea as to whom he might have been fighting? Or where?"

"None." Tod shook his head, positive about this answer if nothing else.

"Has anyone else come to you with unexplained wounds or bruises?"

Again the head shake.

"How many times did you patch him up?"

Tod's chin wrinkled as he thought. "A half-dozen?"

Conall frowned. That was a lot of injuries in only a few months. "And you never questioned him about what he was doing? Why he was allowing himself to get hurt?"

"Many times, but he never answered. When I sewed up his arm I pressed him hard, but when he grew angry, I stopped talking. I wanted him to keep coming to me rather than trying to deal with his wounds himself."

"He was a monk. A scribe. Did you ever suggest he had no business fighting?"

"Oh sure. I also told him it wasn't honorable for him to be sneaking around like this. Harald said—" Tod paused and a thoughtful expression crossed his face, "—he said he couldn't stop. That I was wrong about what was and was not honorable. He said his honor was at stake."

It was on the tip of Conall's tongue to reply that he wouldn't have said priests had honor—or at least not in the way he understood it. But then he thought of Abbot Rhys and realized he was wrong. So he said instead, "Do you know anything about the rest of his life? Did he have any friends other than you?"

"I don't know. I don't know that you could even call me a friend." He shrugged. "Harald kept to himself. On the rare occasions I worked up the nerve to ask him who else might be involved, he wouldn't answer or he would claim he hadn't been fighting and he didn't know what I was talking about. But he had another friend in this, I'm sure of it. At a minimum, someone had to be hurting him." He pursed his lips, hesitating again, though this time it seemed to be because he was thinking about how to explain.

"What is it?"

Tod hemmed and hawed before finally saying, "If Harald hadn't been wounded so often, I would have said all he cared about was books. More than that, he loved stories. Often, while I patched him up, to distract himself he would speak to me of the legends of our ancestors."

Conall's eyes narrowed. "Do you mean his own personal ancestors or your mutual ancestors, the Danes?"

"His stories weren't about real people but were the old stories the skalds tell in the hall. When Harald told them or talked about them, he made them sound real, like he believed Thor at one time walked the earth." Tod shook his head. "He was obviously troubled."

"Is that why you believed he took his own life?"

Tod's head came up, and his expression turned fierce. "I never believed it! Not only is it a sin, but he was not a man in despair."

Conall canted his head. "You're that certain?"

Tod scoffed, telling Conall all he needed to know before he added, "He wouldn't ever."

Then, from underneath his robe, Tod brought out a book, perhaps six inches by eight, and held it out to Conall. "The reason I was late was because I went by my cell. He gave this to me the last time we talked. He was very excited by it and said he was going to translate it into Danish. Would he behave that way if he had any thought to kill himself?"

Conall took the book, which was bound in soft leather, and opened it. It had no title page and consisted of thirty or so loose pages, like it had been part of a book which had been mostly destroyed. The text was in Latin, with illustrations of defensive and offensive fighting techniques taught by a master, referred to in the text as *sacerdos*, and a pupil, called a *scolaris*, translated as *priest* and *student* respectively. The people in the images were armed with swords and shields, and each successive panel moved the reader through a given martial form.

Instinctively, Conall put his fist to his mouth, so amazed by what he was looking at he didn't know what to say. Almost breathlessly he asked, "Do you know where Harald acquired this?"

Tod shook his head. "He didn't say."

It brought to Conall's mind the chest of books he and Godfrid had found in the treasure house of Merchant Rikard, whose murder they'd investigated in the spring. He didn't remember it being among them, but then, at the time he'd been concerned about other things. "May I keep this?"

"That's why I brought it. I hope you will share it with Lord Gareth, if it would help convince him Harald didn't take his own life. I don't want it in my cell any longer anyway. Someone might find it."

Conall closed the book and tucked it under his arm. He was afraid if he held the book in his hand, Tod would see it trembling. "Thank you for your honesty. You have been very helpful."

"Don't tell Brother Godwin. Please, my lord?"

Conall's brow furrowed. "Why don't you want him to know you helped Harald? Your stitching was excellent, and you were doing a service for a fellow monk."

"Godwin decided on the first day I began working with him that I was useless. If he learns someone doesn't think so, he'll take it out on me forevermore." He leaned forward. "He's ill, you know, with a wasting disease. He doesn't have long to live, and when he dies, I will inherit the healing house."

"You want that?"

"I do. Very much. Godwin is set in his ways and refuses to consider new ideas."

It was a common refrain among the young, anxious to replace the old, but in this case, Conall could understand and appreciate Tod's impatience. His stitches *had* been well done. "What if I spoke to the bishop? Or the prior? It could ensure your ascension."

"Or attract censure for physicking out of turn. Or worse, allowing Harald to keep his secret by not speaking of what I knew." But then Tod bit his lip and gave a sharp nod. "Yes. Thank you. I would appreciate it if you would speak to Prior James." He straightened his shoulders. "Best not to lie anymore."

16

Day Two

Caitriona

Since the investigation into Merchant Rikard's death, Cait had ventured down to the docks only rarely at first, but once Brodar had settled into his kingship, she'd been more welcome. One of his first acts, decreed with Bishop Gregory at his left shoulder, had been to abolish slavery in Dublin.

Over the last century, and really since the Danes had become more aligned with the Roman church, slavery in Dublin, and Ireland as a whole, had been on the wane anyway. The Normans had abolished it entirely when they'd conquered England in the previous century, making the slave trade for Danish merchants far less lucrative than it had once been, since an entire market was now closed to them. Conall had discovered an illicit slave trade in Shrewsbury—and almost become subject of it himself—but no Dublin merchant had made his primary living trading in people for at least twenty years.

There had been slaves in Dublin, however, and there were still many throughout Ireland, since the Irish Church had not yet bowed to the pope's decree on the matter. Cait herself had masqueraded as a slave for three weeks, and upwards of twenty slaves had worked for Merchant Rikard.

No longer.

Rikard's son Finn, who'd inherited his business, had been informed of slavery's abolition in advance. Part of the arrangement worked out between Bishop Gregory, Brodar, and the merchants of Dublin was that any slave who wanted to continue as a slave could, working for their former master, with a free living, for the rest of their lives if they chose. The rest would be paid the same wages as free workers and dockmen, already in the vast majority. If the former slave declined the free living, she was then obligated to make her own way in terms of finding a place to live or food to eat. No longer would it be provided for her. Or him, as the case might be.

That said, Finn already had a barracks and kitchen, and he'd set up a system where his former slaves could choose to pay him for food and housing from the wage he paid them. It was in Cait's mind that Finn was actually getting the better end of the deal financially with this new arrangement. Now, he had all of the benefit of slave labor but, except for their wages, none of the responsibility.

Whether Finn and the other merchants hadn't fought the Bishop's request because they'd realized in advance how this might play out, Cait didn't know. For her, the side effect of abolishing slavery was a genuine friendship with several of Finn's former slaves. Lena and Ana had both stayed to work for Finn as employees, since as cook and laundress respectively, they had skills that made them valuable. Finn had needed to pay both a bit more to keep them in his employ.

Cait's other friend was Iona, strangely enough, who'd been openly hostile when she'd learned Cait's real identity. Freedom had transformed her, however, from what might have uncharitably been termed a drudge to a business woman in her own right. She'd been hired to oversee a tavern a stone's throw from Finn's warehouse, and daily she blossomed into her new role. In addition to working at the tavern, Iona was in charge of supplies at Finn's kitchen, so Cait hoped to see her too.

Cait and Gwen had walked several blocks through the streets of Dublin, with Cait's guards (Sitric and Bern) trailing five paces behind, before Gwen finally asked a question that appeared to have been eating at her for some time. "Is Dublin different now that Brodar is king?"

Cait looked at her, genuinely startled by the question. "Can't you tell?"

"I was a prisoner when I was here last, and I was too wrapped up in my own misery to notice much of anything."

Cait smiled ruefully. "I forgot about that. You are so beautiful and competent with such lovely children. It's easy to forget you lived a life before becoming the wife of the steward to the edling of Gwynedd."

Gwen glanced at her. "We have that in common, then."

It took a moment for Cait to realize Gwen was paying Cait's compliment back to her, but then she smiled and added, "It takes some getting used to, doesn't it? A city, I mean."

"I've been to Chester." Gwen's head swiveled this way and that. She seemed curious about everything, without actually poking her nose into anyone's doorway. "That was a big city too. It smelled worse, however, and was full of Saxons and Normans, so not my favorite place."

"You could despise Dublin for being the place to which you were brought against your will."

"That would mean despising Godfrid, which is impossible."

At the mention of Godfrid's name, happiness bubbled up inside Cait. She couldn't *wait* to marry him, to be able to be with him all the time without worrying about what anyone thought. For a moment, she was lost in the anticipation and forgot what they were doing, only to blink and find Gwen smiling at her, eyebrows raised.

Cait shook herself, blushing at Gwen's knowing look. "To answer your question, the city feels like an entirely different place. That we have someone to respect on the throne straightens everyone's shoulders. They know Brodar has everyone's best interests at heart. I think most people knew from the start it was a mistake to put Ottar on the throne, but they did so out of fear."

"Fear of what?"

Cait tipped her head. "Losing what they had? Losing more than they'd already lost? Dublin has been on the decline for years, and while Ottar promised to stem the tide, he never developed a real plan for doing so. He was the one who agreed to fight in Gwynedd for Cadwaladr, seeing only the gold he offered and not the cost to attain it. He thought like a raider, never a king."

"And Brodar is different?"

"Brodar understands Dublin can no longer survive on its own. It is an island of Danes in a sea of Irish. He can either embrace the future or run from it. He seeks to navigate a path forward in alliance with Leinster while maintaining the integrity of Dublin. It won't be easy to do, but if anyone can do it, I think he can."

Gwen guffawed. "Is that Godfrid speaking?"

Cait grinned. "I know more about politics than I ever cared to. But yes, with Godfrid's help, and our marriage, there's real hope for the future here."

"Now you're talking about the O'Connors."

"Leinster and Dublin standing together are stronger than either alone, as was proved at the Battle of the Liffey. And as long as my uncle is king, he has sworn not to subsume Dublin into Leinster." Cait waved a hand. "Danes are unruly and troublesome anyway. Why would my uncle *want* to rule them when he has Brodar to do it for him?"

"That's one way to look at it." Gwen frowned. "We're all slaves, in one way or another, aren't we? We all serve a master. The goal is to have that master be one of our own choosing."

Cait came to a halt in the road. "Do you have the *sight*? A similar thought was in my mind a moment ago when I was thinking about who we are going to see."

"I am no more gifted than any woman." Gwen had walked two paces farther on and now came back to Cait. "You are of the blood, like I am." She tipped her head towards the nearest house. "Not like these Danes. They put their heads down and barrel forward, without looking out of the corners of their eyes. They seem to think only a select few, and those mostly men, have insight."

Her heart suddenly full, Cait threw her arms around Gwen. They were on a slight hill, with Gwen on the downward side, and Cait was taller, so she almost unbalanced them by mistake before she straightened and released her new friend.

"What was that for?" Gwen asked, between breathless laughs.

"Until now, I hadn't realized how alone I felt, with no other woman who truly understood me."

Gwen smiled. "I hoped you would be a kindred spirit. We are lucky to have you."

The two women set off again, glad to be reminded that finding a friend was a little like falling in love, without the thumping heart. They had a sense of each other now—and a trust—that meant they could talk without shielding their true selves.

When Cait and Gwen arrived at the kitchen associated with Finn's warehouse and barracks, Lena was elbow deep in bread dough she'd turned onto a floured table in the center of the kitchen. She had new staff now, paid for their work, one of whom was stirring a pot suspended over a fire while the other sliced cheese in the corner.

"Cait! What are you doing here so close to your wedding day?"

"I don't have anything to do now my mother has arrived. She has it all in hand."

Lena snickered. "I'm sure she means well."

"I am happy to let her have her head." Cait gestured to Gwen. "This is my friend, Gwen, from Gwynedd. She speaks a little Danish."

Gwen bobbed her head. "It is a pleasure to meet you."

Now Lena's smile widened further. "I know who you are. You are the wife of Gareth, Prince Godfrid's friend."

"I am."

Lena looked from one woman to the other. "Does that mean … you are here about the death of that priest yesterday? I thought he took his own life?"

After Cait translated, Gwen ground her teeth. "May I ask who told her that?"

Cait then asked the question for her.

"Iona. I don't know who she heard it from, one of her men, I think."

"Her men?" Cait asked.

Lena gave Cait a sideways glance. "Now she is free, she has many suitors, and she is taking her time choosing among them."

"Did you ever encounter Harald?"

Lena shook her head. "No. We live our own lives down here."

She meant on the north side of town near the dock gate, which Cait understood because she'd lived here too. Being a slave was an entirely separate existence, in large part because a slave didn't have leave to wander Dublin. At the same time, if a dockman appeared in one of the wealthier sections of the city, near Godfrid's house, for example, or the palace, he would be looked at hard by everyone he encountered. It didn't mean he couldn't go there, but he might be asked his intentions more than once.

"Which church do you attend?" Gwen asked.

After Cait translated, Lena said, "St. Mary's parish church, here at the docks. Father Bertold understands us."

Dublin had a dozen parish churches, most of which were small, serving parishioners living in a handful of streets each. Cait could see from Gwen's face it wasn't what she was used to either, but city living was odder to her even than to Cait, who had lived in Dublin since the spring.

Cait nudged Gwen's elbow. "Show her the wooden coin."

Gwen drew it out and held it on her palm so Lena could see it. By the look of awareness that crossed Lena's face, she knew what it was before either Cait or Gwen could ask, "Do you know what this is for?"

"Where did you get that?"

Cait was pleased they'd come to the right place for answers. "From Harald's room."

"The monk had it?" The surprise in Lena's voice was impossible to mistake.

"Does it lead to a brothel?" Gwen asked.

Cait translated, causing Lena to blink. "Is that what you think? No." She shook her head vehemently. "A brothel is no place for a monk either, but that isn't what this is for."

"Then what?" Cait said.

Lena looked away for a moment, gathering her thoughts. Cait and Gwen waited, though Cait couldn't think what could be so momentous that Lena would be this reluctant to tell them. Finally, when Lena couldn't avoid their stares any longer, she sighed. "I know you are aware that some young men are troubled by Dublin's submission to Leinster."

Cait nodded. She did. Of course she did.

"When times are hard, people long for the old ways, before—" Lena made a helpless gesture with one floured hand.

"Before slavery was abolished in Dublin?" Cait said.

Lena scoffed. "They would like to go back to those old ways too, but that is not what I meant or their main concern. They want to bring back the glory days of old. They want to go *a Viking*."

Those hadn't been glory days for Cait's people—nor Gwen's and Lena's for that matter—but she didn't say so. She could feel Gwen listening and watching intently, but she didn't interrupt, understanding, Cait hoped, that Cait would explain everything when Lena was done speaking.

"How does that relate to this wooden token?"

Lena chewed on her tongue for another moment before finally capitulating. "It gains entry to the fighting ring."

17

Day Two

Gwen

Gwen's Danish was rudimentary, but she had learned some basic words and phrases by now and caught the last thing Lena said. "Fighting ring? What on earth is a fighting ring?"

Cait was already asking Lena the very same thing, and received a long explanation, which Gwen did not interrupt. She watched Lena's face, however, and it was obvious she knew what she was talking about.

When Lena wound down, Cait turned to Gwen and explained: "It's a gathering of men who practice their warrior skills together. She first heard of it six months ago. Admission is by wooden coin."

"I'm not sure I understand. Why couldn't they meet openly? Why the coin?"

Cait spoke to Lena again and received a short reply.

"She doesn't know for certain. They change the location of their meetings often, moving around the city and the surrounding countryside. She thinks they aspire to turn themselves into an elite group, like the Dragons."

Gwen could have told them there wasn't ever going to be anyone like the Dragons, but that would have been rude and unhelpful. "Does she know where the next meeting is? Or when?"

"She does not."

"How does she know about all this?"

When Cait asked that question, Lena shrugged. "We may no longer be slaves, but we hear things. People talk in front of us."

"Or we listen in doorways." This was said in Welsh, by a woman who swept aside the curtain that blocked the far doorway to the pantry. She was close to fifty in age, buxom but not unfit, with a halo of red curly hair she didn't appear to be trying to tame, beyond a headband to hold the bulk of it back from her face. She set the wrapped block of butter she was carrying on the table.

"Iona!" Cait greeted the woman with a huge smile and then spoke in Danish, since she herself had no Welsh to reply to Iona's initial greeting.

Iona gave Cait a beatific smile and approached and curtseyed low, also speaking in Danish, but this time something Gwen could understand. "It is wonderful to see you, my lady."

Cait scoffed, indicating this was an old jest between them. "It's nice to see you too."

Iona laughed. "You look lovely."

Remembering her manners, Cait gestured to Gwen and said something along the lines of, *This is Gwen, wife to Sir Gareth the Welshman. We are investigating the death of that monk, Harald.*

"I know." Iona bobbed a genuine curtsey in Gwen's direction and returned to Welsh, "You must forgive my manner. I was cruel to this child when I learned she had deceived us as to her identity. But she more than made up for it by doing what only she could."

Gwen's brow furrowed. "I'm sorry, I don't know what you're talking about. What could only Cait do?"

Iona looked from Gwen to Cait, her own expression puzzled, and said, "Doesn't she know?"

Cait made a helpless gesture. "I-I don't know."

Iona turned back to Gwen. "It is our Caitriona who convinced the bishop and King Brodar to free all the slaves in Dublin." She squeezed Cait's hand affectionately. "She spoke for us when nobody else would."

Gwen translated that into French for Cait, her head spinning at the three language conversation.

"My brother spoke for them too," Cait said in French, obviously embarrassed to be singled out and praised. "As did Godfrid." Then she repeated her words in Danish for Iona.

Iona nodded and then said to Gwen in Welsh, "That may be, but she was the first to say what nobody else would dare." She scrunched some of her curls at the back of her head with a satisfied smile. "What do you want to know about the fighting ring?"

"Anything you can tell us."

"I'll say it first in Welsh and then in Danish, yes?"

"That would be helpful."

Then Iona tipped her head to a table around which stools and benches had been set, and the three of them sat. Lena continued to work at her dough, while another worker was tasked with laying out mead, bread, and some of the butter Iona had brought.

Gwen put up a hand. "May I ask first how you know about it?"

A saucy look crossed Iona's face. "Earlier this summer, I had a lover who was injured during training. He told me what he'd been training for and took me to watch."

"So men train, and then they fight?"

"They train on their own or in small groups. The fights occur every few weeks, on an irregular schedule the men are only told about a few days before."

Iona was as good a witness as it was possible to find. "Please go on."

"Maybe two years ago, before Cait's time, there was an incident down at the docks. Two sailors got into a scrap at a tavern, which isn't unusual, but one pulled his knife and killed the other. A foreman saw it happen and told the sheriff. That was Sheriff Holm's first murder, I think, but since there were witnesses, the murderer was hanged, and that was the end of it.

"Except the foreman got to thinking that the sailor who'd been killed had failed to defend himself properly. These were sailors, who, in previous times, would have been the first on a beach to sack a village. *I* was captured by men such as they. But no longer. This younger generation has never been *a Viking*. The foreman decided he would teach them."

"Is that foreman still the organizer?" Gwen asked.

"As far as I know. His name is Goff."

"Why the coin?"

Iona raised her eyebrows. "Men like their secrets, don't they?" She shrugged one shoulder. "From what I saw, it was well-intentioned. So this monk had a coin, eh?"

"From his bruises and old wounds, he was fighting," Gwen said. "Have you been to a fight since that first one?"

"No." Iona shrugged again and stood up, ready to get back to work. "Personally, I don't see the appeal. Though—when my suitor went to sea he left me his wooden coin." Her smile widened as she saw the surprise on Gwen's face. "I still have it."

The news of the door the coins opened was momentous enough for Cait and Gwen to thank Iona and Lena for their help and set off immediately for Godfrid's house. Iona assured them she would repeat what she knew again to Gareth later if he needed to hear it directly from her—and would surrender the coin if they wanted it. She also wouldn't speak of it to anyone else. Her comment as they departed was, "Who would I tell?"

Gwen didn't want to tell Cait her business, but the fact that Iona had spoken so openly to them about the fighting ring in front of Lena and the two other servants in the kitchen indicated it was an open secret. Those in the upper echelons of Danish society were simply too far removed from the common folk to know what was really going on in Dublin.

As they left the warehouse district Cait stumped along, clearly in a bit of a pique. Gwen thought she knew what was wrong. "There's no way you could have known about this."

"Isn't there? I was supposed to be keeping an ear to the ground about what was going on in Dublin."

"You were supposed to be infiltrating Rikard's organization, which you did. Even if you'd heard about a fighting ring, would you have thought anything of it?"

Cait's eyes took on a faraway look, and she stopped her stomping walk. "I suppose not. And if I had heard about it, I wouldn't have thought it was important. I might not even have known it wasn't a long tradition."

"We know about it now," Gwen said soothingly. "And really, would Brodar or Godfrid have stopped them?"

"Godfrid would have kept an eye on them, but let them be." She nodded sharply. "You're right. If Harald died because of something that happened there, it couldn't have been prevented by us."

18

Day Two

Dai

Dai waved a hand at his mother and Cait, who were heading up the street as he, Cadoc, and Jon were heading down it. According to the blacksmith at the palace, the armorer's shop was one street up and two over from the dock gate, putting it still a few blocks from where they were walking.

The sight of his mother coming towards him with Cait, however, had him wondering what other pieces of the puzzle they were missing. He'd been so focused on learning Danish and the task Jon had given him, he hadn't given much thought to anything else. The two women could have gone to visit a seamstress, but given that Cait was a princess, and a seamstress would come to her, working on the investigation seemed more likely. Especially with his mother beside her.

Jon bent his head to Cait and chose to speak in French, for the benefit of everyone present. "Princess."

"Hello, Jon. Where are you going?"

Even Dai's French had improved so much, just today, that he didn't have to think about what they said and translate into Welsh in his head.

"We are pursuing a line of inquiry, as I've heard Prince Hywel say," Jon replied.

Dai looked at his mother. "Where have you been?"

"Doing the same." She tipped her head. "Should we come along with you?"

Cadoc pursed his lips. "We are going to see a local armorer about Harald's gear."

Gwen made a rumbling sound in her throat that was incipient laughter. "Maybe Cait and I shouldn't come then. I imagine having women along might make him less likely to talk to you three ruffians." She grinned. "For our part, we just learned what door the coin opens."

The five of them had formed a circle in the middle of the street. While Gwen explained what she and Cait had learned, Cait's two guards loitered a few yards away, facing outward. Dai was impressed they knew their job well enough not to abandon their posts out of curiosity. If he had been the guard, he would have been *aching* to know what they were talking about.

"A fighting ring?" Jon's tone was highly offended. "Why didn't I know of it?"

"You're too high ranking," Gwen said. "This appears to be for younger, lower men."

"I'd be interested to learn why Conall wasn't aware of it when he was living at the docks," Cait said.

"He's Irish," Dai suggested. "They might have worked hard to keep it from him."

"The boy is right." Cadoc put a hand briefly on top of Dai's head, as was becoming a bit of a habit with everyone it seemed. Dai knew he meant to be avuncular and tried not to find it annoying.

Dai gestured to Cait's guards. "What about Bern and Sitric?"

Everyone looked at the two guards. They were night and day different in coloring, with Bern blond and Sitric dark, but their build was almost identical: tall and burly. Dai felt like a little boy in comparison. But then, they were already grown men and warriors.

Jon gestured for the pair to come closer, though once there, Gwen urged everyone into the alley behind them. "We're starting to be noticed."

Once the others had followed, Jon, who was Bern and Sitric's commander, put the question to them, in Danish, of course: "Tell me of this fighting ring that is accessed by this wooden coin."

Bern's reply was immediate, "What fighting ring?" but Sitric's denial came just a little too late, and only after a blank look of surprise he couldn't control crossed his face. He was a few years older than Dai and hadn't mastered the impassive look most Danes affected when in public. Even Godfrid, who was so exuberant to his friends, had managed to keep his hatred of Ottar a secret for five years.

Dai wasn't the only one who saw the hesitation in Sitric. Gwen moved closer, the wooden coin in the palm of her hand. "We have one, you see."

She spoke in Danish too, and Dai found himself suddenly proud of his mother. Languages hadn't always come easily to him either, and it had made him appreciate how they often didn't for others. His mother already spoke Welsh, French, and English, as most of Hywel's party did. Instead of being resentful that he wasn't special, he found himself cheering her on.

Sitric stared at the coin for so long, Dai thought he wasn't going to answer, but finally he cleared his throat. "I've been sworn to secrecy. We all take an oath."

"You took an oath to Godfrid," Jon said.

Sitric's expression turned stricken, and now Cait put a hand on his arm. "We already know about the wooden coins and the fighting ring, so we don't need you to break your word. We'll leave it for now."

"Thank you, my lady. I will—" he swallowed hard, "—I will speak to Prince Godfrid when he returns. I will understand if this means I can no longer be in your service."

Jon made an *ach* sound at the back of his throat.

Cait glanced at him, and Jon knew what he'd done and bowed. "My pardon, my lady. I realize it isn't up to me."

She made a dismissive gesture. "None of that. You are a loyal companion and friend, Jon. As is Sitric. You have nothing to apologize for. We will all deal with this when Godfrid gets home. Gwen and I will wait for you at the house." Cait tipped her head to Bern, who was glaring at his companion. Sitric, for his part, could only look at his feet. "Come."

Gwen gave Dai a pat on the shoulder. "Hurry back!"

That left the three men alone again to walk the last hundred yards to the armorer's workshop. As they approached, a Godfrid-sized man opened the door, ducked under the lintel, and departed, an axe resting on his shoulder.

Suddenly, Dai stopped and put the back of his hand to Cadoc's chest. "Let me go in alone."

Cadoc opened his mouth, probably to argue, but then a thoughtful look entered his eyes. Jon stopped too, his expression quizzical. "What are we doing?"

"You and I will loiter over here," Cadoc said, "and then, after a bit, we'll come in, arguing about axes or something equally Danish."

"You don't speak Danish," Dai objected.

Cadoc laughed. "Then Jon can be haranguing me. Anything to disarm the proprietor and make him think you aren't with us."

Jon's eyes turned thoughtful too, and while he considered the wisdom of Cadoc's plan, Dai unbuckled his sword belt and handed it to Cadoc, along with its accompanying knife. "I can't look like who I really am." He also took off his cloak that marked him as a nobleman's son and the jacket he wore underneath. That left him in shirtsleeves and breeches. The cloth used to make them was of good quality, but not the best, and both were hand-me-downs from Llelo, so they were a little too big.

Cadoc took the sword, holding it by the sheath as if he didn't know what to do with it and then bent to the street to gather dust to smear across Dai's cheek. "That's a bit more like the vagabond I know you to be at heart."

With a grin and a wave, Dai left them to enter the workshop.

As the previous customer had done, Dai ducked under the lintel (pleased he had to duck at all), and stepped into the shop—and in his surprise, came to an abrupt halt two feet into the room.

The proprietor, who was standing on the other side of a long counter that ran almost the width of the shop, grinned. "Not what you expected, eh?"

Dai walked forward. "It isn't! From the outside it looks like nothing much of anything." For starters, the shop was bigger inside than he expected, built square with a wooden floor, not rounded like many of the huts around it or oblong like Godfrid's hall. It was warm and dry as well.

Bows, axes, and armor of every stripe hung from the beams that ran from wall to wall three feet above his head. A few smaller items worked in leather, including a fine set of bracers, lay loose on the counter. The swords were to be found on the wall behind the proprietor, too precious to allow just anyone who wandered by to touch.

In appearance, the proprietor was the direct opposite of Gren. He was the same height as Dai, who had just started to grow towards his man's height, with a mostly bald head, a thick mustache but no beard, and a somewhat rotund belly. Dai didn't want to make assumptions, but he didn't think the man was a blacksmith at all.

However, it wouldn't be a bad thing to ask. He reached up and touched a leather sheath hanging above his head. "Where did you get all this? Did you make these weapons yourself?"

The man laughed. "Not me."

"You're a trader?" Dai focused on him directly. "You've sailed far, then? To other lands?"

Dai intended his enthusiasm and questions to be encouraging. But they were also genuine in this instance, so he didn't feel like he was mumming. The man put his forearms on the counter and leaned into them. "You're not from Dublin, I can tell that from your accent, though your Danish is very good. You're not Irish either, I don't think."

"Welsh," Dai said.

"Ah." He nodded knowingly, and Dai realized with shock that the merchant thought he was a newly freed slave. It made a certain kind of sense. "I am Vigo. What can I help you with?"

"I need a blade," Dai said.

Vigo eyed him. "Why would that be?"

Dai made his expression truculent which, truthfully, wasn't hard. He knew his mother had grown weary of seeing it, though things had been much better between them since Dai had apprenticed to the Dragons. He made himself a mental reminder to hug her the next time he saw her.

"So I can fight."

Vigo continued to lean across the counter. The floor where the merchant stood was raised, like a dais, because he was still looking Dai in the eye. "Why would you want to do that?"

Dai straightened his spine and looked steadily back. "Why does it matter?"

Cadoc and Jon chose that moment to enter the store, arguing, as promised, about the merits of swords versus axes. They were speaking in French. Given Cadoc's sword, the decision made sense, and since Jon already knew Vigo—or at least knew of him—there was no chance Vigo wouldn't recognize him.

"Ho!" Vigo straightened instantly and glared at Jon, not a morsel of respect in his demeanor or tone. "What are you doing here?"

Dai backed away to the far right corner of the shop, as he would have done had he really been a former slave.

"We are interested in your weaponry and armor," Jon said in Danish.

"I don't believe you. You aren't interested in my wares." He pointed to Dai's sword at Cadoc's waist. "Not with that weapon."

Cadoc put a hand proprietarily on the sword hilt. Neither man had even glanced at Dai, who was really glad he'd had the forethought to shed the clothes and gear that made him look noble. He'd worn a sword since he had apprenticed at twelve to Cynan, Prince Hywel's brother, before the death of Rhun, and he missed its weight on his hip, even for so brief a time. In addition, when his father had given it to him, he'd looked him in the eye and said, "Do not lose this."

Dai had no intention of losing it. He slept with it tucked alongside his pallet. He never went anywhere without it, not even the latrine, except perhaps in the middle of the night. And even then, sometimes he thought about it before he left it behind. No matter where he was he could be attacked under the cover of darkness, and if he was sitting on the latrine without his sword, he would regret it.

Jon capitulated, though his tone was sharp and his words clipped. "This is about the monk, Harald, who died."

"Killed himself, I hear." Vigo seemed unaffected by the observation.

"That is not certain." Jon tipped his head—as did Dai—both wondering how it was the news had spread so quickly. "Where did you hear of it?"

"Here and there."

Nobody liked to identify their sources of gossip. But while Vigo was as near to hostile as it made no difference, he couldn't refuse to answer Jon's questions. Jon's master was a prince of Dublin. Dai didn't yet have such status, but his father did, and Dai had always been treated well because of it. That was, of course, why he hadn't told Vigo who he really was.

"Did you know him?"

"Did I know who?"

"Harald."

Vigo laughed derisively. "I have never sold a sword to a monk."

And suddenly, Dai found himself staring into the face of an outright lie, and he knew it. *He knew it!* He'd decided last year that he didn't want to be an investigator like Llelo or his father. But today was suddenly *fun*. He'd been feeling just a little guilty at deceiving Vigo, and every man had a right to his secrets, but not when it came to murder. Murder was a violation of a man's right to live. Even King Owain couldn't hang someone without a trial. That was what Normans did. The Welsh were more civilized.

Vigo had looked hard at Jon when he denied knowing Harald, which meant to Dai that he was used to lying. Liars, according to Dai's father, either looked away when they lied or looked right into your eyes and lied to your face. The best ones could do so without the little edge of defiance Vigo showed to Jon. Dai couldn't wait to see how Vigo responded when he asked him the same questions once Jon and Cadoc left.

Jon wasn't done with Vigo, however. He'd brought Harald's sword, and now he laid it flat on the counter in front of Vigo. "I think this is one of yours."

To Dai's surprise, Vigo didn't immediately deny it. He picked it up by the hilt and tipped it this way and that, studying the heft and the shine of the blade. "If I sold it, it wasn't to a man who called himself Harald, and it wasn't in this condition."

The qualifications were interesting, but understandable, since the sword was nicked along the blade.

Now Cadoc stepped forward and said in French. "We are not accusing you of anything. We just want to know if you sold this sword and to whom you might have sold it." Then he pulled a piece of paper from his pocket and showed him a sketch of Harald, which Dai's father had drawn. Dai would have loved to have a similar gift, seeing how useful it was, but his people ended up looking like slugs with heads and his horses like dogs.

Vigo understood the French, clearly, which made sense if he traveled far and wide to trade. Now, he shook his head, and this time his denial appeared genuine. Either he was telling the truth, or he was finding it easier to lie. "I don't know him." He looked into Jon's face. "Was there anything else?"

Jon picked up the sword. "No."

Cadoc replied in French, "Thank you for your time." The door closed behind them without either man ever looking at Dai.

Dai allowed their footfalls to dissipate and then sauntered up to the counter. "What do I have to do to get a sword like that?"

"Work hard."

Dai fingered the bracers on the counter. "It's too bad nobody fights anymore."

Vigo scoffed. "Did you miss the battle against the men of Meath?"

"If it hadn't been for Leinster, we would have lost."

Vigo subsided. "You're not wrong, boy." He leaned against the counter. "So you want to learn to fight?"

"Yes!"

"If you stick around, I might be able to arrange for you to learn."

"You could?" Dai's eyes widened.

Vigo raised one shoulder. "Tomorrow night. Come to me here at low tide."

Dai swallowed. "Would we be going somewhere?"

"We'll see. You're not afraid of getting wet, are you?"

"I do get seasick," Dai lied.

Vigo laughed. "We'll be crossing the Liffey on foot, not by boat."

Dai tried to look unaffected by this news. "You lied to those men."

Vigo's eyes went wide—exaggeratedly so. "Did I?"

"Maybe you didn't recognize the picture of that dead monk, but when you said you'd never sold a sword to a monk, you lied."

Rather than being offended, Vigo laughed. "I didn't lie. I didn't sell the sword, I loaned it. And besides which, it was a priest who rented it, not a monk." He gestured grandly to his shop. "Most men can't afford to buy any of this, but they can borrow it for a time. For a fee." His eyes glinted.

This double revelation shook Dai, but he endeavored not to show it. "Why didn't you say so?"

"Best not to get involved."

"How did you know the man was a priest? Did he come in his robe?"

"No." Another laugh. "He wore workman's clothing."

"Then how did you know he was a priest?"

"You ask a great many questions, don't you?" Vigo grabbed a broom that had been leaning against the wall and handed it over the counter to Dai. "Sweep away their footprints and there's a bun in it for you."

Dai took the broom and went to work, sending a few clods of dirt out the door, which he opened for that purpose. "So how did you know he was a priest?" It was a risk, asking a third time, but Dai thought it was in character.

"I didn't at the time, though I thought I recognized his face when he pushed back his hood. Then I saw him during mass, so, of course, I knew."

Dai didn't know the right approach for his next question, whether to pretend he wasn't interested or to show his enthusiasm. He opted for the latter. "During mass? Where? Who is he?"

Vigo waved his hand airily. "He's one of dozens at Christ's Church." Then he slapped his chest. "But being a curious fellow, I asked around. He's the secretary for the bishop himself." He laughed. "Odd things are happening up at the cathedral, eh?"

19

Day Two

Gareth

*O*dd things indeed.

Dai had told the story of his meeting with Vigo with a gleeful enthusiasm that infected everyone else in the room. How could it not?

Gareth ruffled his son's hair. "I'm proud of you for sticking with it. Not everyone would have known what to say."

"Jon and Cadoc helped." Dai ducked his head. "If they hadn't put up Vigo's hackles, he probably wouldn't have trusted me. I can't believe he sold Arnulf out—to a total stranger!" Then he hesitated. "I guess he didn't mean to because he didn't know who he was talking to. You don't think he's lying, do you? He can't know who I am, can he?"

"I wouldn't think so," Gareth said. "It doesn't sound like it."

"How do you feel about this?" Gwen put her arm around Dai's shoulders. "Lying to him, I mean?"

The old Dai might have shrugged and shown unconcern, but the new Dai was more thoughtful, and he took a moment before he answered. "I felt bad at first. But when he lied to Jon's face, I decided the truth was more important. And if Arnulf rented that sword, then he's been lying to Father this *whole time!*"

Dai's outrage was endearing—and understandable too. They were all working towards a common goal, and it was frustrating to discover people who were supposed to be trustworthy standing in their way.

But it was gratifying too, because this, combined with Gwen and Cait's discovery of the origin of the wooden coin and Holm's conversation with Harald's mother and the existence of his books, gave them a clear indication of where to go from here.

Llelo looked at Gareth. "Can I be with you when you arrest Arnulf?"

"Of course, but I'm not going to do that yet." Gareth's eyes met Gwen's, and then hers widened at what she might have seen in his. "He isn't going anywhere, and I sense he is a little fish. Saying anything to him could alert the bigger ones, like this Goff—or Vigo. I think we need to use him first. And that means letting him run free, as much as it goes against our instincts."

"You're not—" Gwen stopped. "Gareth."

"What?"

Gwen rolled her eyes. "It's a bad idea."

"Is it? You don't even know what I am going to propose."

His wife poked her finger at him. "I was at Shrewsbury too, remember? And Dai—" she broke off, and Gareth's heart clenched at the genuine fear in her face.

"I'm not a child anymore, Mam," Dai said from beside his mother.

"I know." Gwen looked down at her hands.

"I was in Shrewsbury too, Gwen," Conall said gently.

Gwen reached out a hand and put it on top of Conall's. "I know that too." She sighed and sat back, gesturing to Gareth. "Go on. Tell them the plan."

"It is obvious to me we should take advantage of Dai's discovery and have him go with Vigo to the fight, if that's happening tomorrow night." He put up one finger before anyone could say anything. "In addition, we have two coins, which means two more of us may attend the event. Others can be nearby if something goes wrong. We have to think hard about whom we can send openly."

Cadoc looked disgruntled. "It can't be me or Jon, since we are known to Vigo personally now."

"Nor can it be Conall, Llelo, or I," Gareth said. "If Arnulf plans to attend, he would recognize us on sight and know the game was up."

"Whatever that *game* is," Gwen said darkly.

Gareth's eyes swept around the table, seeing his two sons, Gwen, Conall, Jon, and Cadoc, who appeared to be this week's delegate to the murder investigation. In past years, it usually had been Evan, but he and Gruffydd were the leaders of the Dragons now and charged with Prince Hywel's personal safety. Cait, Godfrid, and Hywel were at the palace, each unable to attend because of royal obligations, though all would have wanted to.

Holm was also present, though he'd stayed silent while they talked, likely because he couldn't understand a word they were saying. Gareth had almost surprised himself by including him, but he was the sheriff and, unlike in previous investigations in foreign lands, they didn't need to keep select aspects of their findings to themselves.

"I had a thought we might rope in a few of the other Dragons, if you approve of my plan," Gareth said.

Gwen put up a hand. "My objections aside, which are more for Dai—"

"Legitimately so," Gareth said, wanting to be supportive, and would have been even if he wasn't likely to get what he wanted.

Gwen eyed her husband but continued, "We have two coins and two men to use them. We have a monk who was obsessed with Danish history and mythology—and who died dressed as a knight. I am forced to agree that we have to take advantage of what we've been given. I am wondering, however, if Iona shouldn't keep her coin and use it. Or if women don't need a coin to be admitted, she could go on the arm of one of the Dragons. Having a recognizable person at the fight might call a newcomer less into question."

"Can she go on the arm of Fergus the Sailor?" Conall asked.

"He's Irish. Iona made clear these fights are for Danes."

"None of the Dragons are Danes," Conall pointed out, "and none of them speak Danish at all, much less as well as I do." He looked at Holm and said, "What do you think?" and then translated what they'd just said into Danish.

Holm looked thoughtful for a moment before putting forth his opinion (again patiently translated for those who didn't understand). "Harald had a coin, a sword, and died wearing armor. The idea that he is associated with these fights is an obvious one. I'm sorry to say I know nothing of them, and I too am not one who can go."

Jon translated and then added, "Sitric already confessed to being involved. He *has* a coin himself, so clearly he should go." He rose to his feet. "I'll bring him in."

While Jon was getting Sitric, Cadoc stirred. "The rest of us need to stay close. I, for one, am not going to sit by and wait while the young one has all the fun." He put a hand on Dai's shoulder and shook him.

"We can post men north of the river long before sundown, so nobody will be wondering about a herd of us crossing the bridge at the same time as the participants," Gareth said. "We can also put a man on Goff, to see where he goes and with whom he meets."

"And on Arnulf," Conall said. "Carefully. We don't want to give ourselves away before tomorrow night."

Jon returned with Sitric, who'd already begged Godfrid's forgiveness and was now ready to talk. Although he was dark of hair and eye, his beard was thin, indicating he was probably just twenty, if that. He was large, however, and no longer had the round face of youth.

"Many will not be crossing the bridge. There's a full moon tomorrow night, which makes the tide very low. Under those circumstances, it's possible to cross the Liffey over the tidal flats. The organizers have been very careful to make sure we are never caught, which means the city guards can't be put on alert by so many men leaving the city at the same time after dark."

At low tide, one could also walk across the Menai Strait from Gwynedd to Anglesey before the tide turned, and that was a much farther distance. Gareth would rather take a boat during the slack water at high tide. Less risky, to his mind. But then, he wasn't a huge admirer of the sea, not like these Danes.

"Why do they fear being discovered?" Gwen asked. "That's one of the pieces that's odd to me."

Since Jon had collected Sitric, Conall had been the one translating for Holm in a low tone, and now the sheriff, the Danish symbol of authority at the table, harrumphed. "We have no objection to men training."

Sitric looked down at his hands, and when he spoke, his words were a cross between contrite and sulky. "Men join because it's secret. They think they're getting something they can't get anywhere else. It's like a guild, except for warriors."

Now it was Conall's turn to harrumph. "It's more fun when it's secret, isn't it?"

Jon sat back in his chair, his eyes on his underling. "Stop sniveling over there. So you participate in a fighting club. Why does our discovery of it turn you inside out? Did *you* have anything to do with Harald's death?"

"No!" Finally Sitric shed his mask of reticence and shame. "I had nothing to do with that."

"Then what?" Jon asked.

Sitric was still standing, and now he put his hands on his hips, finally exhibiting a posture that wasn't submissive, just an indication that he was thinking. "It started out as training, but over the last months, since the death of Ottar, the atmosphere has changed."

Gareth waited for Sitric to embellish, which he didn't, so he prompted, "It's different now how?"

"I don't know when it changed, but the meetings are less about training and more about fighting now. The fighters have assumed names and wear masks so nobody knows their identities. There's gambling involved."

Gwen pursed her lips. "Iona didn't mention gambling."

"She went to only one fight. She might not have realized everything that was going on."

"Training was the original intent," Gareth said. "Am I the only one seeing the irony that there now seems to be a profit motive?"

"Gambling." Gwen shook her head. "One of the three original vices."

"Three?" Llelo looked at her quizzically.

"Gambling, alcohol, and prostitution. They are pitfalls for any individual but for the mercantile-minded, they are weaknesses to be exploited. There's a great deal of money to be made in all three."

Conall was looking at her with laughter in his eyes. "Do you have Danish blood in you somewhere? They'll make a merchant of you yet!"

Gwen scoffed. "I didn't say I was going to exploit them! Only that others do. And in this case, if the foreman—or someone else— has organized gambling on the winners of these fights, that could be a motive for murder if Harald was supposed to lose a fight, for example, and he won instead."

Cadoc leaned forward, his focus on Sitric again. "Was there ever a monk who fought in the ring?"

"A monk? No, I don't think so. Really, if that had been the case, I would have mentioned it sooner." Sitric shook his head as if the very idea was ridiculous. But then he stopped and thought again. "But—" his face paled.

Everyone looked at him expectantly.

Sitric swallowed hard. "I have seen the one they call the Templar."

20

Day Two

Gwen

"I am having a hard time envisioning Harald pretending to be a Templar and fighting other men," Gwen said. "Is he really the man Sitric saw in the ring?"

"We won't know until we are able to attend and see for ourselves," Gareth said. "Harald was injured. He'd been fighting someone."

Gwen supposed that was true, though the whole idea of a Templar had always been a strange one to her. Monks weren't supposed to fight. That was the entire point of them. Maybe this was something she could discuss with Abbot Rhys.

Though the questions around Harald's death continued, and it appeared as if all of Dublin now thought Harald killed himself, the bishop steadfastly refused to believe it, and thus Harald was getting a proper burial. That was all he was getting, however: a graveside service on holy ground.

Other than Gareth and Gwen, the only other attendees were a handful of monks and priests and Harald's mother, who sobbed throughout the proceedings. Afterwards, the group dispersed with almost unseemly haste. Bishop Gregory, who'd performed the brief service personally, gestured Gareth and Gwen closer. Arnulf hovered in the background. Gwen found it hard to look at him.

Once they knew who he was, they'd gone through Arnulf's responses to the questions Gareth had put to him word for word as best as they could remember. Few answers had been outright lies, instead being along the lines of *I don't know what else I can tell you* and *I really couldn't say*, which Arnulf had said at least twice. In retrospect, it was hard to tell the difference between actual ignorance and lies of omission. Often that wasn't made clear until after the fact.

"Any progress?" Bishop Gregory said.

"We are making progress." Gareth visibly wavered. He surely wasn't going to speak openly about their plans in the churchyard, not with Arnulf listening. He could lie to put Arnulf at ease, but he couldn't lie to a bishop.

Gwen squeezed his arm. "What my husband is trying to convey is that we *will* find answers. He fears, however, you are not going to like them."

"Are these answers leading to the belief that Harald should not be buried in holy ground?"

Gareth shook his head. "They are not. Not so far."

Bishop Gregory's expression lightened. "I told you to seek out the truth, wherever it took you. Do that, and I am content."

They went their separate ways, the bishop and Arnulf back to the cloister and Gareth and Gwen to the churchyard entrance, having learned nothing of interest at the funeral, in large part because so few people showed up—though a negative was still an answer of some kind. Llelo was hovering in the gateway, waiting for them, with a look on his face that implied urgency.

Gwen found her mouth turning down in anticipation of bad news. "What is it?"

"Prince Hywel requests your presence at the palace."

Gwen checked the sky. "It's almost suppertime anyway. We were just coming."

"You should know before we get there that representatives from Connaught have come." Llelo's long strides ate up the short distance to the palace gate.

Despite the urgency, Gwen halted in the middle of the lane. "Sent by the High King?"

"Sort of." Llelo laughed, though without amusement. It was another sign he was growing up. "Men who support Donnell O'Connor came first, followed within the hour by Rory O'Connor himself, who says he is representing the High King at Godfrid and Cait's wedding."

"Hywel told me they were supposed to be coming," Gareth said. "I apologize for not mentioning it."

"I thought Rory and King Diarmait hated each other," Gwen said.

Gareth took Gwen's hand, and they started walking again. "Since Ottar's death, they have reconciled against Donnell, Rory's brother, who is attempting to gather the other kings of Ireland to him in hopes of bolstering his claim to the High Kingship upon their father's death. This includes Meath and Brega, whom Dublin fought in the spring, as well as Breifne and its king, Tiernan O'Rourke."

Gwen put out her lip. "I thought O'Rourke was Rory's ally?"

"Fifteen years ago O'Rourke led the raids against Leinster in which Rory participated, as a representative of his father." To his credit, Gareth's tone was matter-of-fact, rather than patient with the way she needed to be reminded of what he'd already told her—and what appeared to be such familiar history to him he could recite it at will. "The needs of recent events have superseded old grudges, at least for now. Remember, only a few months ago Donnell tried to arrange for the death of Brodar *and* Rory. Any enemy of Donnell is now a friend of Rory and vice versa."

"Thus making Brodar, as King of Dublin, and Diarmait, as King of Leinster, potential allies instead of enemies." Gwen nodded. "But for Rory to come all this way in person to attend Cait and Godfrid's wedding ..." Her voice trailed off as she thought about all the different things it could imply.

"It means something is afoot," Gareth said.

Once at the great hall, Llelo stepped aside to allow his parents to precede him. As Gareth entered, Gwen could feel a slight stirring amongst the men nearest the door. Regardless of their allegiance, to a man, they nodded a greeting or bowed their heads as he passed.

Gareth wasn't a prince, but he was the steward to the Prince of Gwynedd—and more than that, in the two days they'd been in

Dublin, his reputation continued to precede him. He was *Gareth the Welshman*, as if there could be only one.

Hywel's Dragons had a similar reputation. As she and Gareth advanced down the hall towards the high table, she noted them scattered around the room. Gruffydd stood against the wall behind Hywel's chair, literally watching his back, but the rest were there to watch, wait, and protect.

She caught sight of Dai, near the back of the hall, still in his shirt and breeches, with neither cloak nor jacket, in case anyone at the palace was also going to be at the fight the next night.

Gwen was pleased to see how he'd matured just in the two days they'd been in Dublin. His facility with languages was to be envied and admired. Given the rapidity with which he learned, he might be completely fluent in both Gaelic and Danish by the end of the day. She didn't understand how it was possible for him to be this way, but she could certainly appreciate that he was.

Gwen turned off before she reached the front of the hall. It wasn't her place to approach the high table, and she would rather not call attention to herself. Cait and her mother were sitting at what amounted to a woman's table in the front rank. While Gareth said his greetings, speaking French on the assumption that it was the language the most people at the high table would understand, Gwen took a seat at the far end of the women's table, closest to the wall but adjacent to where Cait sat facing the high table.

"Everything all right here?" Gwen hadn't missed much in terms of a meal, since servants were just beginning to enter the hall with laden trays.

Cait gestured for a servant to pour Gwen a cup of mead. "Nobody has drawn a sword yet."

Gwen took a sip. "The thinking being, if nobody dies during this meal, it will be a triumph?"

Cait's mother, Dorte, snorted into her cup of mead and then came up laughing openly. She'd been so dainty and elegant up until now, that Gwen found herself staring at her.

Dorte put the back of her hand to her mouth. "Pardon me, my sweet. That was so unexpected. I'm going to tell my brother what you said. He will laugh too, a release he desperately needs about now." She eyed the high table, prompting everyone else to look in that direction as well.

Gwen guessed that the dark-haired newcomer next to Diarmait was Rory O'Connor. He sat on the opposite end of the table from the other two newcomers, who were the representatives from Donnell.

She leaned towards Cait. "How do you feel about Rory coming to your wedding?"

"It isn't as awkward as it would have been if Donnell were sitting there. Uncle Diarmait at one point wanted me to marry him." She scoffed under her breath. "As if I could."

"Sometimes we don't have a choice, my dear." Dorte put her hand over her daughter's.

"That wasn't a slight to you, Mother," Cait said. "Diarmait is your brother. You needed to do what he said."

"And you don't?" Dorte's brow arched. "When he spoke to me of your alliance with Godfrid, he implied it was his idea."

Now Cait herself snorted into her cup of mead. "I let him think so."

Dorte wasn't capable of actually grinning, but her smile was a little broader than before. "You are learning, daughter."

A few years earlier, Gwen wouldn't have understood that exchange, even having grown up at court. But her marriage to Gareth and their life of investigating murder had taught her a thing or two about royal politics. She glanced at Dorte. "May I ask how it is you speak such beautiful French? I'm afraid mine is awkward by comparison."

"Of course I will tell you. It's a sad story, really. For many years, Leinster has sought to break the power of the O'Connors. The kings of Leinster, most recently my brother, have sought an alliance with Normans in your country. Learning French as children was an attempt to impress our possible allies with our sophistication. And thus it spread among the other royal households of Ireland." She lifted one shoulder in a dainty shrug. "It didn't work, but I have found the language useful at times. As have Conall and Cait."

"I'm not sorry you learned French, but I can't say I think much of Leinster aligning with any Norman." Gwen spoke matter-of-factly, but her true feelings leaned far more towards outright horror. "In fact, I think it would be a grave mistake. Once they arrive, it is nearly impossible to get them to leave. We know that well in Gwynedd, and even more so in the southern kingdoms of Wales."

Dorte shrugged again. "That may be. It is hard to see how anyone could be worse than the O'Connors."

Gwen bent her head, not knowing how to explain properly to someone who hadn't lived with Normans. Then again, if Dorte *had* lived with Normans, she would be as horrified as Gwen. Things could easily be worse, but it was likely that until the Normans came, the Irish wouldn't know what 'worse' was. Gwen didn't argue, however. As a woman, Dorte very likely had little influence or say in the matter anyway. Diarmait would do what he thought necessary, what kept him in power, regardless of the possible cost. It appeared to be a trait of kings.

For now, Rory O'Connor was an ally, and Leinster and Dublin were safe from any Norman invasion.

Gareth's greetings appeared to have been acceptable, because he was given leave to stand behind Hywel's chair with Gruffydd. But instead of staying on the dais, he spoke briefly with the Dragon captain and then sidled away along the wall to eventually fetch up next to Gwen once again. He leaned down to whisper in her ear. "I know why we were summoned, and it wasn't because Rory is here. Come with me."

Gwen looked up to see a grim look on her husband's face.

"Make your apologies." He brushed his lips past her ear. "Someone else is dead."

21

Day Two

Gareth

Gareth should have known it was a foolish hope to think they could get away with only one dead body in this investigation.

Unlike Harald, whose expression in death was serene, this man had died in pain, with hugely swollen lips, puffy eyes, and a bloody froth around his mouth. He hadn't died here, since he lay with arms above his head, indicating he'd been carried into the storage room off the kitchen—to hide him, it seemed, once someone ran to tell a higher authority what had happened.

Though Gareth crouched beside the body, Gwen sensibly remained near the door, seeing no need to approach too closely. Shelves lined the walls of the room on all sides, laden with stacks of serving dishes, cups, carafes, trays, and the like. As a result, with him, Gwen, Conall, and Jon present, the room was very crowded. Llelo and Dai were keeping watch on the other side of the door, undoubtedly with ears perked in order to hear what was going on inside.

"Just tell me what happened." Gareth looked from Conall to Jon. "And for the love of St. Seiriol, tell me why everyone in the hall is still eating the food, the consumption of which has just killed this man!"

"The food in the hall is not tainted," Jon said soothingly. "King Brodar's food taster sampled it all, and he remains well. King Diarmait himself was adamant that none of the guests become aware someone had died. Right now, he and Brodar are the only ones at the high table who know."

"If all is well, how is this man dead?" Gareth said.

Conall made a gesture with one hand, telling Jon he would talk. "Let me start at the beginning: you are correct to be concerned, but not for the reasons you think. Yes, a half-hour ago, Banan collapsed by the dishes waiting to be carried to the high table. He is King Diarmait's food taster, but even had the entire high table eaten what killed Banan, only King Diarmait would have died. That's why the meal is continuing as usual. Again, King Brodar's food taster had already eaten of everything to be served with no ill effects."

He took a breath. "My family cannot eat shellfish without becoming violently ill. Aversion usually manifests in childhood, initially with less severe symptoms such as a rash and itching in the mouth after consumption. Subsequent meals, however, can mean death. Diarmait's brother died when the same knife used to open an oyster was used to cut his vegetables. One of my great-uncles died after he took a long sniff over a pot where a mixed fish and oyster stew was cooking. Banan was King Diarmait's food taster because he also suffered from the malady, having had his first reaction to a prawn, as did Diarmait, as a child."

"I hope the king paid him well," Jon said dryly.

"He did." Conall toed the heel of the man's boot. "Not that it does him any good now. His family, however, will be provided for."

"What about you?" Gwen looked Conall up and down.

"Of my mother's children, only I am afflicted."

Gareth's breath caught in his throat. "You could have died too!"

"Believe me, I am aware."

Gareth studied their friend. "You're *sure* nobody else is in danger? Dorte and Cait are just in the hall!"

"And they are happily eating without ill effect."

Gareth couldn't stop staring at Conall, and at first Conall almost glared back—before relenting. "I supervised the cutting of fresh meat for my uncle with a newly scrubbed knife and sampled the food meant for their table. Even if everyone at the high table was so afflicted, nothing they eat tonight will hurt them."

Conall's words had started Gareth's mind churning—and his stomach, truth be told. He didn't think *he* would ever be able to eat shellfish again either. "Are you saying just the residue of shellfish on the blade of a knife could be harmful? Or *smelling* it? How can that be true?"

"I don't know how, only that it is." Conall let out a puff of air. "I love my sister and my mother, Gareth. And you can see for yourself that nobody else has died or even fallen ill. Both King Diarmait and

King Brodar have decreed the meal will continue. It is out of our hands."

Gareth knew when he was defeated. "How many people know of the king's affliction?"

"One too many," Conall said bitterly.

Gareth looked at Jon. "Did you know?"

"Not before tonight."

"Which means Godfrid didn't know. I certainly didn't," Gareth said. "King Diarmait didn't tell the kitchen staff?"

"He did better than tell them," Conall said. "He brought his own food taster to supervise their work."

Gwen scoffed. "He didn't do a very good job."

Jon cleared his throat. "King Brodar acquiesced to every request, of course. Our cook was told Diarmait despised shellfish of all kinds and requested we not serve any. Most are out of season anyway, so we complied."

"Or so you thought." Gareth made a *hmm* noise at the back of his throat. "So it isn't common knowledge here. What about in Leinster?"

Conall tipped his head. "Many know. How could they not?"

"Who then are Diarmait's rivals for the throne?" Gwen asked.

"He has sons, of course," Conall said, "but they are hardly old enough to fight amongst themselves as Rory and Donnell do, much less assassinate their father. It would be a bold move for any of them to attempt to take the throne already."

"But not impossible?" Gwen asked.

"The eldest isn't even twenty."

"Is it too much of a coincidence that Rory O'Connor is here tonight?" Jon said. "Or emissaries from Donnell, on the spot, so to speak, at King Diarmait's death, ready to negotiate with Brodar about the future of Dublin?"

"King Diarmait is unsure why Rory would want him dead in this moment, since they are speaking of a mutual alliance to put Rory on the throne over Donnell, whom they both despise. It could be a ruse, I suppose." Conall tapped a finger to his lips. "It's fortunate my uncle trusts nobody."

"Rory would have far more weight to throw around if he brought Dublin into Connaught," Gareth said. "Donnell would find himself at a disadvantage."

"But if Rory was going to arrange for the murder of King Diarmait, would he really be present when it happened?" Gwen shook her head. "Like Donnell, he would have stayed away."

"We can't do anything about the men from Connaught," Gareth said. "We can't even question them without starting a war."

"What about men from Dublin?" Gwen looked at Jon. "Some want to be independent."

"This fighting ring we'll be seeing about appears to be headed in that general direction, but it wasn't my impression from Sitric that they are quite ready for all-out insurrection." Conall's lips twisted. "It is disturbing to me how hated Leinster seems to be. I suppose I shouldn't be surprised."

"It is the reason Diarmait hasn't attempted to rule Dublin directly, my friend," Gareth said, not so consolingly, "and Brodar tries so hard not to appear a puppet."

"We didn't do this," Jon said abruptly. "My prince is a man of honor."

Gareth nodded. "Godfrid and Brodar are excellent dissemblers, but Godfrid loves Cait, and he wouldn't lie to me."

Conall thought about that for a moment. "Nor to me."

Gwen went to the door to gesture Llelo and Dai inside. With the door closed again and all of them crowded around the body, she explained where the conversation had led them.

Llelo shook his head, almost in wonder. "I wouldn't know anything about any of this." Then he looked at his brother. "Do you?" The question was genuine and respectful. The last few days had wrought a change in their relationship too.

There was a pause as a curious expression crossed Dai's face. "I might. Do we know exactly what type of shellfish King Diarmait can't eat?"

"It is hardly something he can determine, is it?" Conall said wryly. "The king avoids all, just in case, along with most fish too, though he claims that is simply because he doesn't like the taste."

If not for the dead body at their feet, Gareth might have laughed at the expression on Jon's face, which implied the very idea of not eating fish at least twice a day was inconceivable.

Dai, however, frowned, his brow furrowing as he thought. "They have a proverb here: *Frisk som en fisk*, yes? Fresh as a fish, which I think is a way of saying someone is feeling well? The English might say *healthy as a horse*."

"Yes," Jon said.

Dai was still frowning. "Yesterday, when I was still figuring the Danish out—"

Gareth managed not to snort laughter at the comment, not wanting to deflect Dai's thought. But one more day had resulted in the boy being all but fluent, at least in the Danish that made up the common tongue. It mattered not at all that he couldn't read a word, though at this rate, Gareth wouldn't put that past him either.

"—someone said those words, and then another man said, *unless you're the King of Leinster*, and they all laughed."

Jon looked at Dai intently. "These were the men in the hall who were speaking of swords and axes?"

"No. This was later, outside. I was coming from the latrine. I'm sorry. I have no idea what they looked like. They were speaking Danish, I can tell you that."

"I don't like it," Conall said flatly.

"Definitely not something to like," Gareth said, "though it could be an innocent comment about the king's dislike of fish."

Gwen tipped her head. "King Diarmait's affliction is the second thing the Danish royal court knew nothing about but appears to be available knowledge to those beneath."

"You're speaking of the fighting rings again." Conall's chin wrinkled in thought.

Gareth hated speculation and said so.

Jon had begun to pace, such as he could, in the small space. "We must do something about the threat from Connaught, even if we can't prevent Rory and Donnell's emissaries from smirking at us from the high table." He stopped, his hands on his hips. "I will send riders to patrol the region around Dublin, starting tonight. At the very least, it will make our ride tomorrow night to seek out the fighting ring less noticeable."

"What good does this do?" Llelo asked.

Gareth took it upon himself to explain. "Diarmait has brought a small army with him, as is his right as Dublin's overlord. Rory has done the same, as a son of the High King. Both are camped in plain view of the city walls. But what about beyond the city? What about north of the river where it appears we must find this fighting ring tomorrow night? Donnell sent emissaries, but what if he has come himself, in force? How would we know if we don't look?"

"If he did any of that, he's getting bolder," Jon said.

Conall tsked. "Someone attacked Diarmait at what effectively is his own table. Short of drawing sword in the hall, you can't get much bolder than that."

"Did Rory know Donnell was sending men to Dublin?" Gwen looked at Conall.

"I don't know." Conall rubbed his chin. "It might be something I can ask, especially now that an attempt has been made on my king's life."

Llelo put his hands on top of his head. "I don't understand how all of you can be so calm about someone trying to murder the King of Leinster!"

Conall spoke through gritted teeth. "Believe me, son, I am not calm."

22

Day Two

Conall

Conall definitely was not calm. In fact, he was in a rage, and the only saving grace for him was that he'd spent most of his adult life hiding his emotions from everyone so as never to appear vulnerable. Otherwise, by now he would have slammed a fist into the wall.

Seeing as the closest wall was made of stone, that would have been a mistake, but it might also have made him feel better to have physical pain to deal with instead of what was roiling him.

He hadn't really known it, or admitted it for many years now, but he loved and admired his uncle. And someone had tried to kill him not an hour ago. It wouldn't have borne thinking about if *not* thinking about it wouldn't have left his uncle wide open to another attempt.

And really, to murder only Diarmait by putting a bit of shell-fish in a dish to be served to the high table took a certain degree of genius. It was horrifying, to be sure, but smart.

It also exposed the culprit in a way he might not have realized. When Gareth and Gwen had asked how many people knew about Diarmait's affliction, Conall had implied it wasn't a secret in Leinster. And it wasn't. The fact that he had a food taster truly should have been common knowledge. All kings did. But either the assassin didn't know about Banan, or he knew so little about the ailment that he was unaware of how quickly death resulted and that Banan could die in the time it took for him to put down his spoon—long before the food reached the high table.

Which meant, at the very least, the killer wasn't a close confidant to the royal family. He was on the outside looking in, which pointed a finger more and more to a Dane or another Irish clan.

The group re-entered the kitchen, and Conall took stock of the staff present. There were at least a dozen people working, several running every which way as the meal was in full swing. Nobody seemed concerned they had a dead man in their pantry, though since he was an Irishman, many might have thought *good riddance.*

Conall put up his hands. "I want everyone to stop." He spoke in his best authoritarian tone and in Danish. While most workers glanced at him, only a handful stopped what they were doing.

Then Jon stepped into the center of the kitchen and barked, "Stop. Now!"

Everyone froze.

Accepting Jon's authority rather than being irritated by it, Conall nodded. "Thank you. If an item is going to burn, you may take care of it. I want the rest of you to look at me and answer my questions."

Thankfully, his Danish had become fluent over the last year, and they all understood and most nodded.

"Am I correct in thinking there was no shellfish dish served tonight?"

A man at a worktable wearing an apron covered in food residue and flour shook his head. "No shellfish dish. It isn't harvest time."

That's what Conall had understood, but to clarify and to get the man talking, he asked, "When is?"

"No harvesting from one moon after the spring equinox to one moon before the autumn equinox."

"What happens if you eat them in the summer?"

The cook turned to one of his underlings and consulted briefly. "They are not as flavorful or plentiful the following years. The summer is the time the females spawn."

"So you *can* eat them."

The man looked as if the very idea was distasteful, but he nodded.

It was the rule Conall had understood as well. He turned to the phalanx of friends behind him and said in Welsh, "Watch their faces."

All of them were experienced investigators, knowing what to do and why he'd asked it of them without needing further explanation. He turned back to the room. "Raise your hand if you have eaten shellfish this summer." He raised his own hand encouragingly.

Most of those facing him did not, but the woman stirring the pot of stew over the fire moved her right hand jerkily, and a boy who'd come in the back with a load of firewood, having missed the initial discussion, put his hand all the way up.

He was behind everyone else, so they couldn't see him. Conall jerked his head at Dai and Llelo, who went straight to him and herded him outside almost before anyone else noticed he'd raised his hand.

Conall went back to his questions. "Did you hire any new workers for the kitchen in the last few days?"

The head cook answered confidently again. "No."

"How about servers?"

"Yes." He bobbed his head. "Two boys and a girl. They are in the main hall now." He frowned. "But they don't come in here. We put the food on the galley, and they take it from there so they don't get underfoot."

"Was the food meant for the high table on the galley or in the kitchen when the food taster died?"

"In the kitchen. It had been set on the worktable for final assessment."

Conall rubbed his chin, thinking of what to ask next.

Jon touched Conall's elbow with his own, indicating he wanted to speak, and Conall gestured that he should.

"What are you feeding the kings now?"

The cook stabbed a finger towards the roasting fireplace. "As you saw, my lord, we cut a new haunch, and it went straight to the table after Edvin ate of it." Edvin was King Brodar's taster. "We took loaves, uncut, and fresh from the oven, and newly pressed butter and decanted honey from the pantry." Finally he indicated a woman sautéing vegetables in a pan. "The parsnips and onions went directly from the pan to the table as well. And, of course, we opened a new barrel of salted herring."

"Of course, you did," Conall said, under his breath. Herring was a Danish staple, and he noted out of the corner of his eye that Gwen's Danish was good enough for her to wrinkle her nose at the mention of herring too.

She had been surveying the table of tainted food, leaning forward and sniffing as he'd been questioning the staff. Into the next pause, she looked up. His audience was getting restive, but he nodded at her. "What is it?"

"I don't see any dish here that smells or looks of shellfish. Am I not understanding what such a dish might look like?"

Conall glanced down at the array of food, frowning. Then he turned back to Jon. "Tell them they can work again." Jon did so, but Conall pointed at the cook. "I need a few more moments of your time."

The cook started to balk, but Jon glared at him. "A man died in your kitchen, eating your food. Don't you think it would be a good idea to find out why?"

The cook immediately modified his expression and posture. "Yes, my lord. Of course, my lord." Maybe he was even sincere, though Conall could understand the desire to put the incident behind him as quickly as possible.

Conall swept a hand out to indicate the table. "Where could shellfish be hidden?"

"That's why you were asking about shellfish? That's what killed him?" The cook frowned as he studied the food. "If any were diced fine, they could be in any of the dishes, though my guess is the chicken and mushroom pie or the stew."

Before Conall could stop him, the cook picked up a spoon, scooped up a bite of the pie, now cooled since it had been nearly an hour since Banan had died, and ate it. Smacking his lips, he said, "Good." He put down the spoon. "I don't taste anything amiss."

"And you're not dead, which is good," Gwen said in an undertone, in Welsh.

They dismissed the cook and trooped outside, Gareth and Jon joined them. Both servants who'd indicated they'd eaten shellfish—the woman, who'd been stirring the stew, and the boy—waited for them. It turned out, perhaps unsurprisingly, they were grandmother and grandson.

"When did you eat them?" Jon demanded, far less polite than he'd been to the head cook.

The older woman bit her lip and glanced at her grandson. The boy, who might have been a man by Welsh standards, simply blinked, as if confused by the question.

Jon glared harder. "What's wrong with him?"

The woman put a hand on her grandson's arm. "Hans is simple. He wouldn't remember when and, even if he could, he can't speak. I am surprised he remembered we ate them at all."

"So when was it?" Jon said. "And what was it?"

She made a dismissive gesture. "Two days ago. We are fed in the kitchen, but I love shellfish, and I don't think they taste bad this time of year—just different."

"So you harvested ... how many?"

She shrugged. "Two dozen mussels, plus a few oysters, and a prawn caught in the rocks. Hans and I ate them in a mixed boil that night."

"Did you bring any here, to the palace kitchen?"

"No." Now that she'd started talking, she was sure.

"Why didn't you want to tell us the truth?"

Her chin jutted out for a moment before she answered, somewhat less defiantly than her stance indicated. "It wouldn't be a bad thing if the King of Leinster died, would it? Even if Prince Godfrid takes that Irish bride, we still could be free."

Conall had been mostly hidden behind Jon's bulk, but now he stepped more into view. The woman's eyes widened, indicating she really hadn't seen him. Her eyes were rheumy, and he guessed she saw well only up close.

"Begging your pardon, my lord." She curtseyed. "I meant no disrespect."

"You did, actually," Conall said, "but I appreciate the truth."

All that remained was to carry the dead man out of the kitchen, a task Llelo and Dai took upon themselves. As Conall held the rear door wide, he said to Gareth, "Here's the difference between you and me. A certain part of me doesn't care whether or not Donnell did it. I believe he did it, and even if you find evidence to the contrary, I still want to kill him."

"You wanted to kill him before," Gareth said reasonably, "so nothing has changed, only the fervor of your conviction." He put a hand on Conall's shoulder. "I feel the same way about Prince Cadwaladr. I genuinely *do* know how you feel."

Conall nodded, supposing Gareth did, at that, and somehow feeling better about his own anger in the process. Gareth hadn't tried to deny or dissuade him from his hatred. He'd acknowledged it and, in so doing, acknowledged his own. "You still wouldn't hang him for a crime he didn't commit."

Gareth scoffed. "You don't know me as well as you think you do."

Conall still thought he did, and thought, when it came to it, that Gareth wouldn't be able to condemn an innocent man—not that Cadwaladr was innocent. He would go to the gallows one day because his impulses would lead him to it, as inevitably as Conall now believed Donnell would die for his crimes against Leinster and Dublin, if not by Conall's hand, then by Brodar's or Diarmait's.

Conall just had to furnish them with the weapon.

23

Dai and Llelo had brought Banan to the palace's laying out room, which had the laundry on one side and the chapel on the other, so it was convenient for both. It wasn't as airy as the room designed for that purpose at Christ's Church, but it had doors that opened in the front and back, which, were it day, would have let in light. As it was, they had brought lanterns, two of which hung above the body, and a third which had been placed on a nearby table.

Gwen had been happy not to stand over Harald's body, but this time she had questions she wanted answered for herself. As Gwen stepped into the room, having returned from nursing Taran and getting both children to bed, Llelo looked up from where he was braced against the wall in a corner. Prince Hywel, interestingly, was in the opposite corner, both men with their arms folded across their chests and an almost identical contemplative expression on their faces.

"Why are you here?" she said to Prince Hywel, perhaps more abruptly than she could have.

He didn't take offense. "A man was murdered by food intended for the high table—food intended for the king, my ally. I have to be here."

"King Diarmait is an ally now?"

"I certainly hope so," Hywel said.

Gwen stepped closer. "Are things that bad at home? You really think you're going to need him?"

"After my grandfather lost his throne to Norman invaders, he retreated to Ireland three times. If I need an army of fighting men, Diarmait has one, and he's more at the ready today than Brodar."

Gwen let it go. Even in adulthood, both married with children by other people, she and Hywel had an abiding friendship that went to the very core of both of them. She could say things to him nobody else could, but she was also aware of the differences in their stations and preferred to use her influence sparingly. To his great credit, Gareth understood without being jealous.

"What did I miss in the hall?" Gareth asked.

"After the meal, King Brodar finally announced that Banan had been killed in an attempt to murder King Diarmait," Hywel said. "He made it sound like it was a question of mistaken identity rather than because of what he'd eaten."

Gwen thought back to her jest with Cait and Dorte about surviving the night without a death and felt a little abashed. "What did Rory say?"

"He expressed shock, horror, and innocence." Hywel shrugged. "Rory is the son of the High King. He can say and do what he likes. And Donnell's representatives are hardly better. They know their safety is guaranteed. I expect we'll get nothing from any of them."

"We need to determine by what means the shellfish poison was introduced." Gareth stood at the head of the table, looking into the dead man's face. "Nobody in the kitchen could tell us which dish was tainted. How are we to discover it, since the only people who could tell us—King Diarmait and Conall—would die in the process?"

Gareth's question had been designed for Llelo to answer, and he obliged. "Is there anything in Banan's mouth?"

Obediently, Gareth leaned forward and pried open Banan's mouth. It was too soon for rigor, but Banan's face was so swollen, the tissues didn't want to move. As it turned out, Banan did genuinely still have food tucked into his cheek.

Gareth frowned. "I'm seeing pastry."

"From the pie as the cook suggested?" Llelo put his head next to his father's. "Could the poison have acted so quickly that he never spit out the food that killed him?" He looked up at Gwen and Hywel. "Has anyone ever seen someone die from poison that fast?"

Hywel uncrossed his arms, interested too. "It wasn't really poison, though, was it? Shellfish aren't deadly to anyone but members of Conall's family."

Gwen wished her stepmother, Saran, was with them. As a healer, she might have had something to add. Before coming over, Gwen had collected her journal that detailed the investigations she and Gareth had conducted, along with those she'd heard of. She set it on a nearby table and started flipping through the pages.

Then, with her finger on a line, she read out what Bristol's healer, who otherwise was a useless drunkard, had told her: "There is an uncommon condition resulting from the sting of a bee where within the space of a few moments the victim's heart begins to beat too fast, his throat closes, his face swells, he develops a rash all over his body, he faints, and then dies." She stopped reading, her finger still on the words. "That describes exactly what we're looking at here."

"What's the relationship between a bee sting and eating shellfish?" Llelo asked.

For a moment nobody in the room spoke, and then Gwen said slowly, "They both introduce something into the body that the body reacts badly to."

Hywel snorted. "Badly is the word."

Gareth's eyes narrowed as he thought. "Once I met a man who said every time he drank milk or ate cheese he experienced diarrhea. I didn't believe him at first, since I'd never heard of it, but he insisted. It obviously isn't the same reaction as we see here, but it is still a reaction."

Earlier, Jon's expression at the idea of not eating fish had been typically Danish; now, Llelo's at not eating cheese was hilariously similar. No Welshman could survive a winter without milk and cheese. "Dai won't eat apples because he claims they make his mouth itch and his throat close."

That prompted his parents to look up sharply. "I didn't know that!" Gwen said.

Llelo shrugged. "He just doesn't eat apples." He gestured to Banan's body. "They don't do *that* to him!"

Gareth rubbed his chin. "But you could see how they might if he ate enough of them or—"

"Or if his body hated them as much as Banan's body hated shellfish," Gwen said, finishing the sentence for him.

Hywel's arms were folded across his chest again as he gazed into Banan's face. Gareth had tried to close the dead man's eyes, but the lids had receded into his head so far he couldn't. Since she arrived, Gwen had been trying not to look at the body at all, so grotesque had it become in death, but now she forced herself to do so. "What are you thinking, Hywel?"

Hywel gave a low laugh. "I'm thinking King Diarmait better find himself a new food taster—sooner rather than later."

24

Day Three

Caitriona

The next morning, while most of her companions were consumed with the whys and wherefores of the poisoning of her uncle's food taster, Cait had remembered the appointment they'd made with Holm to go through the books and other gear Harald had left at his mother's house. Given the crisis at the palace, rather than assist in the work himself, Holm had dropped off a trunk full of books and relics with Gwen and Cait at Godfrid's house and left. He'd been polite about it, but she could see he believed pursuit of the poisoner was far more important and interesting.

Gwen picked up a stack of loosely bound papers from the trunk and set it on the empty table before her. "Everybody is going to forget about Harald now."

"I was thinking the same thing." Cait glanced at her new friend. "We won't."

Now Gwen lifted out a book. "Harald was dressed as a knight and had wounds from fighting. He had the coin. He was involved."

She laid three more books on the table and then put another stack of papers beside them.

The smell of old leather wafted over them. While the leather works, located to the north of the Liffey and thus outside the city, were a blight on the nose if one approached too closely, the smell of leather itself was pleasant—and to Cait comforting. She'd learned to read very young, and it was one of the activities Conall had enjoyed sharing with her.

Then Gwen paused, her head down, having crouched once again to the trunk. Cait noticed and rounded the table to look into the trunk with her. Taking out the last books, Gwen revealed a lower level within the trunk containing a dozen weapons, from slim knives to darts, along with a genuine sword, this one in even poorer condition than the one Harald had died holding, with a rusted blade and a worn leather wrap on the hilt.

"Holm didn't mention these," Gwen said.

Cait gave a little laugh. "He saw books, and his eyes glazed over."

"Harald seems to have been somewhat obsessed with Dublin's martial past."

Cait straightened and returned to the books on the table. Several were quite old, and thus not written by Harald, but two were in Harald's own handwriting: one a work-in-progress translating the Bible into Danish, as Holm had said. The second was a chronicle, with dates and events.

She flipped quickly through the pages. "It's a record of Harald's life."

Gwen looked up from one of the leather folios. "Can you read it?"

She nodded. "My Danish is perhaps not as good as it could be, but it improves daily. It should be good enough for this."

Gwen returned to what she was doing, though Cait could feel her eyes glancing every now and then towards her. Over the next hour, the servants came and went, bringing food and drink for both of them, though if Cait ate and drank, she hardly noticed. She read in fascination—and also, as time went on, with a bit of acid in her belly. Harald seemed overly interested in himself and his own doings. He even recorded what he ate every day, though at the monastery, it seemed hardly to vary from day to day, even when he transferred from the monastery in Ribe to Dublin.

He was quite frank about his grief at the loss of his brother, but very excited to have returned to Dublin. He documented the start of the Danish translation of the Bible, and then, in June, she encountered the first entry which referenced something other than the daily routine of a monk in the scriptorium: *I have today begun to see that my life cannot continue as it has been.*

In the subsequent entries, coming daily over the course of the summer, Harald related his submersion deeper and deeper into a world of legend. He attended his first fight and then began training. Though she could only guess at what his voice might have sounded like, she could almost hear his excitement coming through the pages. He was learning to fight. He was becoming the man he thought he should always have been.

He regretted the death of his brother but felt he was honoring his memory. He detailed his growing relationship with Arnulf, who shared Harald's secret passion for fighting, though Cait never got the sense they actually enjoyed each other's company. Arnulf had been tasked with bringing communion to the elderly throughout Dublin, and the pair used visiting Harald's mother as a way to sneak away to practice. They found an abandoned warehouse by the docks and were soon joined by others. They never wore their church garb to these sessions nor used their real names, relying upon the desire of everyone to keep what they were doing a secret to protect themselves.

Then, on the twentieth of July, came the first mention of Bishop Gregory: *The bishop seeks to unite the Danish church with the Irish. He cannot. It would be a betrayal of our ancestors.*

Cait gave a little gasp at the boldness of the statement, at which point Gwen, who had long since given up on the books and was nursing Taran in the chair Godfrid had provided for her, met Cait's eyes.

"I was wondering when you'd come back to me. The journal is obviously fascinating."

"I have many pages still to read, but listen to this." Cait translated what Harald had written.

Gwen pointed to the table. "I didn't want to disturb your concentration, but look at the top paper in the folio on the left."

Cait did as she bid. The top of the paper had been torn off, but the rest of the paper showed quote after quote from the Bible, all written in Danish. With the paper in her hand, she turned to look at

Gwen. "I read this as possible Danish translations of Latin passages from the book of Luke."

"The quote we found in his room was from Luke."

"And the top of this paper is torn."

"You can even see a bit of ink if you look closely, as if something was written and incompletely torn away."

"Like the quote in his room."

Gwen canted her head. "If we do, in fact, know now where it came from, the question remains *why that quote*? I would ask now too if Harald himself left it there as a message or if someone left it there for him—someone who knew about his books and his writing at his mother's house?" She paused. "Perhaps the man who killed him."

"Arnulf?"

Gwen shrugged one shoulder. "After Gareth is done using him to paint the bigger picture, probably he ought to ask him about this too."

25

Day Three

Gareth

Gareth had known from the start that his day would be completely taken up by the events of the previous evening. He'd stayed up what felt like half the night (though it was really only until midnight) examining the body and then had slept past the dawn long enough to feel a little ill about it. He'd needed the sleep, however, and after a hearty breakfast without too much fish in it and a nice chunk of cheese, he and Godfrid returned to the palace.

As they approached the gate, the look on Godfrid's face was grim. "If you were to remark on the way the streets are eerily quiet today, I would have to agree."

"What are the people afraid of?"

"I don't know," Godfrid said. "A poisoner is a devil you can't defend against. It does no good to post extra men on the wall-walk and in the streets. He is by nature invisible."

"But we post the guards anyway." Gareth sighed. "A show of force is sometimes necessary. We need the people to feel safe."

Jon met them halfway across the courtyard to the great hall. His eyes had black circles under them, indicating he'd slept far less than Gareth.

Godfrid immediately put a hand on his shoulder. "You are relieved. Get to bed. That's an order. We need you fresh tonight."

Jon's mouth formed to say, "What's tonight?" But then his brain caught up, and his expression hardened as he remembered the fighting ring. "You should know, my lord, that the question we have been most asked is if the death of Harald and the poisoning of Banan are related. I've told everyone every time that inquiries are proceeding."

Godfrid sighed. "People want answers. It's understandable. Now, go."

Jon went, and Godfrid and Gareth continued into the great hall. While the streets of Dublin were subdued, as Godfrid had remarked, the great hall was packed to the rafters with diners.

"Is this a show of solidarity and faith, or are people really that trusting about what comes out of the palace kitchen?" Gareth asked.

"My brother told them they were not in danger from the food. It appears they believe him. I'm certain those in the kitchen were up most of the night too, preparing the food for today and making sure it isn't tainted. Gareth—" Godfrid turned to him, "—the wedding is *tomorrow!*"

"You will be at the church on time, and you will marry Cait. All this—" Gareth swept out a hand to encompass the room, "—is not enough to stop it."

Godfrid nodded, seemingly mollified. And it was true. All it took to be married were banns read in advance, which had been done, and a priest to bless them. They could do it in a field if they had to. The point was to be bonded in the eyes of God and men. The rest of it—the guests, the feast, the gifts—were trappings. Lovely trappings to be sure, but unnecessary to the main point.

Gwen had come to Gareth with little besides the clothes on her back. She'd brought him a family, however—something he never thought he'd have again—which was worth far more to him than a patch of land or silver. With Hywel's largesse, he had far more than a patch now too. And it was Gwen who'd been most instrumental in helping him achieve everything he'd accomplished in the last five years.

Godfrid detoured to the front of the hall to speak to his brother and King Diarmait, leaving Gareth to head for the kitchen, initially alone, but then Prince Hywel intercepted him. Gareth didn't bother to dissuade him. He needed a translator, and if it couldn't be Godfrid or Jon, he was happy to settle for his lord.

"You actually look rested," Hywel said by way of a greeting.

"I admit to sleeping longer than I intended," Gareth said. "Are you sure you have time to help with this? I am grateful, to be sure, but don't feel obligated if you have other duties."

"I am here for a wedding scheduled for tomorrow. Diarmait is determined it will happen, but he isn't very pleasant to be around just now. The sooner we complete this investigation, the happier everyone will be."

"Where are the Dragons?"

Hywel lifted one shoulder. "They are being Dragons. Cadoc has gone off with Iago to scout the land north of the Liffey. They dragged Steffan with them to prevent him from drinking too much and then regaling anyone who could understand him with stories of one false exploit after another."

In addition to having a rare facility with knives, Steffan was a storyteller. After music, the next best thing in the evening was getting him to tell a story, either from legend or about himself, often made up on the spot. To have had him on their ship had definitely made the journey across the Irish Sea more pleasant. As soon as they'd learned about the possibility of attending the fighting ring, since Steffan was the Dragon who'd interacted least with the Dubliners, he'd been held back in the hopes of at least one of them remaining somewhat anonymous.

Hywel continued speaking. "Evan is just there—" he gestured towards the kitchen door through which Gareth could make out Evan's bulk settled against the frame, "and the rest are about somewhere."

Gareth had left Llelo and Dai asleep. As promised, after they'd shooed Gwen to bed, Llelo had stayed up late with him over the body, and Dai needed to sleep as long as possible in preparation for staying up all night tonight. In truth, they all were going to need a nap this afternoon. But only baby Taran and Tangwen were probably going to get one.

Conall was already in the kitchen when they arrived, standing over the food that would be served to King Diarmait for his first meal of the day. He turned at their approach, a dolorous expression on his face.

Gareth stared at him. "*You're* the food taster now?"

"It has to be done," Conall said matter-of-factly.

"By the saints, you cannot!" Hywel was equally horrified.

"It does give one a moment's pause, doesn't it?" Conall said, still in that bland tone. "I am not terribly fearful at the moment. I supervised the scrubbing of every dish, pot, and utensil overnight. And the king has sworn to restrict himself to foods that require little preparation." He ripped off a piece of a bun, slathered it in butter and honey, and ate it.

Gareth looked at Hywel. "Yesterday we questioned two servants who'd eaten shellfish a few days ago. What if one of them brought the knife they'd used to open the shells into the kitchen? Banan's death could actually have been an accident."

Conall grimaced. "I dismissed those two because there appeared to be no mal-intent in their manner, and my head was full of hatred for Donnell. Perhaps that was a mistake. As we learned from Arnulf, a person doesn't have to lie outright to obscure the truth." He turned to the cook and inquired where the boy and his granny were today.

"They both worked late cleaning the kitchen, and then I sent them home. Carla was weaving on her feet with exhaustion. Hans does as he's told."

That also didn't sound ominous or threatening. Still, Gareth said, "We should speak to them again." And Conall asked for the directions to their house.

"I probably shouldn't go with you." Hywel made a face. "Somehow, I will have to sit at the table and force down food." He put a hand to his belly. "Good thing I'm hungry."

Gareth didn't say *better you than me*, though his expression must have conveyed some of his thoughts, since Hywel laughed. It was no laughing matter, really, but sometimes a man had to laugh in the face of terrible events. Conall, who wasn't laughing either, motioned Gareth out the rear door, but before they'd gone three paces, they heard a shout from the kitchen, and Evan fell into step beside them. "Can't let you have all the fun."

"Missing our adventures, are you?" Gareth said. "Why aren't you watching Hywel's back?"

"Gruffydd's got it." Evan made a face that was half rueful, half amused. "I could have been content to never investigate another murder, but Prince Hywel sent me in his place." He eyed Gareth. "We know what kind of trouble you can get into. I'm just sorry the prince and I will have to sit out the activity tonight."

"We need to pretend nothing is happening, which means the two highest-ranking Dragons must stay behind."

"I can't say I have ever felt this closely watched before, except perhaps in Bristol. There, however, it was because the members of Prince Henry's court didn't want to stain the ends of their cloaks by associating with Welshmen. Here it's reverence."

"You could view it as a nice problem to have," Gareth said. "And besides, what you said about Bristol isn't entirely true. Prince Henry worshipped you."

Evan's lips twitched towards a smile. "True. We won't ever be sorry to have impressed a possible future king of England."

"One can hope." Gareth certainly wasn't sorry to have found favor with Prince Henry, but found it unlikely the old debt would temper any future actions against Gwynedd. Norman kings and princes cared only for their own personal power. Oddly, both Godfrid and Henry shared blood, being descended from Viking raiders. The pirate in each remained always just below the surface.

Hans and his grandmother were among the poorer residents of Dublin and thus lived to the north of the palace in what could be described as a hut, accessible down an alley near the eastern wall of the city. It was as far from the fresh water source as was possible to get in Dublin. For all that, however, every front stoop in the district was swept clean and the thatching on the roofs was fresh.

As they came closer, however, it became evident that the small crowd of a half-dozen people in the street were standing directly in front of Hans and Carla's house. And they were doing so for good reason.

"I smell blood." Conall coughed.

"I'm glad I left Llelo sleeping," Gareth said. "Inevitably, like all of us, he dreams of dead men. I can't be sorry to spare him one more."

26

Day Three
Conall

The scene inside the hut was worse than even Conall, who'd seen plenty of death and murder too, had feared. Both Carla and Hans had been stabbed. Hans was already dead, but Carla was still alive. Her neighbors had lifted her onto a pallet, and three of them hovered around her.

One of them looked up as Conall and Gareth entered, hope in his face, but then he sagged in disappointment.

"Did you send for Sheriff Holm?" Conall asked.

The man nodded.

"Then he should be on his way. Do you know who I am?"

"Yes, my lord."

"This is Gareth the Welshman. There is no better man for catching whoever did this. Leave us with her, please."

How she was still alive Conall didn't know. There was blood everywhere. But while Hans' throat had been cut, she'd merely been stabbed in the belly. Likely, because it was hard to see in the darkened hut, the murderer had mistakenly left her for dead.

In the face of Conall's authority, the neighbor acquiesced. Conall looked at Gareth for guidance, but he gestured with one hand. "Don't worry about me. She doesn't have much time. Find out if she knows who did this."

Conall picked up Carla's hand to hold it and looked into her eyes. They were bright blue, and she still had enough life in her to look back at him and speak. "Tell King Brodar I'm sorry. I brought shame upon Dublin."

"Tell me what happened."

"A man came to us with coin. He said we were to harvest shellfish—it didn't matter what kind. We could eat some of them, as I told you we did, but we were to chop up several into fine bits and bring them to the kitchen."

"You denied doing that yesterday," Conall said. "You lied to me."

"No." She coughed, bringing up blood. "You asked if I brought the shellfish to the kitchen. I didn't. Hans did."

Conall wasn't impressed with the hair-splitting, but she was dying, so there was no point in chastising her further. "And then what? Banan had pie in his mouth when he died. Is that what you poisoned?"

She nodded. "I'm in charge of chopping vegetables. When the cook was ready to add mushrooms to the pie, I had already mixed in the shellfish."

"It never occurred to you to ask *why* the man wanted you to do this?"

"I did ask. He said he wanted to spoil the meal. I didn't see how adding shellfish could spoil anything, since every type is delicious, but he said *never you mind how*."

"So you took his money."

Carla turned her head to one side, struggling to breathe, but she still managed to answer. "The rest of the hall ate stew. The cook makes pies for everyone only when we have fewer folk present. They take too long to make and need to be watched, so the pie was the one thing at the meal that was only for the high table." Tears leaked out the corners of her eyes. "I didn't know what harm it could possibly do! That poor man! To watch him die in such pain."

She meant Banan, the food taster, though it seemed she was dying in pain too. If Conall had been on a battlefield, he would have eased her passing, but he couldn't do it for an old woman—and worse, he needed information.

"Who was the man? Was he someone you knew?"

She gave the slightest shake of her head.

"Irish?"

Again the headshake.

"So he was a Dane?"

"I thought so. He spoke like one of us. He wouldn't tell us his name."

"Can you describe him?"

Her breathing was becoming more and more labored, with bloody air bubbles on her lips, but she managed to mouth a few last words: "Short. Balding. Middle-aged."

"Did he come back this morning? Is it he who stabbed you and your grandson?"

Her eyes had closed, but she managed one more nod. "I'm so sorry."

Holm arrived, and Conall allowed him to take over. Carla didn't open her eyes again and, within a few heartbeats, she was gone. Conall found Gareth looking at him with sad eyes and made a motion with his head for the two of them to join Evan, who was outside, keeping the onlookers at bay with the few words in Danish he knew. But now that Holm and his men had arrived, he was no longer needed.

Conall led both men a few paces away, farther up the alley, where they couldn't be overheard, though he spoke in Welsh so likely it wouldn't matter, and told them Carla's dying words.

Evan let out a grunt of disgust. "The man she described could be anyone."

"Me included, though my red hair does tend to get noticed." Conall's chin was in his hand.

"You're hardly balding," Gareth said.

Conall grunted. "So says the man with a full head of hair. Perhaps there's a witness among the people who live in this alley. If so, Holm will find him."

"If she'd lived, I could have worked up a sketch," Gareth said. "As it is, we have very little to go on."

"The thing about poisoning that has always bothered me," Evan said, "is it tends to affect too many people or utterly fail. How likely was it really that King Diarmait would have eaten the pie and died?"

Conall shrugged. "Without Banan, the food would have reached the high table. If the king had eaten it, he would have died. Of that I have no doubt."

"But Evan's right that it wasn't a sure thing. I see three possibilities, none of which are necessarily mutually exclusive." Gareth started to tick the items off his fingers. "One, the killer intended to murder the king, but didn't know Banan also had the same affliction and his arrow might hit the wrong target."

"That means he had some knowledge of Leinster's court but not complete knowledge," Conall said.

"And if there's a traitor in Diarmait's court, he isn't very close to the king," Evan added.

"Two," Gareth continued as if he hadn't been interrupted, "he would have been happy if Diarmait died but not so much that he had a clear plan to ensure it. He was willing to use a knife on Carla and Hans, but not to risk his own life to kill the king."

Conall nodded. "I'm with you so far."

"Third, he assumed his plan would fail, so killing the king wasn't the point. He wanted to distract us."

"Which he has done," Evan said.

"You're saying he tried to murder the king to distract us from the investigation of Harald's death?" Conall laughed mockingly. "That's a big leap."

"Not if he fears what we will find the deeper we dig," Gareth said. "What if Harald's death wasn't suicide and instead is only the first line in a much longer song, as my father-in-law would say."

Conall was silent a moment, struggling to see how that could be true, but respecting Gareth enough to consider it. Then they all started walking. Rather than heading for the palace, they made their way to Godfrid's house, where Gwen would be, and where they could confer further in private.

They found Gwen rocking a sleeping Taran while watching Tangwen kick an inflated pig's bladder around the house. Taran appeared to be one of those children who could sleep through anything, a not uncommon trait in a second child. Gareth went straight to his daughter and scooped her into his arms.

She accepted his kiss before wiggling to get down. "Let me go, Tad!"

Then Godfrid arrived too. The joy that filled Cait's face at the sight of him rocked Conall backed on his heels a bit. He knew the two of them loved each other, but the way they clasped hands, as if both had been drowning and now had pulled each other onto the dock had his heart breaking a bit—not for them, but for himself. No woman had ever looked at him like Cait looked at Godfrid. It was a good thing their uncle had agreed to the match. If he'd disapproved, Conall had a strong feeling the pair would have married anyway. Best not to force them into defiance.

Nobody else seemed to notice—or if they did, they gave no sign of it—and the little group gathered around the table in the center of the hall, though Gwen remained rocking steadily in her chair. Conall took in the open trunk, the weapons inside, and the papers and books stacked on the table, and said, "You've been busy."

"More than busy." Cait held up a book. "We found Harald's personal journal."

Conall could feel the sharpening interest of everyone in the room, and Cait didn't make them wait to learn more. "He writes about the fights, about his friendship and rivalry with Arnulf—" she looked at the men darkly, "—and furthermore that Templar regalia was a favorite fighting garb for both of them."

"They were churchmen," Gwen said. "It makes a certain kind of sense.

Cait nodded and continued, "Towards the end, he writes mostly about his regrets. At first, he expresses disillusionment with Bishop Gregory, whom he feels is betraying the Danish Church by uniting it with the Irish bishoprics—never mind that it is at the behest of the pope. But then he pivots to talking about the fighting rings. He was deliberating in his last entry as to whether or not he should confess to the bishop what he'd been doing."

"We have much to tell you too." Gareth told them about the murders of Hans and Carla and their thoughts about the mind of their killer.

"I don't see the connection between Harald and these new deaths," Evan said. "What does the attempted murder of King Diarmait have to do with the fighting rings?"

"Harald writes that the focus of the fighting rings started out being about defending Dublin but had shifted to being more about getting out from under Leinster's yoke."

"I don't like it, but I can understand it," Conall said. "It's essentially what Carla said to us yesterday in the yard."

Cait still held Harald's journal in her hand. "Harald was concerned that, while the sentiment was hardly new, it was becoming more focused and strident. And more recently, the discussion had shifted to the benefits of allying with other Irish kingdoms."

"Did he mention which one?"

"He was secretive even with his journal, as if he was afraid someone would read it." She paused. "But I'm sure we can guess."

Conall felt his anger, which had been banked since speaking to Carla, rising again, and he said into the heavy silence that had descended on the room, "Connaught."

27

Day Three

Dai

Dai munched on the bun, one of two his mother had wrapped in a cloth to sustain him until morning. He'd taken them soberly, knowing his mother couldn't shake her feeling of foreboding and was giving him food instead of a hug in front of the other Dragons, who would have teased him about being tied to his mother's apron strings. They would have meant nothing by it, but she didn't want to risk embarrassing him.

Llelo, too, had looked repressively at him before mounting his horse and riding away with Father, Godfrid, and the Dragons, towards the gate that led to the Liffey. Dai, for his part, was feeling light-hearted and ready for adventure. Maybe that was a mistake, but he didn't sense danger coming his way. He was going to watch the fights. How could he get into trouble?

Aron, the youngest and cleverest of the Dragons, was going as a friend of Sitric, a known participant, who would vouch for him. In the end, Conall had gotten his way as well and took the second coin as Fergus the Sailor. At least he spoke Danish, and his red hair wouldn't stand out among the Danes, since fully a third of them had red hair too.

As Dai reached Vigo's shop and was tucking away the half-eaten bun in the pocket of his coat, borrowed from a collection set aside for the poor at Christ's Church, Vigo stepped out his door.

"Am I late?" Dai checked the sky.

Vigo scoffed. "If you were any later, you would have been left behind. I don't cater to careless youths."

Dai bent his head, suitably chastened, though he also knew he hadn't been late. Vigo had said to wait until full dark, and Dai had set out from Godfrid's house as the sun was setting, settling himself a few blocks away to watch Vigo's door. Llelo and the other riders had left the city before sunset too, ostensibly to visit one of Godfrid's holdings north of the city. Godfrid himself had led them, refusing to be left behind. It was only the five of them: Llelo, Gareth, Godfrid, Jon, and Cadoc. Gruffydd and Evan remained in the city with Prince Hywel, because they couldn't leave him unattended. Steffan had been tasked with tailing Arnulf, while Iago was following Goff.

Dai was genuinely surprised not to see Cait riding beside Godfrid, because she seemed the type to throw caution to the winds and defy convention, but she and Gwen had agreed to act as if nothing was afoot. Since everyone knew Gwen had children who needed attention, she and Cait didn't need to wait things out at the palace. Instead, they had set chairs in front of Godfrid's door, with cups of mead in their hands and a fire burning in a nearby grate for warmth, to enjoy the clear summer evening and converse with Godfrid's neighbors, all of whom wanted to wish Cait well in her marriage.

Glad he could be in the thick of it, Dai lengthened his stride to keep up with Vigo, heading for the dock gate, only a block and a half away. As they approached, however, Vigo put a hand on Dai's arm to stay him, his eyes on the couple ahead of them. With concern, Dai realized it was Conall and Iona, who were just now being greeted by the guard.

Conall's voice echoed in the gatehouse tunnel. "Nice night."

"It is," the guard said.

With a blast of insight, Dai realized the guard thought Iona was a whore and Conall had hired her for the night, which was why he didn't blink twice at a sailor walking to the dock with a woman on his arm.

After giving Conall a hundred foot lead, Vigo sauntered up to the guard, who nodded at him in acknowledgment. "Merchant Vigo."

"Dorn. How are you tonight?" Vigo sidled close, and the two men exchanged a few pennies hand-to-hand before Vigo walked on.

Dai hustled to catch up. "You gave him money?"

Vigo snorted. "Of course." He lifted his chin to point to Conall and Iona. "They must be new, because they didn't." His eyes narrowed.

Dai had a sudden sick feeling in his stomach, which was alleviated slightly when Conall headed towards the shadows of one of the boats at the dock—now completely stranded on the sand—and stood talking quietly with Iona, rather than heading off to the end of the pier like Dai and Vigo were doing. He reminded himself that before

Conall had become the ambassador to Dublin from the Kingdom of Leinster, he'd been a spy—and apparently a good one to have lived so long.

It was full dark, but the moon was bright, and it was easy to see the crossing of the Liffey. During high tide, the channel was easily deep enough for shipping, but during low tide, even though it was a freshwater river, the water receded enough to allow passage across the riverbed. The River Poddle entered the main channel to the east of their location, so its flow didn't affect the crossing of the Liffey at the dock. While there were at least a dozen narrow rivulets snaking their way through the sands, few were more than a foot wide—easily hopped across—and the widest one at the center point had a board placed across it so the travelers' feet would not get wet.

Here, Dai's boots did sink into the soft, water-soaked soil, but after a few quick steps, he was out of the worst of it and back on somewhat more solid ground. The total distance to cross was a hundred yards, nothing like the three-mile journey from Aber to Llanfaes across the Lavan Sands.

For the first time, he wondered how they were supposed to get back without being remarked upon. They weren't going to be able to return the same way. The next low tide would be twelve hours from now when it was full day.

"Don't worry about it," Vigo said.

Dai had been focused on his feet, but he looked at his companion. "Excuse me?"

"We don't have to cross back this way."

"The guards don't mind letting so many people back into the city before dawn?"

"That's what the money I gave the guard was for." Vigo spoke matter-of-factly, and then he shrugged. "Besides, we won't return all at once. Many will sleep here and there, and some will attend mass at the abbey."

Dai hadn't known there was an abbey north of the river. He hadn't realized there was much of anything north of the river, but he'd clearly been wrong. Here was a village in and of itself, and as they came up the bank onto the wharf, he got a strong whiff of leather workings to the east.

Vigo seemed to have a disconcerting ability to read Dai's mind, because he laughed. "Takes some getting used to. We'll be meeting in a glen half a mile north of here, so by the time we get there we'll have left the smell behind."

They continued on, encountering more people the farther they walked, more than a dozen in front of and behind them. A few more strides and they caught up with Sitric, who greeted Vigo courteously.

"Are you going to try your hand tonight?" Vigo asked him.

Sitric lied outright. "I better not. I wrenched my shoulder yesterday. I'd lose. Badly."

Vigo laughed, as undoubtedly Sitric meant him to, and then he looked past Sitric to Aron, the fellow Dragon. "Who's your friend?"

"Aron." It was a name from a Bible, rendered similarly in Welsh and Danish.

"Where are you from, Aron?" Vigo said.

"South. Near Wexford," Aron said in excellent Danish. It just so happened Vigo had asked him one of the few questions for which he'd practiced.

Sitric then clapped Aron on the shoulder. "My cousin is visiting for the week."

"Do you have a coin?" Vigo asked, his eyes still on Aron.

Aron held out one of the coins they'd found.

"Where did you get it?"

"Found it on the street," Aron said, with an insouciance Dai found both admirable and terrifying. "Thought I'd see what this was all about."

Vigo grunted. "Welcome."

They went back to walking, though now Dai found himself shaking inside. He'd been foolish and naïve. He'd misunderstood who and what Vigo was. He wasn't just another attendee of the fights. He was an organizer.

And as they left the road for the clearing where the fights were to take place, Dai couldn't help thinking he'd entered the lion's den.

28

Day Three

Conall

Conall had allowed Dai and Vigo to pass him, which in retrospect had been a wise decision, even though it had been impulsive at the time. He'd glanced back as they'd left the gate, seen Vigo pass money to the guard, and realized he'd made a terrible mistake: the participants in the fighting ring were supposed to bribe the guards on the way out. For one, it was a means of ensuring their silence, but it was also a way of co-opting them into the conspiracy. By not doing so, Conall had revealed himself to be not only a newcomer but possibly someone who hadn't been properly incorporated into the conspiracy.

Bribery had always been an option, but Conall hadn't wanted to risk being exposed if the guard reacted badly. He couldn't risk Fergus the Sailor being revealed to be the ambassador to Dublin. He hoped his mistake wasn't irredeemable. He definitely needed to stay well away from Vigo, so he allowed four or five groups of people to enter the Liffey crossing before joining them with Iona.

He was also starting to think Gwen was right that what they were doing here smacked of Shrewsbury. With Godfrid on their side, they'd had the option of simply descending on the fights with a company of men and arresting everyone they could get their hands on.

But Gareth was right that while this would stop the fights (possibly), it wouldn't get them any closer to their murderer. Secrecy aside, until Conall had seen Vigo bribe the guard, he hadn't been convinced the participants were actually doing anything *wrong*.

Bribery was a sin, of course, but the throne of Dublin wasn't the Church. Sins weren't Brodar's purview. When Godfrid had finally told Brodar what was going on and what they planned to do tonight, the king had looked favorably upon the idea of more of his people learning to fight like the Danes of old.

If that's what they were really doing.

Brodar had encouraged them to find out what was really going on, but not to call attention to themselves if they could possibly avoid it. That had been their intent, but Brodar's particular concern was that he still had to entertain Rory O'Connor and the representatives from the other kingdoms of Ireland, who'd started trickling into the city over the course of the day in advance of the wedding tomorrow. Brodar didn't want anyone to wonder if Dublin was in disarray. Everything was to appear entirely normal.

"I am not overly fond of the sea." Iona had allowed Conall his silence for the initial fifty yards of the crossing, picking her way through the sands beside him.

"I forgot for a moment that you're Welsh. You didn't think to return home after you were freed?" Even this soon after Dai and Vigo had crossed, the water was running a little more freely, and Conall increased his pace.

"That had been my initial plan." Iona hopped over another rivulet that within a count of five had widened from six inches to a foot and a half. "But when it came down to it, I have lived my entire life in Dublin. If I still have family in Pembroke, they don't remember me." She looked at him quizzically. "It is my understanding they are ruled by Normans now."

"That is likely," he said.

She snorted as they came up the bank and caught their breath. "That was well done."

"What was?"

"Distracting me from my fears." She wagged a finger at him like his mother used to do. Dressed as Fergus the Sailor, he thought perhaps it was easy to forget who he really was.

He grinned. "We made it. That's what's important." Then he offered her his arm again.

She tucked her hand in the crook of his elbow, and they began to stroll down the lane. Dai and Vigo were somewhere up ahead, but even in the bright moonlight, Conall couldn't see where. The herd of people coming with them knew where they were going, however, and Conall reflected again on the extent to which the fights were a secret only to those in authority.

It irked him that he hadn't known before yesterday. He used to be better than this.

Iona nudged him. "You're frowning."

He blinked. "Am I?" He rearranged his face. "Just out for a lovely evening watching a bunch of Danes hacking at each other. What could be better than that?"

Iona laughed, a little louder than he was comfortable with, but he'd meant her to, and those around them smiled at their camaraderie.

The fights were taking place less than a mile northwest of the crossing place, on a patch of lower ground in a clearing within a grove of trees. Conall really wanted to know whose land they were on, though some of these tracts hadn't been farmed since the attack by the men of Meath that had killed Godfrid's father two years ago. Anything north of the Liffey was exposed to raids by the Irish. It could also be that only a handful of people knew in advance where the fights were actually being held at any given meeting and the rest just followed, as Conall and Iona had done.

Though it had seemed like a great army of people were walking with them, the number in attendance was a hundred at most. Iona was one of the few women, but she didn't seem to mind, and many of the men knew her, calling her by name. Someone had set up a makeshift entrance to the site to the west of the road, and everyone passing through had to show their wooden coin.

Conall had his at the ready, and he was glad Iona was on his arm, because the man barely glanced at him in favor of looking at Iona. Though her hair was streaked with gray, and she was a few years older than he, she was buxom with a deliberately saucy smile and a glint to her eye. Conall didn't know if that was usual for her when facing the world, but he guessed it might be. She hadn't directed her wiles at him, for which he was grateful.

Then they were making their way around the edge of the crowd. Already in the center of the ring, which was no more than a circle etched in the dirt with a stick, two men with wooden swords and shields were hammering away at each other. While the men might get splinters or bruises, they were unlikely to be seriously injured.

"How is the winner determined?" he whispered to Iona.

She shook her head, not able to answer, but then a tall man, also with red hair, on Conall's other side said, "One man has to yield."

That was an eminently reasonable approach but, in practice, it turned out that Danes are extraordinarily stubborn (not that this should have been surprising) and many refused to yield long past the point when they had clearly lost. The organizer—the man Iona had referred to as Goff—kept motioning for his underlings to throw sand on the blood that had spilled on the dirt of the ring. Conall felt a grumbling in his belly and hoped Iago, whose task it had been to follow Goff, was nearby.

To keep the conversation going, Conall decided to question his neighbor again, even if Conall already knew the answer. "Who is that?"

"You don't know?"

Iona leaned forward. "I brought him. He's new."

"He captained a ship, back in the day. Now he works on the dock. His name is Goff."

The desire for Danish pre-eminence was something Conall could understand. But it was also a way of living in the past. Ireland was never going to accept an independent Danish Dublin again. If they weren't going to be ruled by Leinster, then it would be a different kingdom. Either that, or they would be driven out of Ireland entirely.

Now, with the latest fight ended, Goff stepped again into the center of the ring, arms outstretched. "My friends! Today is a glorious day!"

The crowd's roar of approval was so loud it made Conall want to cover his ears. The sound had seemingly come out of nowhere, and if he were the organizer, he might have feared it could be heard all the way to the palace. Perhaps he didn't care.

Goff went on. "Every time a man steps into the ring, he fights not only for himself, but for his ancestors!" He beat both fists on his bare chest, and his golden armbands glinted in the torchlight. "We are their direct descendants!"

Now he lowered his voice. "For years, I feared they would be ashamed of us, that the mead they drank in Valhalla would be bitter with disappointment and defeat. But today!" He spread his arms wide again. "Today, we are reborn! It is here." He stamped a foot. "Here where we become as our ancestors once were."

He swung a finger as if searching for a particular person in the crowd, but it was merely a rhetorical technique. "Some of you remember those days of glory, before we were cowed by the kingdoms around us. Before we licked Leinster's boots." He clenched his hand into a fist. "I swear to you on the blood of our ancestors that things are going to change. It will not forever be this way. And it is here—" he stamped his foot again, "—our renewal begins."

The roar of the crowd was deafening, which prevented Conall from noting that he and Iona were no longer on the outskirts, but right in the middle of it, and some very large Danes were crowding up behind him.

Suddenly, a hood came down over his head, leaving him able to see only through two slits near his eyes, and someone said into his ear, "The cost of admission is a bit higher for you, Irishman."

29

Day Three
Godfrid

Godfrid had agreed with Gareth that the situation before them called for gentle handling. Rather than swooping down on the fighters, they would watch, learn what they could, and leave the decision to close them down to Brodar. His people had a right to their training. Godfrid thought they had a right even to their gambling.

What they didn't have a right to was murder. Or treason.

And as he and Gareth approached the ring of men from the west, able finally to hear what the leader was saying, he was feeling far more concerned about the latter than the former. Goff wasn't openly saying that Brodar and his family were to blame for their submission to Leinster, but Godfrid *was* marrying Cait tomorrow, forever tying the throne of Dublin to that of Leinster. And the marriage wasn't necessarily bringing with it a loosening of the reins of power on Diarmait's part either.

Leinster was still going to be ruling over Dublin, even if the Danes were allowed their own king. Brodar and Godfrid could pretty up the truth with fine words about cooperation against mutual enemies, but nobody was going to forget any time soon that if Leinster hadn't come when they did at the Battle of the Liffey, the Danes of Dublin might have lost everything.

They still could, especially if this fool had his way.

Gareth crouched beside Godfrid. "What's he saying?"

"Nothing good."

"That's Goff, is it?"

Godfrid nodded. "He fought well at the Liffey. And to think he was already heavily involved in this. I wish I'd known."

They'd left their horses a hundred feet back, and they themselves were a good five hundred feet from the fight, crouched on a rise above the draw in which the fights were taking place. It was a good situation for them, because they could see over the top of the spectators' heads. The organizers of the fight had chosen well too, since the rising earth all around the ring masked some of the light and noise. The two friends had caught sight of a patrol a quarter of an hour earlier and had been moving as silently as possible since then. Godfrid could admit Gareth was better at it than he was, having grown up in rural Gwynedd. These days, most Danes, including him, were city dwellers.

"We shouldn't have split up," Godfrid said. From the start, Godfrid had tried to pair each Welshman with men who spoke Danish, at least in passing, but had needed to split everyone up in order not to call attention to themselves.

Gareth gave a shake of his head. "We talked about this. Trust our friends."

"If anything, it's my fault we don't have more men, but I don't know who of mine I can trust, and Sitric wasn't sure either."

Gareth gave a low growl. "Wasn't sure or didn't want to say? I'm not convinced letting him slide by without giving up the names of his fellows was the best idea."

"When this is over, I will beat it out of him if I have to." He side-eyed Gareth. "In a manner of speaking."

They were good enough friends by now for Godfrid to be sure Gareth knew he didn't mean it literally. A commander who flogged his men inspired fear but no loyalty, and that was precisely the kind of behavior that led to what they were witnessing now.

Brodar was a good commander, and Godfrid had been impressed by the job he was doing as king. But circumstances—and Leinster—had placed him in an impossible situation. He couldn't keep both King Diarmait and his own people happy. So he ended up pleasing one more than the other in most things and no one some of the time. Now, with Cait joining the family, Godfrid was adding to his brother's burden. They could bad-mouth Leinster all they wanted when she wasn't around but, in effect, they were allowing an enemy into their midst.

Or at least that was how the men before them would see it.

Godfrid himself was well-used to the idea of being friends with Irish people. He numbered Cait and Conall among the closest friends he'd ever had. Somehow, he was going to have to reconcile these two halves of his new reality.

"You made sure Steffan understood what to do?" Godfrid said to Gareth.

"I told him to follow Arnulf but stay well back. He knows."

Godfrid grumbled to himself, knowing he shouldn't nag his friend.

"It is Jon, Cadoc, and Llelo who have the most to fear—besides us, I mean. That's why they are together, to leave Steffan free to move about without anyone recognizing him." Gareth glanced at Godfrid with a sympathetic smile. "We sent them east, anyway. They're probably miles away with no idea what's happening. We discovered this clearing only because of the noise."

"I hate that I didn't know about these fights before yesterday."

"I hate that my son is in the middle of it."

Godfrid put a hand on Gareth's shoulder, suitably chastened. "He's a smart lad."

"With far too much confidence." Gareth's growl sounded very much like Godfrid's own. "We should move again. We've been in this position too long."

Just then, one of the patrolling men appeared to their right, his eyes fixed on a point just past where they were hiding. But after a moment, his eyes slid away, and he moved on. Meanwhile, Goff had been conferring with one of his underlings. Then, with a laugh, he held up his hands to quiet the hubbub of the crowd, which had grown restless with no fights to watch.

"We have an exciting change to the program! One of our best warriors has found his way here today and has agreed to give a lesson to a first-timer." He waved a hand and Sitric came forward ... followed immediately by Gareth's son, Dai.

"No." Gareth made a move to rise, but Godfrid put a heavy hand on his shoulder.

"We don't know what this is yet. They aren't going to hurt a boy in front of citizens of Dublin. Even if they know who he is, they definitely wouldn't risk my wrath by harming him."

Gareth subsided and then watched with held breath as Sitric took Dai through the basics of sword fighting. To Dai's credit, he pretended to be far less proficient than he really was, though here and there he showed the flashes of brilliance that had convinced the Dragons to take him on as their squire. Sitric played ignorant too, cursing at Dai in Danish as if he had no idea who he was.

"What do we do?" It was Llelo's voice in Godfrid's ear this time, and he nearly jumped a foot, instantly angry at himself for being so focused on the fight he'd allowed Gareth's son to sneak up on him. Then again, Llelo had been learning from the best. He knew how to move quietly. Who knew how long he'd been watching their backs.

"Nothing, Llelo," Gareth said. "Not yet."

"Cadoc is nearby, and he has twenty arrows in his quiver."

"And there are a hundred men in that clearing, most who have done nothing wrong."

"But it's *Dai!*"

Godfrid, his heart still pounding, lifted a finger. "Not yet."

Llelo put his back to the trunk of an ancient tree to their right. He blended in so well, even in the moonlight, that he was hardly more than a shadow with eyes.

"Where are the others?" Gareth asked.

"Around the other side. They know to remain hidden."

Dai continued to accept instruction from Sitric, and then three more younger men joined the ring, causing Gareth to breathe easier. Goff knew many of the men present were no longer here to learn to be warriors, but to watch while others fought, so soon the lesson ended, and Dai and the others filed out of the ring.

Goff raised his hands again. "Are we Danes?"

The crowd answered with a roar.

"Tonight, our first featured fight pits one of our own against a true contender." Goff made a sweeping gesture with one hand. "We have the Templar versus the Galway Grogoch."

Into the ring walked a man dressed in the regalia of a Knight Templar. While his garb was unnervingly similar to what Harald had worn in death, his face was covered by a full helm, so they couldn't tell his identity, though in size and shape he resembled Arnulf. He was followed by a smaller man wearing a mask over his face with slits for eyes. The disguise couldn't fool Godfrid, however. It was unmistakably Conall.

Gareth clenched his hands into fists. "It can't be a coincidence that three of our own have already been included in the arena. We're blown. We're completely blown." He turned to Llelo. "Get back to Dublin, as quickly as you can. We need reinforcements."

"The guards at the palace gate will laugh at me," Llelo said. "My Danish isn't good enough to explain, and they'll never let me see the king, even if they remember I'm your son."

"Wake Cait," Godfrid said. "They'll let her in without question."

As Llelo scampered away, Godfrid checked the sky, having no real idea how many hours had passed, but thinking it must be getting on towards two in the morning. They were only a mile from the city. If Llelo hurried, he could be at Godfrid's house within the half-hour.

Godfrid just needed to keep whatever was happening here from getting more out of hand—and Conall alive—until Brodar arrived.

30

Day Three
Conall

"Where are you taking him?" Iona grabbed the man's arm before Goff's followers could hurry him off.

"It's the event of the night," one of them said.

Conall put a reassuring hand on her arm. "I'm fine." As it turned out, the sack was really a mask, with slits for eyes, and he could see perfectly well.

Iona looked back at him with concern, but he squeezed her hand and allowed himself to be marched away. Fortunately, the onlookers left her alone, and the red-haired man who'd talked to them gave Conall a nod, as if to say, *don't worry, I'll keep an eye on her for you.*

The big question in his mind was if he was here because he was an Irishman or because he was a very particular Irishman. Conall's only consolation was that neither the man he was fighting, who, since he was dressed like a Templar, Conall assumed to be

Arnulf, nor Goff, the organizer, behaved as if they had any idea who Conall really was. Either that, or both were excellent mummers, an unlikely prospect. He couldn't believe even someone as arrogant and righteous as Goff would deliberately harm the nephew of the King of Leinster.

Unless, of course, the point was to start a war. He hoped his friends were watching but knew better than to interfere, not until they knew more. From the somewhat welcoming pats on the shoulders he received as his guards guided him through the crowd to where the participants waited, his abduction appeared—amazingly enough—good-natured, prompting a tentative sigh of relief on his part.

They didn't know.

He adjusted the hood so he could better see out the slits, and then someone thrust a metal sword into his hand. It was too heavy for him, designed for someone twice Conall's size, which might have been the point. Rather than keep it, he dropped it amongst a pile of other weapons, laid out near where the participants gathered before they entered the ring, and pawed through them until he came up with two short swords—daggers really—and hefted one in each hand.

He could feel the Danes eyeing him with actual interest now. Maybe they'd chosen him for the ring because he was an older Irish fellow, someone to despise, and they wanted someone easily defeated. Suddenly, they were wondering if they'd made a mistake.

Good.

They didn't know it, but Conall had fought at the Battle of the Liffey. Perhaps he hadn't fought *well*, per se, but he'd lived. As he'd watched the men work in the ring tonight, it had dawned on him that the way they were training was all very well and good for raiding, but it wasn't *battle* training. Men on a raid fought one-on-one, usually against less skilled opponents. In battle, the shield wall was all. What they were doing here would be useful once the battle became a free-for-all, but everyone would have to survive the shield wall first.

The Irish were not known for their shield walls, which is one reason the Danes had defeated them time and again. Conall's people were notoriously undisciplined.

He decided tonight he would show these Danes what that meant.

When he'd met Arnulf yesterday, he'd noted his physique. Now in full Templar armor, he loomed over Conall and could have wielded the sword they'd first given him, confirming Conall's suspicion that he was supposed to lose. He wasn't going to forfeit before he'd started, however. He had too much pride for that, and he set his feet determinedly in the ring and forced himself to take even breaths.

He held the daggers as if they were swords. Though he'd taught Cait to fight with the knife reversed in her fist, with the point towards the ground, that was because a woman's strength came from her legs. Conall wasn't constructed like the man who faced him, but Arnulf's mistake was to be wearing so much gear. Maybe if they'd both been wielding a two-handed sword, as in battle, it would have made sense. But Conall had brought knives to a sword fight, and he knew the identity of the man who faced him. Arnulf hadn't been born to the life as Conall had been, and that knowledge told Conall to act first.

He dove forward, somersaulting the eight feet between himself and Arnulf, and came up on one knee with his knives crossed in front of him. Arnulf parried, but the intersection of the knives caught the blade. As Conall rose to his feet and flung his arms wide, he ripped the sword out of Arnulf's hand. A moment later, Conall had hooked his right foot around Arnulf's left knee and brought him to the ground. And a moment after that, he had his knives to Arnulf's throat.

A gratifying silence descended on the crowd. Then a few people started to laugh.

Conall said, "Do you yield?"

Arnulf had both hands up. "I yield! I yield!"

"Take off your helmet."

From the sidelines, Goff said, "That isn't our way—"

But Arnulf was already fumbling with his helmet. The face revealed, however, was not one Conall recognized. This *wasn't* Arnulf, but a different fresh-faced young man with dark hair and darker skin, whom Conall had just humiliated for no reason.

Conall stepped back, dropped both blades to the ground, and walked out of the ring.

31

Day Four

Dai

"You were rooting for the Irishman. I could see it." Vigo nudged Dai and spoke low in his ear. "Why?"

Dai blinked before coming up with an answer on the spot that wasn't even a lie. "He was so much smaller than the other man, I didn't think it was fair. I'm not so big myself yet." He bit his lip. "The Irishman was very good."

"He was good at street fighting, typical for an Irish sailor. Perhaps he wouldn't be so good in battle." Vigo tapped a finger to his lip as he watched Conall greet some men who approached with their congratulations. Conall moved towards where Iona waited for him, tugging off his mask and putting on the hat he'd worn to the fights. Pulling it down low over his eyes, he put his arm around Iona's shoulders and walked off into the darkness.

Dai was thinking that *Vigo* should be thinking that there were too many foreigners at the fights tonight. He also remembered where he'd seen Goff before: coming out of Vigo's shop right before Dai himself entered it. He hoped Cadoc and Jon were close enough to notice and remember too.

For his part, Vigo had already lost interest. He tugged on Dai's elbow. "I don't know how it was that Fate brought you to me yesterday. As it turns out, I have need of you. Come."

Dai didn't argue. He was here as Vigo's guest. He thought he'd performed well in the ring, especially given that it was unexpected. At first, he hadn't liked pretending to be a worse swordsman than he was, but he'd managed to find a perverse sort of pleasure in being very bad—and then suddenly improving there at the end, so Sitric, and thus Goff, could feel he'd taught him something.

His parents had worried when he was younger how easy he found it to lie. Dai could see, maybe, he could be a little bit concerned about it himself—except today, it had been very important he be good at it. And Conall, effectively, had done the same thing. Now that he was a man, Dai saw the difference between lying to protect the role he was playing or the people he loved and lying to his parents.

They left the crowd, with a new fight starting behind them, and walked north through the woods, over a rise, and came out next to a byre for cattle, set on the edge of a field. A split rail fence ran around the lean-to that protected mounds of hay from the weather, but was open to the elements on two sides.

No cattle were in it at the moment. Only Steffan, on his knees with his hands bound behind his back. A man Dai didn't recognize stood before him with his arms folded across his chest and a glaring look on his face. A younger man with a shock of white-blond hair stood a few feet away, looking somewhat worried. Horses and men were clustered off to one side, dressed in Irish fashion, but most of the men around the byre were Danish.

Vigo touched the younger man's shoulder as he went by. "Thank you, Arnulf. You can go now."

Dai tried not to gape as a look of relief crossed Arnulf's face, and he nodded. "Yes, sir."

Unless this was an elaborate ruse to entrap Dai, Vigo really did trust him with details he might not mention to anyone else. It did really seem that Vigo didn't know he'd sold Arnulf out. At the same time, Arnulf's respect for Vigo was clear, along with the fact that the two of them knew each other well.

"Why are you here, Donnell? I thought we talked about this. You weren't supposed to come tonight." Vigo spoke in fluent Gaelic, Dai's other new language. This was another surprise, and Dai tried not to stare. This couldn't be Donnell, the prince of Connaught ... could it? Regardless, Vigo's words were not respectful, as befitting a prince.

"And where else should I be?" Donnell replied. "I've been curious as to whether you would keep your end of the bargain. I'm wondering now if you haven't betrayed me too."

Vigo scoffed. "I have not."

Donnell gestured to Steffan. "You say that, but you allowed strangers in your midst." Both men's accents were similar, but slightly different than Conall's. "And Diarmait is still alive."

Dai dropped his head so nobody could see his face. He wasn't supposed to know Gaelic, of course, and he was glad he was standing out of either man's line of sight, a few paces behind and to the right of the two men so he could see their faces in profile. Dai's father had spoken of the political situation among the Irish clans, and the hatred Diarmait held for Donnell and Rory, who themselves were locked in a battle for edling to the throne of Connaught and the High Kingship. If this was Donnell, who did that make Vigo?

The prince turned his head and lifted his chin to indicate Dai. "And now you've brought another!"

Vigo motioned for Dai to come forward. "He's a newly freed slave. Welsh. He can translate."

Donnell grumbled, but he gestured Dai towards Steffan. "Tell the captive who I am."

Dai was saved by how hard he'd been working to keep his face impassive, along with the time needed to translate the Gaelic into Welsh. As it turned out, Donnell hadn't been speaking to him but to Vigo.

Unaware of the emotions roiling Dai—or that he spoke Gaelic too—Vigo said to him in Danish, "This is Prince Donnell, heir to the throne of Connaught—and the High Kingship, he would have me tell you. He would like you to translate our words into Welsh for the benefit of this cretin." He kicked out a foot at Steffan's thigh.

Steffan winced but then immediately smoothed his expression again.

Dai nodded quickly, not having to feign that he was genuinely overawed. His eyes went to Steffan, who raised his head to look up at him. Steffan had an abrasion on his jaw, perhaps from a ring when someone had backhanded him across the face. His nose wasn't broken, which was some consolation, and Steffan's brown eyes gazed calmly back at his captors.

Really, Dai had decided long ago that he wanted to be Steffan when he grew up. But first he had to get him out of this. He glanced at Vigo. "Who is he? Why is he captured?"

"He is one of the Welshmen who came with Prince Hywel from Gwynedd. A member of the patrol caught him in the woods, spying on us."

"He's a Dragon?" Dai made his eyes go wide. "You're sure? Maybe he's a former slave like me, wanting to learn how to fight?"

"With that gear?" Vigo shook his head. "He knows how to fight already. Besides, I saw him in the street when they arrived. There is no chance he's here just to watch, and I want to know why before—" he broke off, and made a gesture. "Enough! You ask too many questions. Tell him to whom he is speaking and ask him why he's here."

"What's this? What are you saying?" Donnell was impatient with the Danish, which he apparently didn't speak at all.

Vigo put out a calming hand and reverted to Gaelic once again. "The boy asked if the man before us is one of the Dragons."

Donnell looked extremely put out.

Dai took in a deep breath, not having to pretend to force himself to calm and to think. Then he did as Vigo had first bid, explaining to Steffan about Donnell and adding, "They want to know why you're here."

"Tell them I'll talk if they tell *me* what gave me away. My guess? Someone back in Dublin sold us out, either someone in Godfrid's house or Conall's. Someone working for this *mochyn*."

Dai shook his head. "I can answer that right now. Vigo recognized you from when we arrived."

Steffan looked pained. "I thought his shop was off the main street?"

"It is," Dai said. "He still saw you."

"So why doesn't he know you?"

"I don't know, and I don't want to ask."

"Find out what they want."

Donnell was looking fierce. "What is he saying?"

Dai hastily spoke in Danish to Vigo. "He wants to know why you captured him. He was doing nothing wrong."

Vigo's eyes narrowed. "Why was he in the woods?"

Dai obediently translated into Welsh for Steffan.

"Tell him I overheard sailors talking about the fights and thought I'd look in. Tell him I'm a sailor, not a Dragon. I was merely walking into Dublin with Gareth. I don't work for him!"

Dai translated this for Vigo, who did the same for Donnell with Gaelic. It was both a brilliant and awkward way to communicate, and Dai had to make sure, when Vigo and Donnell spoke, that he kept his eyes unfocused, as if he was waiting to be spoken to again.

Donnell slammed his fist into the palm of his hand, his anger barely contained. "Your fighting ring is a distraction we don't need. I told you it was going to get out of hand. I don't find these fights as amusing as you do."

"They have been useful. It's through them that unrest against Leinster has spread throughout Dublin. Keep a man entertained; keep him fed; and he'll do anything you want. Each man out there is a spark just waiting to burst into flame. Ottar never understood the people he ruled. I do."

Around Dai, none of the Danish men appeared to react to the disdain in Vigo's voice. Either none spoke Gaelic, or they were so loyal to Vigo they didn't care how little respect he had for their people.

"Too bad we couldn't have figured out a way for Ottar to survive the battle," Donnell said. "He was more malleable than Brodar has proven to be. I regret the need for you to kill him."

Vigo's chin jutted out. "It is a deed for which I am still waiting to be fully compensated."

Donnell frowned. "Patience, dear brother. The throne is within reach. If Diarmait had died, like he was supposed to, we might have taken the city today and be one step closer to total victory. Brodar would have listened to reason, stopped the wedding, and renounced Dublin's subjugation to Leinster."

"Brodar might not have believed Connaught's rule would have been any better."

"He would have if I promised him autonomy for Dublin." Donnell made a disgusted gesture with one hand. "Now we have to start over."

"Perhaps."

It was what Donnell had tried to negotiate with Ottar, through the men of Meath, though the death of Merchant Rikard had exposed the plot and forced Ottar to march on them instead of becoming their allies. This new scheme appeared somewhat more straightforward than the first: kill Diarmait, maybe kill Rory too, and take advantage of the chaotic aftermath. With those deaths, Donnell's path to the throne of Connaught and the high kingship would have been clear—and Dublin could rule itself.

If Dai were Danish, he might think it was a good deal.

As steward for Prince Hywel, Dai's father was heavily involved in the running of Gwynedd. Hywel had many brothers, though so far there'd been no infighting to speak of amongst them. Within the Dragons, it was Aron who thought about political strategy the most, and with whom Gareth consulted when he had a problem he couldn't immediately solve. Or, more often, when he knew how to solve it, but wanted to talk through the repercussions of his decisions and actions. Dai wished fervently that any of the other Dragons were here, because this was too big of a problem for him to solve alone.

Vigo turned to Steffan. "I'll ask one more time, why are you here? Is it at the behest of this Gareth? Or someone else?"

Dai kept on translating.

"I am just here to see the fights."

"He's lying," Donnell said.

"Of course he's lying," Vigo said mildly.

"We should kill him. Bury him in the woods where nobody will ever find him."

"We could do that," Vigo said, patience evident in his voice, "but he is a Dragon and servant to the edling of Gwynedd. He might have told someone where he was going, and when he doesn't return, this Gareth person will start asking questions—questions you don't want answered. We are not ready yet."

"You don't want them answered either, brother." Donnell visibly ground his teeth, his temper building again. "We can't let him tell what he knows. He has seen me."

"I did suggest to you earlier that you shouldn't come here tonight," Vigo said, again in that mild tone.

Now Donnell turned on him. "It's too great a risk to keep him alive. Get it done quickly and quietly."

"No."

Donnell's eyes narrowed. "You are disobeying *me*?"

"You are not my liege lord, *brother*." Vigo spat out the word. "We are in this together, for what we both achieve if you inherit the throne from our father." Then he put up a hand and softened his tone. "Why waste good Welsh muscle? Ever since Father put a stop to our raiding, our income has dropped precipitously. I have buyers in the north who would pay well for these two."

Vigo gestured to Danish men behind Dai. And then, between one heartbeat and the next, two of Vigo's men had Dai against a pillar. A moment after that, his hands were tied in front of him, with the rope looped around his neck.

Vigo had a smirk on his face. "There. That's better."

Dai was shocked—and ashamed—to have been taken so much by surprise. "What-what are you doing?" he stuttered in Danish.

Steffan had surged to his feet with a look of horror on his face.

Vigo's face was a mask of hostile amusement. "Tell him as long as he behaves, you will live. If he fights or tries to escape, we will first hurt you, and then kill you."

Dai managed to translate through his mounting horror, and though Steffan glared ferociously, he didn't fight when the man who'd tied Dai wrapped a rope around his wrists too.

When Vigo next spoke, his tone was full of satisfaction, and his words were for Donnell, since they came once again in Gaelic. "Just as I thought. A Dragon."

Donnell frowned. "What's that supposed to mean?"

Vigo motioned with his head for them to lead Steffan and Dai out of the byre, which their captors did. Once outside, they were both forced to their knees. "It means our prisoner is so stuffed full of honor he values the life of a Welsh boy he only just met. He will behave if it means I don't hurt the boy."

Donnell looked Steffan up and down and laughed. "You always did have the luck of the devil, brother. Send word to me when Diarmait is dead. It better be soon. I'm tired of waiting."

He strode to his horse, and the half-dozen men he'd brought with him sprang into action. Within a count of ten, the whole company had ridden away north, leaving Dai and Steffan beside the byre, with four heavily armed guards around them.

Vigo made another motion with his head towards Steffan. "Take them to the steading. I'll arrange for their transport tomorrow."

This time Steffan came up from his knees a little stiffly, which Dai hoped was an act but feared was not. "I don't understand what you're doing."

"Translate!" Vigo grasped Dai by his hair and hauled him to his feet too.

Dai obeyed, trying to breathe evenly like Steffan was. Of course, Vigo was right that Dai made an excellent hostage to Steffan's good behavior, just not entirely for the reasons he thought.

"I'm making a calculated choice." Now that Vigo had the true upper hand, he appeared to be even more talkative and willing to answer questions.

"In allying with Donnell, you're exchanging one master for another," Steffan said. "How can that be a calculated choice? You are Danish, aren't you?"

After Dai translated, Vigo tsked. "Half-Danish."

Dai hadn't yet explained to Steffan that Vigo and Donnell were half-brothers, both sons of the high king. and there wasn't time now either because Vigo ordered his men to tie the other end of the ropes that bound Steffan and Dai to the saddle of one of the horses. At least neither had a sack over his head, so they could still see and hear.

When they were both secured, Vigo said, "Your only concern is to do as I ask, when I ask it."

Dai translated.

"How do I know you won't kill him anyway?"

"I give you my word."

Steffan scoffed. "Why should I believe you?"

Vigo laughed. "He is worth more to me alive than dead. As long as you behave, you both will live."

"To be sold," Dai added bitterly.

Steffan paused. "My fate aside, am I correct in thinking this is about overthrowing Brodar?"

Dai knew it wasn't now, but rather than explain to Steffan, he translated in order to hear what Vigo had to say.

In reply, Vigo scoffed yet again. "If Brodar is the practical man I think him to be, he can keep the throne. Once Diarmait is dead, Leinster will be weak. Brodar knows what it means to be a real Dane. He just has to be reminded."

"What do you get out of it?" Dai was genuinely curious. "Donnell becomes High King and King of Connaught and you get ... what?"

"Leinster," Vigo said with satisfaction.

"Do you really think Donnell will give it to you?"

"He has to. He knows I have the power to destroy him."

"Then he could just have you killed." At this point, Dai figured he had nothing to lose and would ask questions as long as Vigo would answer.

Vigo sneered. "He can try." Then a genuinely pleased expression crossed Vigo's face. "You are a smart boy, aren't you? I might have to keep you."

"Slavery is illegal in Dublin," Dai said instantly.

"Not for long. And not in the rest of Ireland. Many things will change when Donnell is crowned High King."

And when Dai translated this last bit for Steffan, it was the first moment Steffan looked genuinely shaken.

32

Day Four

Cadoc

C adoc's Danish was very bad, but his Gaelic was excellent. He was close enough to the byre to have heard a few names bandied about, *Donnell* and *Connaught* being the most momentous, and to see that things had gone awry very quickly down below him. He'd found a perch in a tree not far from where Dai and Steffan were being roped to the back of a horse, but now he couldn't come down without risking exposure.

He would have just shot them all. Part of him thought there was no reason not to, and it would have solved a great many problems. But it might have created a great many more.

He *could* kill the heir to the High King of Ireland. That was as simple as nocking an arrow and loosing it.

None of them might survive the aftermath, however, least of all Dublin itself.

Still, if Dai and Steffan had been in real danger of being murdered on the spot, Cadoc would have thrown caution to the winds and shot everyone anyway.

But as it was, he did nothing, just watched the villain Vigo lead his friends away.

Unfortunately, once they were gone, Cadoc faced a real dilemma whether to track them through the woods now or get help and then track them. Steffan was more than competent, and likely had a knife his captors hadn't found tucked into some piece of clothing. He could free himself and Dai if he could live long enough to get to it.

But Cadoc couldn't leave them alone for that long, so, after they left, he made his way down from his tree. Vigo's men had taken the torches with him, but the full moon and clear night meant Cadoc could still see. After listening for a count of thirty, during which time Cadoc settled his heart and his breathing to a manageable level, he started after them, though he quickly realized the pace they were setting was near to crippling. Dai and Steffan would have to be running to keep up, an uncomfortable prospect tied to the back of a horse.

Initially, the trail was easy to follow, but once they came out of the woods and reached a crossroads, Cadoc was forced to stop and reassess.

He couldn't see or hear them. So many people had passed this way recently that hoofprints couldn't be read as meaningful either. He didn't know which way they'd gone.

But then, on the path north, a bit of pale fluff caught his eye, followed by a second and a third farther on. As he bent to the first one, he saw it was a crumb of bread, as were the others.

He straightened, looking west, which was the only other real option for where Vigo could be taking Dai and Steffan. If Cadoc were Vigo, he would have gone west, into Irish lands. But these men were Danish, even if allied with Donnell. North made sense too. He hoped too that Vigo wasn't going to take his prisoners far, not at three in the morning.

Once Cadoc committed to the road, he was able to move fast enough that it took less than a quarter of an hour to catch up, aided by the trail Dai had left behind. Cadoc heard them before he saw them, giving him time to take a shortcut through a patch of woods that cut off some distance due to a bend in the road around a hillock. They'd come maybe two miles from the crossroads. It wasn't so very far in actuality, but it was a long way to run behind a horse.

Which is perhaps why the entire company had come to a halt. As Cadoc crouched behind a tree on a little rise above the road, he saw Dai on his knees, his head down and breath coming hard. From the marks behind him, the horse had dragged him twenty feet before the group stopped.

Cadoc's heart warmed to the boy. He could be tired. But as Dai bent over, his forehead almost to the dirt, his bound hands went to the pocket of his coat.

Then his captors hauled him to his feet again, and they set off, at a slower pace, with Dai continuing to stumble along behind them. Somewhere along the way, Vigo had taken a different turning, leaving only four men guarding Dai and Steffan.

When they had reached a point fifty yards ahead, Cadoc stepped into the road and bent to the cloth Dai had dropped. It was hemp, rough woven and designed to hold food for a journey—in this case, the bun from which Dai had been scattering bread. Cloth in hand, Cadoc started after them, though again making sure he remained well back. He was less afraid of losing them now than being spotted.

Fortunately for everyone involved, Cadoc included, the company turned off the road a short while later, this time into a more substantial holding than the lean-to, consisting of a thatched-roof hut with outbuildings. Smoke rose from the hut, but Steffan and Dai were taken to the adjacent barn, which significantly larger than the house. White sheep dotted the adjacent field. They'd arrived at a working farm.

To whom the farm belonged could wait until Cadoc had figured out the more important issue of what to do next. Dai and Steffan had been brought to the farm by four men, all on horseback, which was an indication of the money and status of the people involved. Ordinary peasants had cobs—horses to pull wagons and plows but untrained for riding the way these horses had been ridden. That made the men around Vigo warriors of a sort. They could be common Danishmen, but Cadoc thought they might be higher ranking than that, more on the level of a *teulu*, a personal guard.

He was rising from his hiding place to move closer to the barn, in hopes of hearing what was happening inside—and preventing something bad, if he could—when two things happened at once: Vigo rode into the clearing with three more men—and a hand came down hard on his shoulder. "Stay still."

He turned to find Aron, followed closely by Iago, stooping low just behind him. A rush of gratitude flowed through him to see two more of his fellow Dragons in his hour of need. They were brothers in a way he'd never known before, and a fellow brother was in trouble— not to mention their brother-in-training.

"How did you find me?"

Aron grinned. "We never lost you."

"You can run, I'll give you that." Iago grunted. "A few times I was afraid you'd get too far ahead, but Aron here—" he elbowed the younger man, "—has a good nose for the forest. Who knew?"

Aron ignored Iago's compliment entirely, his eyes focused on the house and the barn. He knew his own worth.

"What do you see?" Cadoc said.

"Too many men." Aron grimaced. "We may not have a choice about going in, however. I overheard the bit about selling Steffan and Dai as slaves. I don't like the look of these newcomers either, and I don't trust Vigo not to change his mind and kill them outright."

Cadoc could only agree.

33

Day Four

Gwen

"My lady! Your son is here!"

Gwen swept her cloak over her shoulders and came to the edge of the railing that overlooked the main floor of Godfrid's house. Cait was already heading down the stairs. Her long night braid hung over one shoulder, but she was fully dressed. She'd slept in her clothes as Gwen had, having stayed the night, heedless of questions of propriety. But of course, Godfrid hadn't come home.

Gwen looked down to the fire to see Llelo looking up at her. "Mam."

She was down the stairs by the time Cait reached Llelo. She would have flung her arms around her son, but the warning look in Llelo's eyes told her to wait. "What has happened? Just tell me."

In a few sentences Llelo explained what he'd seen, ending with, "Dai was well, last I saw."

Gwen put her hand to her heart and looked to Cait. The plan, upon which everyone had agreed before Godfrid and his men had ridden north, was not to engage with the fighters, but simply to watch and learn. Nobody had thought the gathering would be this extensive, or that Dai and Conall would be roped into fighting. And because of the secrecy involved, they hadn't let the watchmen on duty in the city or palace know what was happening until it happened.

Fortunately, Godfrid's house wasn't far from the palace and, with Llelo in tow and Cait's remaining bodyguard, Bern, jogging beside them, they arrived in the courtyard to find a dozen men and horses already preparing to ride. Hywel himself was tightening his horse's girth.

Gwen ran up to him. "How did you know to be ready?"

"I didn't. I woke early and couldn't go back to sleep. I had what I thought was an unwise idea to ride out with Evan and Gruffydd, perhaps to greet Gareth and the other Dragons returning. I met Brodar crossing the hall."

"As it turns out, you're needed." And she explained why and where, as Cait was doing with Brodar.

"I can lead the way," Llelo said in Welsh, "but I left my horse at Godfrid's house."

"We don't have time to fetch it." Gruffydd put out a hand to Llelo, who took it and swung onto the horse behind him.

Brodar actually grinned down at Cait and Gwen. "My brother is capable of getting into the most amazing kinds of trouble. Have no fear. I will rescue him once again." He tipped his head towards the hall behind him. "We've made quite a commotion. Perhaps the two of you could do me the favor of convincing O'Connor and your uncle that nothing is amiss."

And, before either woman could either protest or agree, he urged his horse after Gruffydd and Llelo, through the gate and into the street.

Within a dozen heartbeats, the rest of the company followed, leaving Cait and Gwen alone again.

Cait huffed. "I am not overly fond of being left behind. And I really don't like this task he set us."

"You are about to be a princess of Dublin," Gwen said. "This won't be the last time it is you who are sent to appease your uncle."

"I'm sure you're right." Cait looked towards the hall. "In defense of my family, I would do anything."

34

Day Four

Dai

"It's going to be all right," Steffan said.

The pair of them had been left in the dark in the barn. It smelled of hay and horse, not entirely unpleasantly. Dai's hands were still tied in front of him and the other end of the rope had been wrapped around a beam above his head and knotted. It meant his arms were raised above his head, stretching his shoulders and putting him on his toes. It wasn't comfortable.

Twenty feet away, Steffan had been subjected to a similar arrangement. Neither could get to the other nor help the other.

"How exactly is it going to be all right?" Dai tugged on the rope for a moment, but it served only to tighten his bonds further.

"Well, it won't be if you keep doing that." Steffan spun in a circle at the end of his rope, surveying what little they could see of their surroundings.

The barn had been well-maintained, with no cracks in the walls. Summer was the time when fresh daub would have been applied. The only reason they had any light at all was because the door to the hayloft was open, perfectly framing the moon. That wouldn't last long, but it was cheering for now.

Steffan turned back to Dai. "We need to be ready when Cadoc comes. That was good work dropping those bread crumbs."

Dai rubbed at his right cheek with his shoulder. "You saw that? Do you really think Cadoc is on his way?"

"He'd posted himself in a tree overlooking the byre."

The feeling of relief that flooded through Dai was like sinking into a hot bath. "You're sure?" And then at Steffan's wry look, he apologized for doubting. "Of course you're sure."

Steffan scoffed. "Vigo has no idea who we are."

"They know you're a Dragon."

Now Steffan grinned. "But they don't know you are too."

It was the nicest thing Steffan—or maybe anyone—had ever said to him. Dai wanted to be worthy of the title. But then he frowned. "Why didn't Cadoc rescue us already?"

"Think about it, Dai. Prince Donnell is in league with Vigo, supposedly a Danish merchant of some prestige and repute, but clearly far more than that."

"He's Donnell's half-brother."

Gratifyingly, Steffan's jaw actually dropped. "You know that for certain?"

Dai nodded.

Steffan snorted. "You might have told me sooner. As your mother would say, *when were you going to step onto the stage and sing?*"

Dai felt genuinely apologetic. "I meant to back at the byre, but with all that was going on I didn't think of it again until just now. They called each other *brother*. Vigo's mother is Danish, that much is clear. Perhaps he's illegitimate because I hadn't heard the High King had a Danish wife."

"Now I understand why he thinks Donnell will follow through and give him Leinster." Steffan gritted his teeth. "All the more reason for Cadoc not to have acted right away."

"I don't understand."

"What would be the consequences of killing the High King's sons?"

Dai deflated. "War."

"Vigo's involvement in the fighting ring was never more than a pretense to leave the city and meet with his brother."

"That might have been how it started, but it became more than that to Vigo." Then Dai told him everything he remembered about the conversation in Gaelic between Vigo and Donnell.

Steffan listened intently, breathing normally throughout, which was calming also to Dai, and when Dai finished, he bobbed a nod. "Good. I'm glad you told me. Remember everything you said because you'll have to repeat it to Prince Hywel and Prince Godfrid."

Dai frowned. "What about you?"

Steffan's expression turned bleak. "Chances are, I won't be rescued with you."

"What? Why not?"

But before Steffan could explain, the door to the barn opened, and Vigo entered with three other men, one of whom pointed to Steffan and said in Danish. "That's the one!"

Dai had no idea who this man was, but Vigo walked up to Steffan, looking up because Steffan was taller and he was slightly suspended in the air. "You lied to me," he said in French. "You speak French more than well enough to understand me now. My friend Tomos here tells me all the Dragons speak French." Then he gestured to the other two men. "Cut him down."

"Why?" Dai asked in Danish, real panic in his voice. "What do you want with him?"

Vigo shot Dai a dismissive look, but he answered the question anyway. "Now I know he can understand me, he can be made to talk without need for you."

"Just be glad they learned it, Dai," Steffan said in Welsh as his feet settled on the ground. "If Vigo had hurt you, I would have talked. I wouldn't have had a choice."

Dai started to struggle against his ropes, even though he knew it was futile. He believed Steffan about Cadoc being close by—or was trying to believe him—but that didn't mean either would survive being separated. Somehow, however, Steffan had known what was coming. "Where are you taking him?"

"Never you mind that, boy." Vigo slapped Dai upside the head, though it wasn't hard enough to make his ears ring, which told Dai he still didn't know Dai's identity. Steffan was right that Vigo would have used it against them. "You should look to yourself." Then he jerked his head to the two men who held Steffan. "Bring him."

They dragged Steffan from the barn, leaving Dai in darkness.

35

Day Four
Conall

Conall was nearly beside himself watching the events of the evening unfold, made worse by the arrival of Sitric, sent by Aron with word of the capture of Dai and Steffan, and that he and Iago would follow Cadoc. "I didn't know any of this was going to happen! Truly I didn't!" Sitric appeared genuinely worried that Conall—and thus Prince Godfrid—would think he'd drawn them into an ambush.

"We have larger concerns now," Conall said, not so soothingly, but with some understanding.

Then Jon arrived on Conall's other side, wearing a hat much like Conall's, but pulled even lower down over his face to disguise his identity. The three men plus Iona retreated to the edge of the ring. The last fight of the night was winding down, and to celebrate another successful event, the fight's organizers had begun to pass around alcohol, one whiff of which told Conall it was *water of life*. Whiskey.

Sitric accepted the flagon and took a long slug. To do otherwise would invite notice and censure. After Conall too had drunk and passed it on, Sitric said, "Pardon my omission, my lord. I forgot we drank whiskey at the end."

"We will remember it, but Harald's death is of far less concern in this moment than what is going to happen to this mob once it has more whiskey in it."

"Should I do something about Arnulf?" Jon nodded towards the priest, who had his arm across the shoulders of the young man Conall had fought. They appeared to have been at the whiskey sooner than the rest of the crowd. Either that, or it really worked that fast.

"First, we need to find out what has become of the others," Conall said. "Hopefully they are close enough that they realize what kind of trouble we're in."

And then the foreman, Goff, made everything that much worse. He stepped into the ring, both arms held in the air. "I wanted to share a message from King Brodar himself." He produced a paper and flourished it. "He warns us that our enemy is at our gates! Rory O'Connor has not come to Dublin to celebrate Prince Godfrid's wedding. He has brought an army, and our king needs our help to defeat him!"

With each successive sentence, the shouts of approval grew louder until they became a roar.

"What in the name of St. Ansgar is happening?" Sitric stared at Goff, a man he'd once admired.

"Nothing good." Jon's hands were clenched into fists and he seemed moments away from exposing himself and them, so Conall gripped his upper arm.

"Wait."

Jon clearly didn't want to, but the rest of what Goff might have said was drowned out by a sudden roar from beyond the crowd, and Godfrid himself bounded out of the woods, his sword held above his head.

The crowd roared their approval back at him. Even with all the upheaval of the last months, and despite the general resentment against Leinster, Godfrid and Brodar themselves remained personally popular among the citizens of Dublin. The common people had always been very clear in their choice.

"Godfrid! Godfrid! Godfrid!" Someone off to the right began the chant, and Sitric instantly picked it up, his hands cupped around his mouth. Such was the way of a mob that the chant quickly spread and, with Godfrid's arrival, Goff had no choice but to accede his place in the center of the ring.

Conall spied Gareth circling around the outside of the crowd and tugged at the others. "Come on."

They snaked their way amongst the chanting onlookers and converged in the gathering place for the fighters. With Godfrid now the center of attention, Goff had retreated there, and Jon immediately went up to him. "You have either been used by villains or are a traitor. Either way, I expect you to support your prince."

"What?" Goff gaped at him. "What traitor?"

Jon snorted. "You have been listening to the wrong people."

- 301 -

"Rory O'Connor is our enemy."

"That may be, but King Brodar did not write that message, as Prince Godfrid would tell you if he was speaking to you instead of to your acolytes." Jon lifted his chin to point to where Godfrid stood, still trying to quiet the crowd. "The king has no problem with you training the next generation of fighters. Murder and treason, however, are another thing entirely."

Now Goff's mouth fell open. "You have this all wrong!"

Conall's lip curled. "So you don't know that Vigo met this evening with Prince Donnell of Connaught, with whom he is allied?"

"N-n-no!"

Conall tsked. "Maybe you really have been duped."

Goff swallowed hard. "I swear to you—" But then he cut himself off and swung around to where Godfrid had finally quieted his audience.

Godfrid's arms had been up, the sword above his head, but now he dropped them and stood before the crowd of people, silent all of a sudden as the full impact of Godfrid's arrival among them hit home. A prince of Dublin was standing in their midst. He was a true warrior, *of* them but not *one of* them. He was, in fact, what every fighter among them aspired to be.

So they listened as he spoke.

"Our ancestors came to Ireland seeking wealth because it was through silver and gold that honor was gained. For centuries, our people lived by raiding other peoples. We settled in Dublin not because we had suddenly become farmers and merchants but as a base from which to raid even farther and wider.

"It wasn't just the Irish we raided either." Here, Godfrid flung out a hand towards the east. "We sacked settlements on the shores of Wales, England, and France. We went anywhere the land was rich and the people ill-prepared to counter us."

Now he dropped his arm and gazed at the men and women looking back at him. "Friends, those days are over. We grow just as fat and rich by allowing our neighbors to grow fat and rich and trading with them. We do better selling them goods than by taking what they have. We do better by building than destroying. We have discovered we would rather live peaceably with our neighbors than make war against them."

The people listening could have been disagreeing, but Conall didn't read that in their faces. They appeared riveted and suddenly subdued, where before they'd been raucous with blood and whiskey.

Godfrid moved to head off any objections anyway. "I am not saying what you are doing here is wrong. My brother, when he learned of what Goff has built, was proud. They sailed together to Gwynedd, as some of you may recall, and fought together just last spring at the Liffey."

Nods came from all around. Conall had never heard Godfrid speak before, not like this. He hadn't known he *could* speak. Godfrid had lived in Brodar's shadow the whole of his life. He'd gone where his father and then his brother pointed, fought where they told him to fight, and never once complained.

Maybe this was the same Godfrid, and it was just Conall who was seeing him with new eyes.

"There is a need still for men to wield sword and axe. We saw that at the Battle of the Liffey, where the warriors of Dublin fought to defend our city and our people against the men of Meath. Ottar fell that day." He gave a little laugh. "God knows he and I had our differences, but I never questioned his prowess in battle. Today, however, we face a different threat."

His listeners stirred at the change in Godfrid's tone, and even Conall, an Irishman, felt his spine straighten, knowing he was about to hear something different.

"The threat against us isn't about Danes versus Irish. It isn't about us versus them. It is about our very survival." He punched a fist into his open palm. "Tonight I am here because I learned Prince Donnell of Connaught has come to Dublin, not to pay his respects, not to celebrate my wedding to my Irish bride, but to collude with those who look at Leinster and see our traditional enemy, not realizing that in trading Leinster for Connaught we'd merely be exchanging one overlord for another even more brutal.

"I have no love for Leinster, believe me. And while I do love Caitriona and see the possible benefit of a closer alliance with the throne of Leinster, do not mistake me: I would never—" he paused and then emphasized, "—*ever* compromise Dublin's sovereignty.

"But that is what we face tonight. Brodar would not have me tell you this, but we went to war against our allies when we fought the men of Meath. King Ottar himself plotted with them and Prince Donnell O'Connor of Connaught, the High King's son, to murder both my brother and Donnell's brother Rory, who sat at our high table this very night."

If Conall had been asked, he would have counseled against revealing Ottar's treachery, but he hadn't been asked, and he understood both why Brodar hadn't told anyone about the death warrant earlier, and why Godfrid did now.

Regardless, the revelation swept through the crowd like a sudden gust of wind, leaving mouths open and grown men gasping.

Beside Conall, Goff stuttered his protest, prompting Conall to turn on him. "This is also something you claim to have known nothing about?"

"I knew nothing! Nothing, my lord!"

Godfrid, however, wasn't done, and he held up his hands for quiet once more. "Some of you are already warriors. Some of you are in training to become warriors. All of you may be needed, if not today then one day." He put a hand to his heart. "I share your hopes and dreams for Dublin. One day, God willing, we will return our city to its rightful place on land and sea. We will speak more in the coming days. For now, know that my brother and I stand with you." He clenched his fist and held it above his head. "For the glory of Dublin!"

"For the glory of Dublin!"

It wasn't a cheer Conall had ever heard before, but every man's fist was in the air in mimicry of Godfrid.

And then an accompanying shout came from all sides of the clearing. It echoed so loudly, floating above the trees, that Conall had to fight the urge to cover his ears. The crowd had been won over by Godfrid's speech, and it was as if a wave was cresting on a beach as each man fell to his knees at the sight of King Brodar himself riding into the clearing, followed by twenty of his men. Prince Hywel and the other Dragons hung back, but the fighting ring was now surrounded by warriors.

At the sight of his brother, Godfrid also went down on one knee. Brodar dismounted and the crowd parted for him. As he reached Godfrid, he held out his hand for Godfrid to rise, and the two men clasped forearms. "I see you've been busy saving my kingdom for me ... dare I say *again*."

"Everything I do, I do for Dublin, and you, my lord."

Beside Conall, Goff too had gone down on one knee.

Conall had bent his head but not knelt, and he looked down at the back of Goff's head. "You really meant to overthrow your own king, Goff?"

"Please believe me, my lord. I didn't know." Then Goff gave in to a moment of weakness. "Is it death for me?"

"Help us rescue our friends. And then we'll see."

36

Day Four

Dai

Dai jumped at the sound of a wooden board being shoved out of position, and he twisted towards the back of the barn. His arms were aching beyond anything he'd ever endured before, and he felt tears pricking the corners of his eyes as first Cadoc's head and then his whole body came through the hole he'd made.

His face full of concern, Cadoc went first to untie the rope that kept Dai suspended. As Dai dropped his arms, he genuinely wondered if he would ever be able to raise them again. Cadoc struggled for a moment to untie the rope that bound his wrists and then gave up and simply sawed at them with his knife, which was sharp and deadly. A moment later, both men had slipped through the hole again and, whether out of a sense of order or to leave no trace of his passing, Cadoc reached through the hole to set the loose boards in place again.

Dai wasn't so much weepy anymore as light-headed, relieved beyond measure to be free, but terrified of what might be happening to Steffan. As they reached the trees where Aron and Iago waited, he said urgently, "Did you see where they took Steffan?"

Aron put a finger to his lips. "We saw."

Dai had made sure his voice was no more than a whisper and added, "What are we going to do?"

"There *are* only four of us," Aron said dryly. "Even the mighty Iago has his limits."

Iago was used to Aron talking this way and ignored him, his eyes focused on the little hut. "Why did they take him into the house?"

"To get information from him," Dai said.

"What information can they get from him in the house that they couldn't get in the barn?" Iago said.

"I don't know. They discovered he spoke French, so they didn't need me anymore. Steffan said that was a good thing."

"He's right," Cadoc said.

Dai nudged Aron. "Tell me what is happening. If I am to become one of you, I have to know."

Again, it was Cadoc who answered, his voice full of sympathy. "Are you aware of what has gone on between not only Leinster and Connaught but within the household of the High King himself?"

"You mean the way they fight amongst themselves?"

"That's exactly what I mean. The O'Connors actually encourage it." Cadoc indicated with a flick of his finger the hut into which Steffan had disappeared. "Vigo is the High King's son. So is Rory. So is Donnell. Vigo, however, is illegitimate, but even that wouldn't matter if he could prove himself to be the strongest."

"By which Cadoc means the most ruthless, the most willing to do anything to achieve an end," Aron said. "Vigo needs to know what brought Steffan to the fight tonight. He is desperate to learn how much of his plot is known. They have been thwarted once. His brother might not take another loss well."

Dai's hands clenched into fists, and he looked at Cadoc. "You should have shot Donnell and Vigo when you had the chance."

Cadoc didn't dignify what was obviously not true with an answer.

Aron wasn't done with the explanation, though now it was more than Dai wanted. "O'Connor encourages his sons to fight each other, but if someone else were to harm any of them, the reaction would be immediate and devastating."

"That's what Steffan said too." Dai's shoulders sagged. "So we can't kill Vigo."

"No, we cannot." Cadoc's tone was grim. "But that doesn't mean we can't do something."

"Set up over there." Aron tipped his head towards a bit of rising ground to their left.

Cadoc studied the spot. "I'm going to shoot anyone who gets close to you, no matter who he is."

"You do that." Aron gestured that Iago should go to the right, and Iago left them at a running crouch, moving around the edge of the property. He disappeared behind the barn, only to reappear a moment later on the other side of the main house, a shadow amidst other shadows cast by the moon.

Vigo had posted only two guards, who stood talking quietly a few feet from the house's front door. They hadn't moved when Cadoc had rescued Dai and showed no signs of moving now. Their night vision was ruined by the torch stuck in the ground a few feet from the front door.

"What are we doing?" Dai asked.

"Rescuing Steffan."

Someone inside the house screamed. It was an awful sound.

Dai made to stand, but Aron caught his arm. "Wait."

A light flamed at Cadoc's position, something the guards couldn't miss, though they stared disbelieving rather than doing anything about it. Apparently unconcerned that his position could now be determined, Cadoc loosed an arrow at the thatched roof of the house, which instantly caught fire. He sent a second flaming arrow into the roof of the barn.

By the time he loosed his third flaming arrow, one of the guards had shouted a warning and both had started towards Cadoc, swords drawn. But Cadoc's next two arrows caught each in the chest before they'd gone twenty feet. Aron had forbidden Cadoc to kill Vigo, but everyone else was fair game.

Aron gripped Dai's shoulder. "Shout *fire!* in Danish."

Rising to his feet, Dai cupped his hands around his mouth and shouted, by which time Aron was running towards the house, and Iago had also left his hiding place. Dai would have gone too, but he didn't even have a knife on him, and he knew better than to think he could accomplish anything with his fists other than a momentary deferment of his own death.

By the time Aron reached the house's front door, the roof was fully aflame, aided by several more flaming arrows Cadoc had put into it. Aron set himself to the right of the door. A moment later, the first of Vigo's men burst through it. Aron grabbed the man by the arm, spun him around against the wall of the hut, and put a knife into his back.

A second man had come through the door on his heels, but Cadoc shot him in the chest. His sword bared, Iago hit the half-open door with his shoulder and went through it with Aron right behind him.

Dai couldn't abide hiding a moment longer. He raced towards one of the guards Cadoc had shot, picked up the man's sword where it had fallen to the ground, and leapt into the house after Aron and Iago.

The smoke was choking, and he instantly ducked to get below it, which may have saved his life, because someone had stepped out from behind the door and taken a swipe at his head. Dai stabbed out blindly with his borrowed weapon and, by sheer luck, managed to connect with the knee of his attacker, who yelped and leapt away. The reprieve allowed Dai to grab the edge of the door and slam it hard, driving the man towards the wall.

Dai leapt up and had his sword to the man's throat before he realized his assailant was Vigo himself.

"Don't kill him, even if he deserves it," Aron warned from behind him.

While Iago dispatched the remainder of Vigo's men, Aron passed Dai heading for fresh air, his arm around Steffan's waist, helping him walk. Steffan's left hand was wrapped in a bloody cloth.

Meanwhile, the thatch continued to burn, dropping cinders all around them. Iago stopped beside Dai, breathing hard.

"What do I do with him?" Dai asked.

"You can't kill me." Vigo smirked. "I'm the son of the High King."

"You're right; we can't." Dai looked at Iago and motioned *go ahead*. "But he can do something."

"My pleasure." Iago punched Vigo with a hard uppercut, snapping his teeth together and sending him first into the wall and then to the floor. Then Iago flung Vigo over his shoulder and carried him from the house.

37

Day Four

Gareth

On the ride back from the clearing, they'd wrested more of the story from Goff—the part Goff knew, anyway. He seemed desperate to clear his conscience—and avoid the accusation of treason.

In a way, what he had to say was hardly more than Gareth had known already: Goff had started the fighting ring under Ottar in an attempt to bring old-fashioned Danish values back to Dublin. As a Welshman, Gareth wasn't necessarily in favor of some of them, including the ability to hack a man to pieces with a dull blade. But those of honor and loyalty were timeless and, under Ottar, they had not been prized sufficiently.

They got the rest of the story from Dai, whose language skills had proved invaluable: Vigo had been Donnell's eyes and ears in Dublin before Ottar's death—and he'd been the man who stabbed him in the back at the Battle of the Liffey. After Brodar's elevation to king, Vigo and Donnell had hatched a new plan to murder Diarmait and their brother Rory to ensure Donnell's inheritance. Vigo would then step to prominence, bastard or not, in Leinster, which then, like Dublin, would be a client state to Connaught.

In a way, Brodar should consider himself lucky not to have been a target, but even Vigo and Donnell seemed to have realized the Danes would never accept direct rule by either of them.

On the ride back to the city, Godfrid had told Vigo that trusting Donnell to follow through once he'd gained what he wanted was foolish. As Vigo had been gagged and thrown over the back of a horse at the time, he couldn't reply, and Gareth had agreed to leave the questioning of him to Brodar and Godfrid. As a son of the High King, bastard or not, even tying him up was dangerous, and Gareth was perfectly happy to steer clear of the political winds that might blow from Connaught when the High King found out.

That left Arnulf, whom Gareth placed in a penitent cell at the church to think about the error of his ways. Gareth hadn't even stopped to bathe and change, only grabbing an apple and a bite of cheese after leaving his horse at Godfrid's house.

"You should be with your sister." Gareth eyed Conall, who intercepted Gareth as he crossed the churchyard. Workers were picking up every stray leaf and twig from the surrounding grass, laying out the woven reed mat Cait would walk upon from the gate to the church door so as not to dirty her dress, and scattering flower petals, which Gareth and Conall skirted so as not to undo their good work.

"She is with our mother and Gwen. If I were smart, I'd be drinking a warm cup of mead—or better yet, sleeping—but that would leave this last task to you alone. Trust you not to shirk it and to finish what you started."

"In the wake of the night's events, I expect few others except Bishop Gregory to remember what we were here for in the first place."

"Haven't you heard? There's an important wedding today," Conall said.

Gareth gave him a wry smile. "Oh, I know, and the murder of an unpopular monk is hardly as exciting as uncovering treason. But Harald deserves justice, in whatever form that might take."

"What if Arnulf can't tell us what happened to Harald?"

"He will tell us," Gareth said grimly, "or he will point us to the person who can."

"If he's smart, it will be someone who died tonight."

"I'm praying he isn't that smart."

Arnulf sat on the low bed in the cell, hunched over with his elbows on his knees and his head in his hands. Bishop Gregory was just leaving, his expression one of sadness. "I'll be in in the little chapel, praying for the souls of all who've died this week." He shot Arnulf a glance. "And for those still living. Please come find me after you've finished with him."

"You are welcome to stay as witness," Gareth said. "There will be no hurting him."

Bishop Gregory smiled gently. "I know you won't. That's why I can leave you to it."

At the arrival of Gareth and Conall, rather than trying to stonewall them, Arnulf chose to go on the offensive and started speaking the moment Gareth walked into the room. "I just explained everything to Bishop Gregory, and I'll tell you too. I didn't kill Harald."

"Then tell us what happened, preferably from the beginning."

Arnulf gripped the wooden siderail of the bed so hard his knuckles turned white. Now he'd started, he was reluctant to continue. But continue he did: "You can't know what it means to be born Danish, neither of you. From birth, every boy is taught to be a warrior. Except now, few are given the opportunity to become one." He'd been looking down at his feet, but now he looked up. "It is our birthright, and the kings of Dublin have squandered it for years."

Gareth didn't bother to argue the point since Arnulf was past listening.

Now the priest waved a dismissive hand. "Oh, I know Ottar sent men to Wales to fight for Cadwaladr, and we fought against the men of Meath just last spring. But we weren't *prepared*. There was a time when *every* Danish man was a fighter." He plucked at his robe. "Not this."

Conall canted his head, keeping his voice level. "You regret taking the cloth?"

Arnulf's mouth twisted. "I am a younger son. My father died when I was a boy, and I had no one to train me. I joined the Church because my mother wanted it, and it seemed the better of my options."

"When did you enter Goff's company?" Conall asked.

"Near the beginning."

"Which was when?" Gareth said.

"Two years ago?" Arnulf didn't sound sure, but Gareth didn't feel the need to press that particular point.

"What about Vigo?" he asked.

"He supplied us with weapons. Goff listened to him and was a good teacher, but not so good at speeches—or rather, he had one good speech and gave it every time, the one you heard, in fact."

Gareth could see how that might be. "And Harald?"

"He came later. His brother was the soldier, not him. He came home to Dublin because Tiko had died and, as far as I could tell, Harald could think of little else but emulating the heroes of the past." Arnulf's expression turned doleful. "He tried hard, but he wasn't very good."

"You fought with him?" Gareth said.

Arnulf nodded. "We were thrown together, as you might expect, given our shared secret. At first, I was angry with him for joining, because I feared he would betray me. But he was on fire with Dublin's warrior past and furious with Bishop Gregory and Brodar for not standing up to the Irish." Suddenly his expression, which had become momentarily animated, turned sad. "A week ago things changed. He came to me with a story about how Vigo was really the bastard son of the High King and was set on betraying us with his brother Donnell, who'd been behind Ottar's death and the war last May."

Conall straightened in the doorway. "How did he know?"

"He'd followed Vigo to a meeting with Donnell. I have no idea how he found the time or what prompted him to do it. The risk he took!" Arnulf shook his head. "At the time, I didn't see how it could be true and told him so. He railed at me, Vigo, and Goff so much it was as if he'd lost his mind. He wasn't making sense."

Arnulf paused, and when next he spoke, his tone was heavy with guilt. "I went to Vigo about it."

Now they were getting to the meat of the matter. "Talk us through what happened the night he died."

From behind Gareth, Conall added, "If you didn't kill him, you have nothing to fear."

Arnulf bent his head anyway. "It isn't fear I must live with, but shame."

Gareth let the silence lengthen, knowing Arnulf couldn't help but fill it.

Finally, Arnulf sighed. "Vigo invited Harald to a private lesson, just him, me, and Harald. Full armor, as you saw. We fought hard."

"Which is why his sword had untreated nicks in it," Gareth said.

"Yes. He always endeavored to polish those out, but—" Arnulf looked down at his hands.

"But he died before he could. Tell me about that."

"After the lesson, we drank toasts to our ancestors, as we always do. Vigo kept urging more drink on Harald, chiding him, accusing him of not being as tough as his forefathers. I thought Harald had been drinking before he arrived. Even after our training had sweated some of it out of him, he still wasn't entirely sober, and he became even more belligerent, as some drunk men do, over the next hour. Finally, before the neighbors got involved, Harald and I left together.

I was relieved, in truth. I was afraid of Vigo by then, and I feared—" he stopped.

"You feared what?" Gareth wasn't going to let him end there.

Arnulf sighed. "I feared what Vigo might do to Harald if I left them alone together."

"Harald was sober enough to walk?"

Arnulf nodded. "In retrospect, I should have steered him to his mother's house, but we went home instead."

"Did you see him to his room?"

"I told him he needed to get out of his armor, but he refused my help or to help me. He said he wanted to pray, and since I was hardly sober myself, all I could think about was getting caught out of bed. I left him heading towards the church. He was walking on his own, and I thought—" Arnulf stopped and swallowed. "I hoped prayer would be the best thing for him, and he would have forgotten all about his grievances by morning. I managed to claw my way out of my own armor and went to bed with a lighter heart."

"Until the bishop found Harald dead in the chapel," Gareth said, "in full armor."

Arnulf nodded. "Until then."

"Do you know why Harald died in the chapel?"

Arnulf had a look on his face that implied he'd thought of little else since the body had been found. "Harald was angry, betrayed— first by the bishop and then by Vigo. He was angrier at Vigo than with Bishop Gregory, however. Now that I've had a chance to consider, I don't think he meant to profane the chapel."

"Why else would he go there? Why lie on the altar?" Conall said.

Arnulf looked up, tears streaming down his cheeks. "In his mind, he was a monk and a warrior. In his drunken state, what better place could he have found to pray?"

"Or to lie?" Gareth said.

Arnulf nodded miserably.

From behind Gareth, Conall said in Welsh, for Gareth's ears only, "There but for the grace of God go how many of us? I've rarely been that drunk, but when I was, thank all the saints I had better friends to watch over me than poor Harald."

They'd been focused on Harald and his motives, but that didn't mean Arnulf himself was off the hook, and now Gareth said, "Tell me about the quote on his bedside table."

Arnulf's expression turned sheepish. "I left it there."

Gareth had guessed that, of course. Conall finally left the doorway and came closer. "You wanted us to think Harald killed himself? That was your idea?"

"Sort of."

"What does that mean?" Gareth said.

Now a sulky look crossed Arnulf's face. "When Bishop Gregory sent me to find you, first I stopped by Vigo's shop and told him Harald had died and where his body had been found. He thought it would be enough to start the rumor. People love to gossip, so it didn't take much."

Gareth could only agree with that. "Where did the note come from?"

"Harald and I had been discussing the translation of the Bible into Danish he'd been working on. He had asked me to help him with some passages, so I knew where to find the paper. On the way back from speaking to you, I stopped by Harald's mother's house, tore the bit from the top of the paper, and left before his mother returned from the market. It seems I should have taken the whole paper and burned it. Bad luck, I guess."

"I wouldn't have thought a priest would believe in luck, bad or otherwise," Conall said, though in an undertone.

If he heard, Arnulf ignored him, lost in his own story and misery. "It was the best I could do on short notice. Vigo hoped the note would stop the investigation before it started and thought it was better to have Harald condemned than for the bishop to find out about the fighting ring." His shoulders fell. "Not that he didn't find out anyway. Vigo was furious with me for not forcing Harald to remove his gear before we parted." Then he snorted, mustering a bit of righteousness. "It was Vigo's own fault for making Harald so angry. Normally we left our gear with him between bouts rather than trying to find a good hiding place in our rooms."

"It was you who spread the rumors, though," Conall said, pressing the point. "Despite the bishop's determination to keep the cause of Harald's death a secret, you made sure it was known, to the point that it got back to his own mother that same day."

Arnulf's eyes were on the ground again. "Yes."

"And Vigo?" Gareth said. "By now you must have realized Harald was right, and yet you attempted to cover up what Vigo had done—and was doing."

Arnulf still didn't look up, and his shoulders hunched again.

"You wanted to protect yourself and your position that badly?"

"I was in too deep."

Gareth suddenly put a few more pieces together. "You were in debt to Vigo, weren't you? Maybe not just for the armor. Had you been gambling on the fights? And losing?"

Arnulf nodded dully. Then he put his face into his arms and began to weep. "I wish I could take it all back. I wish I'd helped my friend."

38

Day Four

Gwen

Gwen had her arms wrapped around her son, refusing to let him go. He was taller than she was, but she weighed more. She hadn't known Dai was in real danger and, in a way, that made her need to hug him even more fierce.

Still, Dai's gentle pats on the back eventually encouraged her to release him, and she loosened her hold. He was past the age where her love embarrassed him, and these days he could even say *I love you* back to her. Now, even though she'd let him go, he brought her into the circle of his arm again. "I'm all right, Mam."

"They could easily have done to you what they did to Steffan."

At her words, they both turned to look at the Dragon in question, who was sitting on a bench, being seen to by Tod, the healer's apprentice, who himself was being assisted by Aron.

Once he'd dragged Steffan into the house, Vigo had pulled two of the fingernails from Steffan's left hand, demanding Steffan tell him what he knew. Steffan had refused, of course—and refused even to let him know he really did understand what he was saying to him. He'd been aided by the fact that he'd passed out briefly after Vigo had ripped off the second nail.

Setting fire to the house had the beneficial side effect of leading the search party right to them. They'd been mounting Vigo's horses, in preparation for returning to Dublin, when their friends arrived.

They'd entered Dublin in the gray light of morning, before the city was truly stirring, and since Vigo had ridden in thrown over a horse, with a sack over his head and a cloth binding his mouth, nobody outside their small circle knew they had a son of the high king locked up in their shed. The question remained what to do with him.

Gareth had Goff and Arnulf continuing to consider the error of their ways in side-by-side penitent cells within Christ's Church. It seemed the best way to prevent news of what *really* happened north of the Liffey from spreading throughout Dublin—and worse, reaching the ears of either Rory O'Connor, who was camped with his men to the west of the city, or Donnell, wherever he might be.

Rory had to know by now that something untoward had happened in the night that had required the king to leave the city. Cait had done an impressive job deflecting King Diarmait's questions, implying it was merely a training exercise that had taken the Brodar outside the city so early in the morning.

"On the day of his brother's wedding?" Diarmait had asked.

Cait had merely shrugged and offered him a shellfish-free breakfast.

"I'm really fine." Steffan held up his hand. "I confess to have never been so afraid in my life as when he brought out the pliers. I thought he was going to remove one of my fingers whole—or take my eye."

Cadoc dropped a hand on his shoulder. "We would have been too late to stop him. I'm sorry."

"It's my fault for getting caught. It's embarrassing, really."

"You were caught because Vigo recognized you as a Dragon," Dai said. "There was nothing you could have done about that except not go—and at the time you didn't know you'd be recognized."

Steffan growled. "No way I wasn't going."

Gruffydd grinned. "Tod here will bandage you up, and you can tell the girls you were bitten by a wolf before you killed it."

Steffan's eyes lit. "I had to let him have my left hand so I could strangle him with my right."

Cadoc sighed dramatically. "It also means you probably won the bet, though young Dai here could argue he gave you a good run for your money."

Gwen lifted her head at that. "What bet?"

The faces of all the Dragons bore an identical sheepish expression. After a quick glance at the others, Gruffydd flicked out his fingers. "We wagered on which one of us would be of most service to the investigation. Too bad we can't pay Steffan his winnings in fingernails."

It was a macabre jest, but everyone laughed. Gwen, however, turned to her boys, her eyes troubled. "That was closer than I like to see my sons to real danger."

Atypically, Dai didn't brush off the concern. "I was scared, Mam. I really was." Then his brow furrowed. "But I didn't let it stop me from doing what had to be done."

Evan walked over and looked Dai in the eye. "Iago tells me it was you who captured Vigo."

Dai allowed himself a pleased look. "Iago knocked him out. I'm glad I didn't realize he had pulled out Steffan's fingernails himself or I might have been angrier and done something stupid."

"I don't believe you would have, but credit to you for wondering that about yourself." Evan tipped his head towards the door. "Go get cleaned up. All of us must. And pretend like nothing is in any way amiss!"

As it turned out, that was easier than Gwen had thought it might be. The sight of Cait in her wedding dress was enough to dispel everything else from her mind. And when Cait walked into the churchyard an hour later, the look of stunned surprise on Godfrid's face told everyone he couldn't think of anything but his bride either.

Godfrid had insisted Gareth stand up with him, in addition to Conall and Brodar, so both Gareth and Gwen stood at the church door with them. Taran had fallen asleep in Dai's arms, and Llelo had swung Tangwen onto his shoulders so she could see above the heads of everyone in the crowd, even the tallest Danes.

Even Steffan had come, though his hand was bandaged, and Aron and Iago hovered over him. His hand would heal, but their attentiveness was because torture couldn't—and shouldn't—be so easily dismissed. With everyone at the church, Brodar had sent his own men to guard Vigo in the shed, hoping that having guards around Godfrid's home wouldn't be viewed as odd, given that he was getting married today.

Church bells rang above their heads, and the street and churchyard were packed with citizens of Dublin. On the arm of King Diarmait, Cait progressed along a woven reed mat to the church door, where Godfrid and Bishop Gregory waited.

Although the Danes themselves were not known for their musical talents, they appreciated song and, after gory and tragic battle sagas, love songs were among the most commonly sung. Gwen and Hywel moved together to one side of the steps, and everyone turned to look at them. Hywel leaned down and hummed the starting note in Gwen's ear, since he had perfect pitch and could always get it exactly right, and they began:

As far as the wind dries,
and the rain moistens,
and the sun revolves,
and the sea encircles,
and the earth extends
By the truth of Heaven,
I am yours,
Name what thou wilt.
And I will grant it
For my heart warms unto thee ...

There was no applause after the singing, but Dorte was weeping, so Gwen knew she'd done her job. She returned to her family, finding herself alive in that particular way a performance that went well could make her. Hywel's eyes too were alight, and she suspected he, at least, would be called upon to sing again in the hall at the celebratory feast—and would be happy to oblige.

The ceremony itself was short, conducted half in Latin, which Gwen understood, with key moments in Danish, which she didn't. What was supposed to happen, however, did, and when Godfrid put his ring on Cait's finger, Gwen found tears welling up in her own eyes. She wished Gareth was beside her because she could have clasped his hand, remembering their own wedding nearly five years ago.

Then the church doors opened and the entire company entered for the nuptial mass. Gwen herself was delighted about the marriage, of course, but she couldn't help thinking of Harald and his journal, protesting the loss of Danish sovereignty, which Godfrid's marriage to Cait only solidified. The church itself was full of summer flowers, sweet scented and full of light, a fine counterpoint to the darkness of the last few days.

Now that Cait and Godfrid were married, Gareth too was surplus to requirements. Leaving Brodar, Conall, Rory O'Connor, and King Diarmait to kneel and stand with Cait and Godfrid, Gareth appeared at Gwen's side, just about the point that Taran, who'd been asleep, started to fuss. Once she relieved Dai of his burden, and

Gareth took Tangwen from Llelo, the four of them slipped out a side door into the churchyard.

"Too many people in too small a space," Gwen said.

"If both of you weren't so sweet, I wouldn't have put it past you to have pinched Taran to make him fuss," Gareth said, "just so you could leave early."

"I would never do that!" But Gwen was smiling as they navigated through the crowd of citizens who didn't fit in the church but still wanted to wait to greet their new princess, and down a deserted side street. If any residents of Dublin weren't at the church, palace, or lining the road between the two, they were staying inside.

Godfrid's house lay in the opposite direction, west of Christ's Church. But as soon as they were within sight of it, Gareth put out a hand to stop Gwen, and then tugged her and the children towards a nearby alley. "Something's wrong. The guards are gone."

Gwen clutched Tangwen's hand, and the three of them waited as Gareth walked through the gate, into Godfrid's yard, and into the house. The wall around the complex was only three feet high, designed to keep children and pigs inside, not to deter intruders.

After what felt like an hour, but likely was really a fraction of that time, Gareth returned. "I don't know how or why, but Vigo is gone."

39

Day Four

Gareth

The post-wedding feast was winding down, even as it had spilled into the streets. Brodar had opened his stores, and the mead flowed freely to one and all. Holm and his men were already being kept more than busy. It was the reason the wedding and feast had taken place early in the day rather than in the evening. Many Danes were belligerent on a good day, but darkness and drink made them mean.

Godfrid and Cait had long since disappeared to Godfrid's house. To give the newlyweds privacy, an hour ago, Gareth had sent Gwen and the children to sleep at Conall's home, escorted by Dai and Llelo, who were told to stay to guard the door, just in case.

"You don't look happy." Hywel descended from the high table and settled on the bench opposite Gareth.

Gareth lifted a cup of mead to him in a silent tribute. "Do you know why?"

"Of course." Hywel took a sip from his own goblet he'd brought with him. "You don't like the fact that King Brodar arranged for Vigo to be sent to Ottar's father on the Isle of Man without consulting you."

That was the entirety of Gareth's problem in a nutshell. "Did you know in advance what Brodar was going to do?"

"No. I wouldn't keep something like that from you, even if Brodar wanted me to. But I can't say I'm surprised. You shouldn't be either."

"I know. He's the King of Dublin and can do what he likes. I shouldn't allow it to upset me."

"You like wrapping up an investigation and tying off the ends. You can't do that here."

"I investigated at Bishop Gregory's request. I found Harald's murderer. Why can't I be satisfied with that?"

Hywel took another sip of his mead, savoring it on his tongue before swallowing. "Because you care about justice." It wasn't a question. "And you're right that Vigo should be punished, maybe even hanged, since he killed not only Ottar in battle but the servants who poisoned Banan. Brodar asked me to assure you Vigo has only punishment in store for him at the hands of Ottar's father."

Gareth managed a snort of mocking laughter. "Vigo did like to get his hands dirty, I can say that for him."

"Did you hear what he said when Godfrid pulled out the gag?" Hywel looked up from his cup to meet Gareth's eyes. "No, you wouldn't have understood since it was in Danish: *if you want something done right, you have to do it yourself.*"

"It would have been nice to have witnesses attest to that fact at a trial. He'll never get one now."

"Well, that's the thing, isn't it?" Hywel said. "He wouldn't have no matter to whom Brodar gave him. Welsh law doesn't apply here. If Brodar gave Vigo back to Donnell or his father, they'd let him go immediately, probably with a pat on the head and a thanks, and he would continue to wreak havoc on Donnell's behalf, just not in Dublin or Leinster. If Brodar gave him to Rory, he would have been tortured and killed, just for the fun of it. If he gave him to Diarmait, he could be used as leverage against the High King and all of his sons. And even if Brodar kept him himself, a trial would still have been out of the question."

"When you state it so plainly, I feel naïve. I wouldn't have been happy with any of those choices, even Diarmait, who, as Brodar's liege lord, would be the natural choice." Gareth's chin was in his hands, feeling more morose than ever.

"Vigo did try to kill him," Hywel said, with a wry smile.

"So I imagine he isn't happy either."

"Not very," Hywel said, though he didn't sound concerned by it.

"What happened to our fear that the High King would retaliate against Dublin or Leinster for harming his son?"

"Rory knows the truth now. Brodar showed him the warrant and allowed him to speak to Vigo. It would have been one thing if Donnell had succeeded killing his brother, but now ... the High King objects more to failure than to murder. Besides, you have to admit Brodar's solution is ingenious. Vigo will disappear into the dungeon of the one person who has the greatest claim on his life, and who will hate him most, once he learns he should. Even Diarmait cannot argue with sending Vigo to the Isle of Man. Vigo stabbed Ottar in the back. He said so himself, in front of witnesses. Ottar's father does have the greatest claim."

"You're right. I see it too." Gareth took a long drink and set down his cup, feeling a bit better about how the day had gone.

Hywel put a hand on Gareth's arm. "Be content. We have done our duty here. More than that, we have showed all of Dublin that Gwynedd stands with their king and prince, now and always. And we have showed Leinster we can be trusted."

"You want Diarmait to turn to us instead of Pembroke, if he needs help against his allies, don't you?"

"I don't relish losing Welshmen in a foreign war, but neither do I want to see either Leinster or Dublin fall to a Norman army. When Diarmait betrothed Caitriona to Godfrid, Diarmait gained a larger family than he realized."

Gareth settled back in his seat, his eyes on the high table, more at ease in this moment than he'd been since they'd arrived in Dublin. Then he looked back to his prince and grinned. "Just as long as Gwen is never again called upon to cross the Irish Sea."

"Never that." Hywel laughed. "Caitriona and Godfrid will just have to come to us."

The End

Historical Background

B efore I learned of the Danish role in the assassination of Anarawd, King of Deheubarth, I had no idea that the Danes had ever conquered parts of Ireland.

The Danes, as a group, were part of a vast migration of men of the North to other regions of the world, initially for plunder and eventually for settlement. Coming from regions that now make up Norway, Sweden, Finland, and Denmark, these men went *a Viking*, and created widespread settlements: to the south, in Normandy and Sicily; to the east into Russia; and to the west in England, Ireland, Iceland, Greenland, and the coast of Newfoundland.

The Dublin Danes were part of that tradition, and Ottar and Brodar were real people as described in *The Viking Prince*, both ruling Dublin in the mid-twelfth century. Brodar and Godfrid were part of an extensive lineage of rulership of Dublin called the Mac Torcalls, whose hegemony was briefly usurped by Ottar, but then reestablished. Scholarship is confused about some of the specifics, but it is clear that members of their clan ruled Dublin until the arrival of the Normans under the leadership of Richard de Clare (Strongbow) and ultimately King Henry, who defeated the Danes and expelled them from Dublin for good in 1171 AD.

The ruling family of Gwynedd, as led for most of the twelfth century by Owain Gwynedd, had both Danish and Irish ancestry. Through Gruffydd ap Cynan, Owain's father, Prince Hywel is descended from both Sitric Silkbeard, King of Dublin; and Brian Boru, High King of Ireland.

About the Author

With two historian parents, Sarah couldn't help but develop an interest in the past. She went on to get more than enough education herself (in anthropology) and began writing fiction when the stories in her head overflowed and demanded she let them out. While her ancestry is Welsh, she only visited Wales for the first time while in college. She has been in love with the country, language, and people ever since. She even convinced her husband to give all four of their children Welsh names.

She makes her home in Oregon.

www.sarahwoodbury.com

Made in the USA
Middletown, DE
20 July 2019